# These
# Things
# That
# Walk
# Behind
# Me

# Praise for
# These Things That
# Walk Behind Me

"David Surface's stories are organic and unstoppable, an itch that has to be scratched, and it's more than an itch, something other, and you're not quite sure what it is, but it's growing, possibly in response to your attention, but you can't stop scratching, no matter how hard you try to ignore the change arising from within, and your complicity in what is about to happen. Simply put, these are horrifically beautiful stories. Savor them."
**Eric Schaller, author of *Voice of the Stranger***

"What makes these stories so powerful is Surface's commitment to the realistic and the strange, and his understanding that they are adjacent and intertwined. These are nimble and satisfying stories that take the best qualities of literature and genre to create a creature that is its own dark thing."
**Brian Evenson, author of A Collapse of Horses**

"In These Things That Walk Behind Me, David Surface gathers dark and haunting tales that explore the thin line between nightmares and daydreams. From unsettling encounters with the past to eerie whispers of otherworldly beings, each story lingers with a sense of dread and anticipation. A chilling exhibition you won't want to miss."
**Christopher Barzak, Shirley Jackson Award-winning author of Before and Afterlives**

Copyright © 2024 by David Surface
Published by Lethe Press | lethepressbooks.com

ISBN: 978-1-59021-765-8

Introduction © 2024 by John Langan

Typesetting: Ryan Vance
Cover: Ryan Vance

# These Things That Walk Behind Me

David Surface

With an introduction
by John Langan

 LETHE

# Contents

# Introduction:
## The Strange Darkness of David Surface

1.  There's no one behind you.
2.  Nothing behind you—sorry.
3.  You may be reading this on a plane, a train, a bus, or even in a car. You may be sitting on a living room couch or a favorite chair, in a booth at a diner, or on one of those long rows of plastic seats they have in airport waiting areas. You may be crossing a bridge, entering a tunnel, or sitting absolutely still. And, of course, in any of these scenarios, someone may be seated to your rear, maybe a family member or friend, scrolling through their phone while you read, maybe a fellow traveler, sharing the ride for a few stops, or possibly all the way.
4.  That isn't what we're talking about, though, is it?
5.  David Surface has described his terrific stories as "strange" and "dark;" he's identified some of them as ghost stories, quite deliberately constructed

as such. To use the word strange in the context of the kind of fiction Surface writes is to evoke the example of the great Robert Aickman (1914-1981), whose application of the adjective to his own idiosyncratic compositions single-handedly set up a new stall under the big, billowing circus tent of horror. As all such namings inevitably do, it organized a constellation of writers around itself: Franz Kafka, Jorge Luis Borges, Walter de la Mare, M. John Harrison, Linda Rucker, Simon Strantzas, and Michael Wehunt, to name a few. To the extent that any kind of compositional principles might be extrapolated from reading and studying the work of Aickman and these others, three elements stand out:

– First is the selection of a reasonably quotidian protagonist—as often as not male—of a reasonably quotidian sensibility. No raving Lovecraftian lunatics here, nor Dunsanian poets, nor Howard-esque strongmen. This is room, though, for post-Freudian neurosis. Plenty of room. (In this regard, these stories participate in the larger generic trend of featuring more down-to-earth protagonists.) (I suppose you could argue that fits with the even larger literary focus on such characters.) For the protagonists of these strange stories, essential portions of their psyches are obscure, perhaps by choice, perhaps not.

– Secondly, this type of character is brought into similarly occluded situations, whose entireties elide full perception. Generally speaking, these situations center on buildings—houses, hotels, apartments, fair tents, churches—which are never fully seen, experienced only as fragments.

- Finally, the occluded characters and occluded situations are moved through one another. Here, Aickman's stories—and those of the writers working in this vein—achieve their particular effect. In a traditionally constructed horror narrative, the protagonist and the situation in which they're involved collide, resulting in a transfer of metaphor, whereby the situation becomes a trope for the character. (Think Jack Torrance and the Overlook Hotel in King's The Shining: the hotel with its rooms of ghosts and boiler on the verge of exploding embodies the man full of his own ghosts and on the verge of exploding.) (Or think Straub's Ghost Story, in which Alma Mobley and her monstrous kin draw power from their ability to reflect the protagonists back to themselves.) This transference results in a moment of illumination, in whose glow the text's depths are made more distinct. In Aickman's work, in contrast, the character and situation flow into one another, become entangled, and then pull apart without such a clear symbolic exchange. Instead, the situation sprawls and metastasizes, spilling over the bounds of a more straightforward relationship with the protagonist. You could say that what comes into (partial) view is the situation's unconscious, the parts of itself of which the situation, even in its figurative dimension, is unaware. The result of the meshing of the insufficiently (self) aware protagonist with the occluded aspects of the situation feels deeply strange and disorienting, in part because we still recognize in the unfamiliar elements of the situation traces of what they are replacing. When all is said and done—but that's just the point. At the end of the story, nothing is said and done, not with the definitiveness that trite expression implies. We're left with strangeness humming through our brains.

6. There's still no one—nothing behind you.

7. It is, yes, a bit of an indulgence on the part of someone writing an introduction to a book of short stories to spend so much time on such a technical description of another writer's technique. Yet it seems necessary to me in order to avoid the accurate but insufficient shorthand of comparing David Surface to Robert Aickman and leaving it at that. ("The Aickman of Cornwall-on-Hudson." "Aickman's Hudson Valley Successor." "Aickman with Better Hair.") What Surface achieves in a significant number of the stories collected here (and in his excellent previous book, Terrible Things) is to understand and employ Aickman's narrative strategy in the composition of his own striking fiction. This accomplishment informs Glen Hirshberg's description of the "disturbingly contemporary sense of bewilderment" Surface's work evokes, the feeling of "a world tilting out of true."

8. Were my desire to avoid spoilers not stronger than the desire to discuss how Surface's stories bring forth their particular strangeness, there is a great deal we might say. In addition, a decent discussion would take us beyond an introduction to a critical essay. While Surface's work invites and deserves such detailed attention, it exceeds my remit here. (That said, as you read these stories, watch out for bridges and tunnels, both literal and metaphorical,

and spend some time thinking about the way that things flow in both directions over such passages and how sometimes things get stuck on them, too.)

9. Before bringing this introduction to a close, there is one more subject for us to return to, and that is the other word Surface has used for his stories: dark. Even in the context of strange and ghostly stories, it's an elusive term. Unlike "strange," there is no specific writer or group of writers who use the word to delineate their aesthetic. Rather, it's a modifier we might apply to all the entertainments grouped under horror's big tent, as well as to work under a number of adjacent marquees. Whereas an appreciation of "strange" benefits from bringing an analysis of Aickman's stories into consideration, Surface's choice of "dark" requires (re)reading his fiction.

10. Nothing behind you. No one, either.

11. Ironically, an immersion in Surface's work returns us to the strange, with its emphasis on the unconscious areas of characters and situations—to those parts of both that remain unilluminated. Yet where the darkness of the typical Aickman protagonist is based on unacknowledged drives, the darkness in Surface's characters arises from incomplete and even repressed knowledge, knowledge of those spaces of the self and the world that are troubling and disturbing. Darkness within is, in part, a response to darkness without, a failure of recognition, if not an outright evasion. In his lexicon of horror, The Darkening Garden (2006), the critic John Clute listed amnesia as among the key markers of the field, and darkness as it applies to Surface's characters is of a piece with Clute's idea.

The narrative mechanisms of these stories might be described as a character being brought into a situation that disturbs them but whose full outline remains obscure for reasons having as much to do with their psychology as with how the situation occurs. The tension their continuing interaction with the situation generates escalates until something, some important element of the situation, is brought into view. But this revelation only reveals how much more darkness lies beyond the end of the story, inside the protagonist and out. Mystery solved yields a mystery still more profound.

12. So strange stories, yes, and dark, too. Stories with fine prose and sympathetically drawn characters give them an emotional heft and resonance not always found in this fiction stripe. Stories that follow you.

13. Nothing—no one behind you.

14. But there will be.

*JOHN LANGAN*

# Give Me Back My Name

WHEN ROB WOKE, the room was pitch dark, with nothing for his eye to hold onto. His brain flashed through a series of other bedrooms he'd slept in, other houses, apartments, and motel rooms, each quickly dissolving into the next while he lay still and waited for the objects around him to become clear. The familiar shape of a bureau to his right. The solid rectangle of a framed picture on the wall. Carrie's body breathing next to his.

He lay there for a moment longer, letting the relief of knowing where he was soak into him, then got out of bed and went downstairs to start the coffee.

This was his favorite part of the day, the quiet in-between time before anything had started when it felt like he was the only person in the world. He enjoyed this morning ritual, filling the kettle, striking a match, lighting the blue flame on the stovetop, and setting the kettle on it. Then, the patient waiting for the flame to do its work while the blackness outside the windows turned blue.

The coffee was ready and waiting in the two big mugs by the time Carrie came downstairs, bleary-eyed and carrying her big shoulder bag stuffed with students' homework. She took the mug from his hand, dropped onto one of the kitchen chairs, and took a deep and grateful sip.

"God, that's good," she whispered.

"Ready for another big day at school?" he smiled.

Carrie rolled her eyes. "Yeah... I gotta tell the kids a ghost story today."

"Really? I thought you liked ghost stories."

"I do. But the school wants me to keep telling the same one every year. You know, where the dead woman keeps saying, *Give me back my golden arm.*"

"You mean the one where you're supposed to yell at the end and make everyone jump?"

"Yeah. The husband steals his wife's golden arm, and, at night, he hears her calling, *Give me back my golden arm. Give me back my golden arm.* It's so stupid. I mean, who has a golden arm?"

"I don't know..." he said, "Will the kids even think that's scary? A golden arm?"

"Maybe I should update it or something. *Give me back my iPhone Six!*"

After Carrie left, Rob went out and raked the front yard to let the cold October air wake him up. He spent the rest of the morning washing the dishes from breakfast, then sweeping and dusting. He liked to keep moving when he was alone. It kept his mind focused and sharp.

At twelve, he took a break to eat lunch and check his email and saw a message from a job he'd applied for. *We'd like you to come in for an interview after you've agreed to submit to a routine background check.* He deleted the email without responding, stood up, and went back to cleaning the house.

Rob had dinner on the table as usual when Carrie got home from school. Pasta primavera with marinara sauce and crusty bread. They ate while Carrie told Rob about her day.

"So, how did the ghost story go? Did you scare the hell out of those poor, defenseless children?"

Carrie took another sip of wine before she answered. "Oh, sure. Scarred them for life. *Give me back my golden arm.* Actually, I think I saw a couple of them jump at the end."

"What does a ghost need with a golden arm?" he asked. "I mean, it's not like she can go out and *spend* it or something because she's dead, right?"

"I don't know." Carrie shrugged. "Maybe it's like... the principle of the thing. You know. You take something from me, now you have to give it back."

They were clearing the table after dinner when she asked him, "So, have you heard back from that security job yet?"

"Nope. Not yet."

"Jeez," Carrie said, "What's taking them so long? Are they doing one of those background checks or something? They probably just want to make sure you're not a serial killer," Carrie grinned. "You're not a serial killer, are you?"

"No," he managed a wry smile, then bent down and kissed her forehead. "I'm not a serial killer."

Rob usually looked at all the requirements before applying for a job. Whenever he found one that required a background check, he'd cross it off his list and move on to the next. He must have missed this one—he'd have to be more careful next time.

A simple job—that's what he'd told Carrie he needed. One where he could work in peace and quiet without anyone breathing down his neck. And as usual, she'd agreed. *People should do what they're good at,* she'd said. He was good at being alone. Low-profile jobs were the best. Construction. Maintenance. Security. Carrie didn't seem to mind. It was one more reason he felt safe with her.

*You must have been a shepherd in a former life,* she'd said once. He'd smiled but felt the sting. His former life was gone. In fact, it wasn't even his life anymore.

WHEN HE'D LEFT the house that morning twenty years ago, he hadn't known he would disappear. He was just going to go for a long drive to clear his head after another terrible fight with Ann. He was twenty-three years old back then; their divorce was almost final, and the future was a horrifying void. The legal bills and demands for support confused and terrified him.

*They can't make you give what you don't have,* a friend had told him. What his friend hadn't said was what they could do to him. He was stunned when he understood how bad things really were, but it made a terrible kind of sense. Ever since he was a child, Rob had been haunted by the feeling that something bad would happen to him one day. Something he didn't have the power to stop. Now he knew what it was. He was going to prison. Not today, not tomorrow. But someday. It was going to happen.

By the time he realized how far he'd driven, he'd gone nearly two hundred miles. The landscape around him had started to change, the look of the trees and houses. Even the sky seemed different. It was the feeling of *newness* that overcame him. He could feel his old life falling away, like the pieces of a cocoon he was shedding. Ann's anger, the divorce proceedings, the lawyer bills. The threat of prison. They were all there in his rear-view mirror, like storm clouds gathering, but a storm that was happening somewhere behind him. He could outrun it.

*I could just keep going.* That was the thought that rose in his mind and took hold of him. It was true. He could just keep going.

He'd done none of the things he should have done first to make disappearing easy. The fake IDs and social security number, the new name. He had to learn about all of it on the run. He'd thrown his cell phone into a river—he knew enough to do that—then found a library that would let him use the computer. It amazed him that he could go online and find complete instructions for how to assume a new identity. It had been written for women escaping dangerous, abusive husbands or boyfriends. He was surprised and reassured by how much of it applied to him. He realized you didn't have to be a bad person to disappear. It was something that happened to good people, too.

He spent three days in a dusty cubicle, just taking notes in a spiral notebook. When his eyes and brain got tired, he'd look out the library window at the bright green lawn outside and the orderly white houses. Once, the door to one of the houses opened, and a man stepped outside. Rob watched the man walk to his mailbox and get his mail. An older man with graying hair, he was reasonably trim and fit and wore what looked like a blue track suit. Rob watched the man flip through his mail, then turn and walk back into his house, his movements unhurried and confident. The thought crossed Rob's mind that this was how he'd like to look one day. An unhurried, confident man with attractively greying hair and no worries.

Twenty years later, that's exactly what he was.

He'd never told Carrie about Ann. Or his real name. That was one of the rules for disappearing. *Do not tell your new partner about your former life, no matter how much you are tempted.* After they'd been together for about seven years, he'd felt tempted for a brief while, but the feeling had passed. After all, he was a new person now. The old one no longer existed.

One night, they sat outside, drinking and talking. Carrie was worried about her sister, who'd just separated from her husband. "I really hate it," Carrie said. "It's so sad. They used to be such good friends."

"Yeah, well, that's how a lot of marriages start out," Rob said. "You think you're *such good friends* with someone. Then one day you don't even know who they are..." He felt himself descending into a familiar spiral but stopped himself. He was more drunk than he'd realized. When he looked up, Carrie was staring at him, her eyes growing wide with shock.

"Rob, were you...? Oh my God. You were married before. You were, weren't you?"

He froze. A sudden panic twisted in his chest, like a wild animal caught in a trap. He wanted to lie, but he knew it was too late. She'd seen him.

"Yes. I'm sorry. But... it was a long time ago. I was just a stupid kid. It only lasted a few months."

It was dark outside, but he could see her face turn pale. "Jesus, Rob, why didn't you tell me?"

"I don't know. I guess... I guess it was just too painful."

"Why? What happened?"

"She died." The words surprised him. He didn't know he was going to say them, but once he did, he just kept going. "It was cancer. Ovarian."

He could see her struggling with what he was telling her. "I'm... I'm sorry," she finally said. "That must have been awful."

It killed him how quickly she'd turned from shock to sympathy. She believed him. Relief rushed through him, mixed with shame. He hated to lie to her, but he did it to protect her. To protect them both and their life together.

Carrie waited a moment, giving him some time, he supposed. Then she asked quietly, "What was her name?"

For a second, he almost said *Ann*. There was no reason not to. Then, almost before he knew it, the caution he'd drilled into himself took over.

"Hannah."

He saw the impact that hearing the name made on her. The name made it real. He could almost see her flinch. Now, it was his turn to wait and give her a moment. When he thought she looked ready, he continued.

"I'm sorry I never told you. I just… I mean, it was a long time ago. It was a really hard time, and I guess…I guess I just didn't want to think about it. I'm sorry." He was pushing his luck, he knew, but he asked anyway. "Forgive me?"

She looked at him for a long time before answering, and for a moment, he was afraid she'd seen through him. Then she sighed. "I guess I'll have to, won't I?"

That night he dreamed that he murdered Ann.

All the planning and plotting he'd done in real life to erase his marriage, to erase *her*, came into play in his dream, and he moved through it like some kind of faceless killer, perfectly executing every detail of her death in the most cold-blooded, methodical way. In his dream, there was a box he had to put her body into. The box was too small to hold her body, so he started folding her in half, then again, and again, breaking her down and pushing the parts together until they fit. The box was made of clear plexiglass, so he could see the different parts of her inside, pressed up against it—a whorl of long brown hair, one flattened cheek, the fingers of one hand splayed against the glass like a starfish. He didn't want anyone to see, so he took the box out into the middle of the ocean and dropped it in where it sank without a trace. Instead of waking up with his heart pounding or in a cold sweat, he woke feeling oddly satisfied and accomplished. Almost proud.

HE BEGAN TO notice Carrie acting strangely, a little preoccupied and distant. He knew she must be thinking about "Hannah" and the story he'd told her. Of course, it made sense—how could he expect her not to think about it? He supposed it would take a while for her to get used to the idea that he'd had another wife before her. Eventually, the thought would lose its rawness, and become part of the fabric of the past. Knowing she was alive somewhere would only make it worse. Carrie would dwell on it for months, maybe years. It was better to say that "Hannah" was dead. He'd actually done her a favor.

Then the thought occurred to him—how did he know that Ann *wasn't* really dead? It was possible. After all, it had been twenty years—a lot could happen in twenty years. Cancer. Car crashes. All kinds of things. Why shouldn't one of them happen to her?

He began to think of Ann as *gone*. Truly gone. At first, he felt a twinge of the old regret, but that faded, and he almost came to believe that it was true. Not only that, but that he'd somehow *made* it true. By telling that lie, it was the same as if he'd killed her.

One day, Carrie asked if she could talk to him about something. She never asked if she could talk to him unless it was something difficult and important. This time she seemed nervous, more nervous than usual. He stroked her arm and told her it was okay, she could ask him anything, while he braced himself of whatever she was going to say.

"I just wanted…" She stopped herself and then started again, "I was wondering if you can tell me… if you don't mind telling me… about Hannah. Where is she buried?"

He froze. Of all the things she could have asked him, this was one he did not expect. He struggled to find something quick to say.

"Idaho," he blurted out. He was going to say Indiana, but that felt too close. Idaho was farther away. Idaho was perfect. He watched Carrie take in this piece of new information.

"Because…" she began again, "If you… if you ever wanted to visit there… I mean, visit *her*… for any reason, you should do that. I mean, there's no reason for you not to do that now. If you want to. Right?"

The awfulness of it, her selflessness, how good she was trying to be for him, hit him like a blow. He closed his eyes, waiting to recover from it. He thought of what it must look like to her, that he was overcome. He was, but not in the way she thought.

"Thank you," he said, "But, I don't… I mean, it's been so long…"

Carrie stepped forward, put her hand on his shoulder and gently rubbed him. "That's okay," she said. "Just… if you ever want to. Whenever you're ready."

For the rest of the night, he felt shaken. The lies he'd had to tell Carrie over their years together had actually been very few. His name, where he was from, not much else. His marriage to Ann had always been a lie of omission. He'd simply never brought it up, and Carrie had never asked. Until now.

Why hadn't he just denied it? That would have been the end of it. But part of him knew that Carrie would always have that doubt in her mind. Saying yes had been his way to get around that. Now it felt like a crack was forming in the ice under his feet. And every question she asked and every answer he gave felt like a hammer blow, making the crack spread faster.

The next night, Carrie asked him, "Did you and Hannah... did you have any children?"

"No," he said. He gave a silent prayer of thanks—not for the first time—that at least this much was true. Then he remembered. When he and Ann were first married, they'd bought a cute stuffed dog as a "pet" because they couldn't afford a real one. Sometimes he thought it was a substitute for the child they hadn't had yet. They'd lay in bed and tease each other with it, making it talk in funny voices, playing together like children. A few years later when their fighting had become ugly and violent, when he was packing to leave, he'd found that stuffed dog in the closet, preserved carefully in a white shoebox wrapped with a gold ribbon. It was the only time that he'd actually wept, falling to his knees on the floor with the toy in front of him, sobbing like a parent grieving the death of a child.

The next day they drove out to the country to pick up some garden supplies. On the way home, the traffic slowed down to almost a standstill, and they crept along at five miles an hour. "What's the hold up?" Rob grumbled. He craned his neck to see if he could spot construction signs or police lights ahead, but the long line of cars disappeared around a curve; whatever was causing the holdup was hidden.

Something on the right side of the road caught his eye. It was one of those little shrines made of tinfoil and painted wood. It seemed like he saw them everywhere lately. All those names and brief sentimental messages. *Kristal— Forever in Our Hearts.* Crosses with artificial flowers, sometimes real ones, held in place with twisted wire.

"I don't understand why anyone would want to do that," he said. I mean, why would you want to commemorate the spot where someone was killed? That's horrible."

"Well, they do it on battlefields, don't they?" she said. "Like Gettysburg and Antietam."

The traffic crept forward slowly, then stopped. He glanced over at the little shrine again, the typical, white-painted cross with fake flowers and some kind of stuffed animal tied to it. As they got closer, he could see it was a stuffed dog. He noticed the eyes, sad and droopy, the large brown pupils turned upward in a look of supplication, like a saint at prayer in an old painting. They were the same eyes that their stuffed dog had. His and Ann's.

He looked closer. It was the same toy. The same one.

Panic flooding his brain, he pulled the car over onto the shoulder, pushed the gas pedal to the floor and sped alongside the other cars toward the exit far ahead, gravel crunching and spitting under the tires.

"What are you doing?" Carrie yelled, but he kept going until he pulled off the highway and eased the car onto a two-lane road.

"Why the hell did you do that?" Carrie asked. "What's wrong with you?"

He knew he should tell her something, offer some kind of explanation. But he couldn't.

When he thought about it later, he realized how foolishly he'd behaved. That toy dog he'd seen by the side of the road—they must have made hundreds of them. Maybe thousands. There was nothing strange about it. Nothing at all.

That night he told Carrie he needed to go for a walk. She looked up for a moment, her eyes red from the onions she was chopping. "It's going to rain, isn't it?"

"I don't know… maybe," he said, heading for the door. "I'll make it quick."

"Supper's at seven, okay?" he heard her call out behind him. He headed down the driveway to the street, turned left and started walking as fast as he could. All the stress and anxiety he'd felt building since his talk with Carrie, it was all chemical, he knew. Just hormones. Fight or flight. It would fade in time. Everything would fade in time. Carrie's shock over finding out he'd been married before. Any lingering suspicions she might have. They would all get worn away under the steady, grinding pace of their daily lives. No matter how upsetting something might seem at first, there was nothing that time wouldn't take care of.

He'd only gone a couple of blocks when felt a cold drop hit his forearm. He took a quick glance up at the sky saw heavy gray clouds rolling in, then started walking faster to beat the rain and to get his heart rate up to clear the poisons out of his system.

It seemed like more cars than usual were speeding past him. People on their way home from work, he guessed. Not too many people out walking like him. Just the old man across the street who never smiled, trimming his hedges. A young boy with a backpack getting home late from school. A woman standing in the middle of the street.

He paused and peered ahead at the woman, wondering what she was doing there. At first, he thought she must have dropped something while crossing the street, but she didn't appear to be looking for anything. She was just standing there on the white line in the middle of the road, staring straight ahead in his direction. She was too far away for him to get a good look at her face, but there was something familiar about the outline of her body and the way she was standing that made him feel uneasy.

As he watched, the woman tilted her head to one side as she looked at him, the way Ann used to do. A cold feeling crept up inside of him. *It can't be,* he thought. *She's dead.* It took him a second to remember that wasn't true. Still... how could it be her? It wasn't possible. He felt frozen in place like an animal seen by a predator. He didn't dare to move or breathe.

He heard the rain before he saw it, the sharp popping in the leaves of trees, slow at first, then faster, more cold drops hitting his arms and neck. He saw the old man put his clippers aside and hurry indoors, but the woman didn't move. She was still standing in the middle of the street with the rain falling all around her. His own shirt was already wet and clinging to his skin, but from a distance it looked like the woman's hair and clothes were still dry.

The hiss of car wheels in the rain came fast from around the sharp curve behind him, and he stepped out of the way as a red SUV blew past, spraying water as it hurtled toward the woman. He braced himself for the terrible thud, for the sight of the broken body flying through the air. But when he looked again, the car was speeding on its way around the bend, and the woman was still standing in the center of the street. Still looking in his direction.

That was when she began to walk toward him.

He turned and started walking toward home, not looking back. When he couldn't stand it anymore, he broke into a run and didn't stop until he burst in through the kitchen door, wet and breathless. Carrie was still standing at the oven, stirring the onions. She looked up, an alarmed expression on her face.

"Jesus... what happened to you?"

"Nothing," he panted, "Just trying to get out of the rain..."

He waited till she wasn't looking, then locked the door behind him.

\*

LATER, HE FOUND Carrie at her desk, peering intently at her laptop screen.

"What town did you say Hannah was buried in?"

He'd just come to ask if she wanted a cup of tea or something, but her question stopped him cold.

"What are you doing?" he asked, trying to keep his voice as normal as possible.

"I just want to see where it is."

*Why?* That was what he wanted to ask. But he didn't. If he asked *why,* she'd know he didn't want to tell her. Still, he had to say something.

"Carlton." It was the first name that popped into his mind. A half-second later he realized it was the name of his high school English teacher. He listened to her fingers clicking busily on the keys, then pause.

"It's not here."

"Well, it was a really small town," he said, hoping that would sound reasonable. Her fingers clicked some more. Then she leaned back and frowned at the computer.

"I can't find it."

"Really? That's weird." He didn't know what else to say. Then he remembered why he'd come into the room. "You want me to get you some tea?"

She looked up at him, still frowning. "Yeah," she finally said. "That would be nice."


LEAVES BEGAN TO pile up in the yard and choke the gutters that overflowed like waterfalls, but he stayed in the house. There was plenty of work to do indoors, he told himself. The truth was that he didn't feel safe outside. It reminded him of how he'd felt when he'd first come here years ago, when every person on the street looked at him a little longer than he thought they should, and every police siren went right through him like a knife. He felt that way now.

"I've been thinking about going to visit my aunt in Portland," Carrie said one night.

"I didn't know you had an aunt in Portland."

"Yeah. I thought we could go out there for a visit. You know, see some of the sights. It's really beautiful out there."

He felt an alarm go off somewhere inside his body. "I don't know... You know I don't like to fly." He didn't really mind flying. What he didn't like was having his ID checked so many times. He'd done it before when he had to. But there was no point in pushing his luck.

"No," she said, "I thought we could drive."

"To Portland? How long a trip is that?"

"Only three days. There's a lot of pretty land between here and there. "I mean..." she paused and put her hand on the back of his. "You seem a little stressed. I think maybe you could use it, right? A little time away from here"

And just like that, he felt a door open somewhere inside him. *A little time away from here.* Thunder rumbled somewhere in the distance. He could hear the rain tapping at the windows again, trying to get in.

"Sure," he said, taking the hand she'd offered into his. "That sounds nice."


THE FIRST FIVE hundred miles are the longest.

That was the joke that came into his head as they crossed the state line from Iowa into Nebraska. He didn't say it, because he was afraid that she might see what he was seeing—the long days and nights he'd spent on the road twenty years ago when he'd left his old life behind. It unnerved him, how much it looked the same. The same flat, colorless fields. The same ribbon of blacktop stretching all the way to the horizon.

Carrie liked to stop at odd little restaurants and shops she found along the way where they'd sample the coconut creme pie and buy corny postcards. He could tell she was trying to make this a fun trip to relieve some of the pressure of whatever had been bothering him. But to him, her efforts felt stiff and forced. There was something else on her mind. He couldn't tell what it was, but he didn't want to ask. He just wanted to get through this trip and then make it back home.

The next morning after breakfast, Carrie insisted on driving. He'd driven most of the way yesterday, she pointed out, so it was only fair. He agreed, reluctantly. He liked to drive, it was true, but more than that, he didn't like being driven by someone else, sitting in the passenger seat with nothing to do.

When they crossed the state line into Idaho, Rob felt a stir of some nameless anxiety in his chest but couldn't figure out what it was. Carrie, who was usually talkative in the car, had been unusually quiet. About an hour after they crossed into Idaho, he was surprised when she took an exit off the interstate onto a smaller state route.

"Where are you going?" he asked. She said nothing, but he could feel her gathering her words, trying to find the right ones.

"We're going by Carlton," she said. "I just thought... since we're so close, we might as well drop by there. Just for a minute."

*Carlton?* He tried to remember where he'd heard that name—then it hit him. It was the name of the town

GIVE ME BACK MY NAME

where he'd told her his first wife was buried. The one he'd made up.

*There is no Carlton,* he wanted to say. *It doesn't exist.* Instead, he did his best to swallow the panic rising inside him and tried to control his voice.

"Why... why do you want to go there?"

"I just thought..." she stopped to swallow and take a breath—clearly, this was difficult for her. "I just thought we should stop, just for a minute, and... pay our respects. To your wife. To Hannah."

His mind went blank for a second, then the urge to rage at her, to jump out of the car or take the wheel from her hands, all overtook him.

"Jesus, Carrie. I can't..." he began, trying to summon up the anger he needed to distract her and throw her off. "I can't believe you're just doing this without telling me. Why the fuck... why would you do this without telling me? Without talking with me about it first? What if I don't *want* to do this? Did you ever think about *that?*"

"Of course, I thought about that," she said, her voice rising. "I know you don't want to do this, Rob, but I think you should. I think you need to. Ever since you told me..." She stopped, and he realized she was trying not to cry. "Ever since you told me about Hannah, about you and Hannah, you haven't been the same. There's something wrong, Rob. I don't know what it is, but I can tell. Something's wrong. And, I don't know, maybe I'm wrong, maybe I don't have the right. Maybe I'm crazy, but I just think if we do this, it might help you. It might help both of us."

That was when he understood. This had been her plan all along. To fix him. To fix the two of them. It was horrible. What would she do when she realized that the town wasn't there?

He was trying to summon up the courage to tell her the truth when a road sign appeared in the distance and moved past them. CARLTON.

His mind went blank as he read the letters. What was happening? How was this possible? Could there be a real town with the same name he'd made up? What were the odds? Had he seen the name somewhere before and forgotten it?

He heard the *click click click* of the turn signal and felt the pull of the car as she slowed down and turned off onto the exit.

He stared out the passenger window at the broad, empty streets lined with old buildings and chain stores. When Carrie pulled over at a market, he thought she was going in to use the bathroom, until she emerged a minute later holding a small bouquet of yellow flowers. His heart hurt when he saw them.

They turned off the main street and made two more turns. Then he saw the cemetery.

Carrie drove the car through the iron gates and proceeded to roll through the rows of headstones as if she knew where she was going. He pictured them searching through the headstones for hours, then finally giving up. He'd tell her that he wasn't sure it was the same cemetery, that *it was so long ago.* She'd understand. She wouldn't be happy, but she'd believe him. And that would be the end of it.

Carrie finally parked the car and turned off the engine. She sat for a moment, then looked at him, her eyes full of concern. "Are you ready?" she said quietly. He realized his heart was beating very quickly. He felt dizzy and short of breath. She would probably take it for emotion. He nodded, then they both got out and started walking. Carrie held the bouquet of yellow flowers in her hand.

He quickly scanned the cemetery and tried to gauge how big it was. He was trying to calculate how long it would take before she gave up, when she stopped suddenly, and a strange little sound came from her throat.

There to the right of them, no more than four feet away, was a shiny headstone engraved:

HANNAH MARTIN.

Rage—that was the first thing he felt. A wave of rage surging through his veins. Who was doing this? And why? It was horrible, some kind of cruel, sadistic joke. He looked wildly around as if there might be a camera crew hiding behind a tree, recording his terror and humiliation. But the cemetery was empty——they were the only people there.

He looked back at Carrie, half-expecting to see an evil grin on her face—*is she in on this?* She was staring solemnly down at the grave. She looked up at him and he was stunned to see tears glittering in her eyes. Then she held out the little yellow bouquet toward him.

"Do you want to…" she said in a soft whisper. He stared in horror at the yellow flowers and shook his head. "It's okay," she said softly, then stepped forward herself and leaned down to prop the little bouquet up against the gravestone. At that moment, he would not have been surprised to see them vanish or burst into flame. She stood with her hands folded respectfully in front of her, still gazing down at the grave. He tried to imagine what was going on in her mind but couldn't—his own mind felt like it had exploded and was a jumble of fragments now, jagged pieces that couldn't connect.

He became aware that she was saying something. From the tone of her voice, he could tell it was a question, but he didn't quite understand it. She had to say it twice before the words made sense to him.

"Are you ready?"

*Ready? Ready for what?* She stepped back and nodded toward where they'd parked the car and he understood.

"I mean..." she said, "We can stay a little longer... if you want to."

*"No."* It was the first word he'd been able to speak. He turned and started walking back toward the car, his mind still spinning. A touch on his arm made him jump; it was her, of course. She'd come up to walk silently beside him, one hand resting gently on his right arm, like they were leaving a funeral.

The drive to the motel was long and mostly silent. Carrie drove. This time he was glad. He didn't feel quite capable of driving yet. His mind was still in a turmoil. What was happening to him? Had he seen the name of that town on a map or in a book somewhere, forgotten that he'd seen it, then had it echo back to him when he needed it? And the other name. The one on the gravestone. How was that possible? How many Hannah Martins could there be in the world? He knew that a Google search usually turned up a long list of even the strangest name. How strange was it, really, to find a gravestone with Hannah's name? Then he remembered—there was no Hannah Martin. It was the name he'd invented when he needed something to tell Carrie, the way he'd invented a new name for himself when he'd first disappeared years ago. *Robert Martin.* For years it felt fake on his lips. Now it was who he was. For a terrifying moment he couldn't remember what his real name used to be.

"Are you okay?"

At first, he wasn't sure if he'd heard her correctly. He turned and saw her glancing over at him with a concerned look on her face.

He tried to answer but couldn't. His mind had stopped working. They drove along in silence for a moment. He could feel her gathering her words again.

"I know…" she started, "I know that was hard for you. I just thought it was something we needed to do. You and me."

*You and me. Rob and Carrie Martin.* There was no Rob Martin, but that was who he was now. And what about her? Half of her name real, the other half not. He wondered if she could feel it.

The motel was a few flat buildings scattered at the edge of the highway. It was right out of an old movie, with its near-empty parking lot and old purple neon sign with one letter burnt out. It looked, he thought, like the kind of place that a person might come to end their life.

He got out of the car and squinted at the single harsh floodlight above that was surrounded by a halo of moths and other insects swirling round and round endlessly. Looking around, he felt as though he'd been here before. It was the kind of place he'd stayed back when he'd first gone on the run, holed up in a musty room with the shades drawn, cutting up his driver's license and credit cards, shedding the last traces of his old life.

They opened the door to their room, the smell of mildew covered with a thin veneer of disinfectant rolled out to meet him, and the anxious feeling of being trapped rose up inside of him. For a moment he wanted to turn and leave, ask her to find someplace else. But he was so exhausted by everything that had happened today, he wasn't sure if he could even make it back to the car. All he wanted was to lay down, close his eyes and turn off the panicked thoughts that were still racing through his mind. He took a deep breath and walked inside.

It was worse than he'd imagined. The awful striped wallpaper, the ugly brown carpet worn thin by decades of lonely, pacing feet. As he looked around the room, a terrible feeling stirred inside him. He knew this room. He'd been here before. Twenty years ago, when he was first on the run. But that was in another state. Like the name of the town, and the name on the gravestone, it wasn't possible. *Motel rooms look the same,* he told himself.

Then he saw it—the jagged tear in the ugly wallpaper, there in the same place near the cheap digital clock. The torn place looked like the shape of a hand. Twenty years ago, he'd spent hours looking at it, afraid of what it might do if he turned out the light.

Carrie was already in bed. He locked the door, snapped off the lights so he could no longer see the awful striped walls, but the smell of rot and chemicals was still there, hovering all around him in the dark. He closed his eyes and breathed deeply, trying to put himself to sleep. To hurry the morning light when they could leave this place.

"Rob," she said, her voice in the dark startling him. It took her a long time to speak again. At first, he thought it was because she couldn't tell if he was still awake. For a moment, he thought of pretending to be asleep, but there was something in her voice that told him she wasn't going to let this go; she was going to keep going until she'd said whatever she had to say.

"I'm glad I know about Hannah now. I wish you'd told me a long time ago, but that's all done now, and I'm glad I know." She paused again, but only for a moment. "If...if there's anything else, anything you haven't told me, you can tell me about that too. It doesn't matter what it is. You can tell me. You know that don't you?"

Laying on his back, he shut his eyes tight against the dark, against the feeling rising inside his chest. He could feel her waiting.

"And if you don't want to tell me..." she continued, "Whatever it is, whatever the reason. If you don't want to tell me, if you never tell me, that's alright too. Rob? Do you know what I'm saying?"

He dug his fingers into the sheets, clutching them tightly like he was trying to stop himself from falling. After a while, he heard her sigh and roll over, and a few minutes later, her steady, even breathing.

He'd been exhausted, but now a nervous energy flooded his veins. He got up as quietly as he could and slipped into the bathroom to relieve himself. He didn't turn the light on, but even in the dark, he could see that the toilet seat was metal, like in an army barracks. Or a jail cell.

*She knows,* he thought. Or, if she doesn't yet, she's close to it.

Moving back into the bedroom, he felt too wired to go back to bed. He watched Carrie breathing long enough to make sure she was really asleep. Then he pulled on his pants and shoes and stepped outside, taking care to close the door quietly.

The night was colder now, the stars sharper and more distinct in the black sky above, and he could feel his pulse quicken to pump warmth to all the parts of his body. Somewhere a generator or an electric light was humming; the steady sound almost felt like it was coming from inside of him. It was on a night like this when he'd left, twenty years ago.

He could do it now. If he wanted to. He could get in the car and just start moving the way he had back then. Part of him was repelled by the thought, but the simple fact of it, the fact that he *could*, called to him.

He didn't have to leave, he told himself. He could just go for a drive. Just a short drive, to clear his head. He'd be back in an hour, maybe two. She didn't have to know.

He started to walk toward the car when he noticed a figure standing across the parking lot in the space between two of the buildings. It was a woman, he could tell, silhouetted by another light somewhere behind her. He kept expecting her to move, but she didn't. She was just standing there, facing in his direction. He realized she was watching him, and a cold, trapped feeling rose inside of him.

The woman slowly cocked her head to one side like a curious, hungry bird, and he knew who she was.

*What do you want?* he wanted to scream. Before he could, she was flying toward him like the ground rushing toward someone falling, her face flooding his vision, so huge that he couldn't make it out, but he knew it, like he knew the voice howling inside of him like a raging wind that nothing can stop or keep out.

*Give me back my face.*
*Give me back my name.*
*Give me back my life.*

# Little Gods
# to Live in Them

I<small>T WAS BEFORE</small> dawn when the noises started. Steady, rhythmic, so distant they were almost inaudible, but with a feeling of great pressure behind them, the way her own blood felt throbbing in her ears when she'd climbed too many stairs. Lying in bed alone in the dark, Jane pressed her fingers to her wrist to find her pulse. When she found it, she could tell that there were two separate rhythms: similar, sometimes overlapping, but not the same.

Downstairs, the noises were even louder. Pulsing, steady as a heartbeat, they rattled the dishes in her cupboard, and made the panes of glass in the window frames buzz like wasps.

Jane opened her laptop and saw that the community newsgroup was already crowded with questions. *What is that noise? Are you all hearing this? Is there construction going on somewhere? Has anyone called the police?*

When she closed her computer, the sound was still there, a steady, low-level throb, all the windows and hinges in her house humming like insects to its rhythm. The early morning light filtering through the windows seemed strangely muted, like there was something wrong with the sun.

Instantly, Jane remembered a morning when she was a young child, waking up and wondering why the house was so dark. She'd found her mother standing on a stepladder, covering the last window with a heavy wool blanket. Her mother had told her there was going to be a solar eclipse, that an eclipse was when the sun turns black in the middle of the day, and that it was very dangerous to look at it. Jane's mother reassured her that it was all perfectly natural, and that there was nothing to be afraid of. Jane did not believe it, and cried and begged her mother to make it stop. But her mother could not stop it—no one could. So, Jane hid inside her darkened house while the sky outside turned black and poisonous. When it was over and her mother had taken all the blankets and towels down from the windows, Jane asked if it would ever happen again.

*Yes,* her mother said, *but not for a long, long time.*

Jane walked into her kitchen for another cup of coffee and saw a smear of red on the polished wood floor. Casper was watching from the marble island in the middle of the kitchen, sitting up straight and staring at her with his unblinking pale green eyes.

"Shit, Casper... what did you do now?"

A mourning dove, wings askew, lay in the corner by the dishwasher, a few torn-out feathers scattered around, its beady eyes already frosted-over.

"Goddam it, Casper..." she began, then stopped. What was the point? He was an animal, doing what animals do. Bringing his prize-kill home to her. Why should she expect him to behave any differently?

Jane got the broom and swept the dove into a dustpan. Casper, still staring at her from his perch, blinked once and yawned. She could see pieces of bloody feather still inside his mouth.

Jane took the dove outside and dropped it into the garbage can, making sure the lid was on tight. Away from the rattling and buzzing noises in the house, the pounding seemed to come from everywhere at once.

"You hear it too?"

Jane turned and saw her neighbor Maddy peering over her rosebushes.

Jane nodded. "Woke me up this morning at five-thirty. Probably some kind of construction..."

"What if it's not construction?" Maddy said.

"What do you mean?"

"I don't know..." Maddy paused for a moment, peering intently at the treeline. "Like... sky quakes."

"*Sky* quakes?"

"They've been reported in India," Maddy said. "Along the Ganges River. The North Sea and Japan. New York too. In the Fingerlakes. They're like sonic booms. Always near water."

Jane kept her expression relaxed and attentive, the way she always did whenever Maddy was going on about things like crystals and auras and chakras, things Jane knew and cared nothing about.

"So, that's what you think it is? Sky quakes?"

Maddy frowned and shook her head. "Too rhythmic. And it's been going on for too long..."

Jane listened. The low, throbbing sounds she could feel in her bones were coming from somewhere behind the trees.

"Sounds to me like it's coming from the river," Jane said. "Let's go see."

Maddy's violet-colored eyes grew wide behind her huge glasses. "You mean... right now?"

"Sure," Jane said, forcing a smile she didn't feel. "No time like the present."

Maddy wouldn't come, so Jane climbed into the big white SUV and started down Route 9. She turned left onto Old Harbor Road and began the long slow drop down toward the river. The sound was definitely coming from that direction. She could tell, even with the windows rolled up. Trees crowded-in around her, thick and dark.

When she turned the corner, something huge and grey rose up in the road ahead. She slammed on the brakes and stared out the window at the thing in front of her. It was one of those concrete construction barriers, the largest she'd ever seen. At least ten feet tall, it stood grey and silent in front of her, blocking her way.

Pushing the SUV door open, she climbed out and walked up and down the length of the barrier, looking for the name of a construction company, a phone number, anything that could tell her who'd put this ugly thing in her way. But the gray wall rising in front her was blank and immoveable as a granite cliff.

When Jane got home, she threw her keys onto the kitchen counter, closed her eyes and took deep breaths to calm the pounding of her heart. When she opened her eyes, she noticed something on the ceiling above her. At first, she thought it was a spider web. Looking closer, she saw a fine web of cracks running through the plaster, cracks she knew had not been there yesterday.

The house was old, the oldest in town. Built in 1795, it satisfied her desire for stability and permanence, and she displayed the date proudly in big brass numbers over the front door when they'd first moved in. Robert had worried that people might mistake *1795* for the address. Over the years, it became a kind of joke she told at his expense, the kind that wives tell about their husbands. *Silly Robert. Silly man.* Now Robert was gone, but the house was still here. It was all she had left.

Jane listened to the distant steady pounding, anger rising in her chest. *A permit,* she thought. There had to be a permit somewhere for new construction. She opened her computer and spent a few minutes searching the town website, but there was nothing about a new construction project. If they were too lazy or stupid to update the website, she'd just have to go there and find out herself.

Jane was on her way to the town hall when she saw a large sign in the window of what had been a vacant store.

UNIVERSAL BUILDERS ASSOCIATION
COMMUNITY RELATIONS

Jane stopped to look more closely at the sign. Near the top was an abstract logo that looked like a cross between the towers and cables of a bridge and the wings of a bird in flight. No email, no website, but there was a phone number at the bottom.

Pulling out her cell phone, Jane punched in the numbers and waited. After two rings, there was a click and a warm male voice spoke.

*"Hello, Mrs. Westmore. This is Bradley Smith, Universal Builders Community Relations rep for your area…"*

"How…" she began, but the voice cut her off—she realized with a flash of annoyance that she was talking to a recording.

*"I'll be glad to meet with you in person to discuss any questions or concerns you may have. I'll text you a*

*suggested time and the address of a meeting place near you. If it's agreeable, simply reply yes, and I'll look forward to meeting you."*

The phone buzzed in her hand. Jane was startled to see it was the address of her favorite coffee shop, just two blocks away. The meeting time—twelve pm, one hour from now.

JANE KNEW THE coffee shop was busy on Saturdays, so she arrived a half-hour early. At precisely twelve o'clock, the door opened, and a tall man stepped inside. He was wearing one of those tan canvas coats with too many pockets, the kind of hunting-jacket designed for men who've never been hunting. When he saw her, his face lit up in a broad smile.

"Mrs. Westmore? Bradley Smith." It was the same warm, smooth voice she recognized from the phone message. He extended his hand, and she took it. His grip was cool and firm.

"You…" she said, releasing his hand. "You're with Universal Builders?"

"Community relations," he smiled. "I'm like the unarmed emissary they send out front with a white flag. Pleased to meet you. May I sit?"

She didn't like his joke. It was inappropriate and made her think of invading armies. "So," she began, "Your company is doing some kind of major construction by the river?"

"You mean the bridge."

"What bridge? I haven't heard anything about a new bridge."

"Well, they put a lot of effort into keeping it quiet. Looks like it worked," he smiled. Again, his attempt at humor riled her.

"Why haven't I heard about this? Why all the secrecy?"

"Well," he smiled apologetically, "I'm not really part of all that. Basically, my understanding is that it's some kind of Homeland Security thing. Any major public work like this, especially where transportation is involved, nowadays they prefer not to spread the word too far and wide. It's just a whole different world we live in now, unfortunately."

She looked closely at this man sitting across from her with his long legs stretched out casually in front of him. The skin on his face was tight and tanned with wrinkles around his eyes when he smiled. It was the kind of face you get on ski slopes and sail boats, she thought. His jeans were faded, but his Italian loafers with their gold buckles and soft blood-red leather were the kind that cost a fortune.

"So, that noise I've been hearing," she said. "That pounding..."

"The pile drivers," the man nodded.

"It woke me up this morning. It rattles the dishes in my kitchen. And this..." She pulled out her cell phone and opened it to the photos she'd taken. "Those cracks. They appeared in my ceiling this morning."

The man stared intently at the photos for a few moments, a concerned frown on his brow. "Can you send me these?" he asked, handing her phone back to her.

"Then what?"

"I can have someone come to your house and survey the damage—"

"You mean you send someone who tells me what it's going to cost, then I have someone else look at it who tells me it's going to cost five times what your guy says. Meanwhile, you keep hammering those big holes in the ground and destroying people's homes..." Jane was horrified to feel tears rise into her eyes and turned away to quickly wipe them away. When the man spoke again, his voice was low and gentle.

"No one's out to destroy people's homes, Mrs. Westmore. Why don't you let me talk to my people. Then we'll take it from there."

ON HER WAY home, Jane was embarrassed and furious with herself for crying in front of the man. All those lies about women using their tears to control men—they were meant to make women seem weak. Besides, it wasn't weakness that had made her cry. It was the frustration of losing control, of being outmatched by something bigger and more powerful than herself.

When Jane pulled up to her house, she saw Maddy kneeling on the ground by the side of the road, laboring over a small wooden structure, the size and shape of a child's doll-house.

"What's that?"

Maddy glanced up at Jane. Her eyes, behind her huge black glasses, were startled, then cautious. "Just something I've been working on..."

"Is that a dollhouse for your grandkids?"

Maddy went back to work, leveling the ground under the little house with a garden trowel. "No. It's a hokora."

"A what?"

"A hokora. A Shinto shrine."

Jane knew Shinto was some kind of Japanese folk religion. She examined the structure more closely. It was made of plywood that Maddy had obviously painted by hand in bright colors. It did not, in Jane's opinion, look very Japanese at all.

"What's it supposed to be for?

"People in Japan have been building them for thousands of years," Maddy said, still digging and smoothing with her trowel. "For spirits to live in. Spirits and gods. *Little houses by the side of the road, with little gods to live in them.*"

"So," Jane said, "Is it supposed to protect you or something?"

Maddy kept working and didn't look up when she answered. "Maybe."

Jane watched Maddy working on the little shrine for another moment, then went back to her house and poured herself a glass of wine. As she took her first sip, she glanced out the window and saw Maddy still working in the dirt. She wondered if Maddy knew how foolish she looked, a grown woman on her knees building a home for invisible spirits. She remembered the "prayer wheel" Maddy had made for her when Robert had first gotten sick. Jane had hung the ugly thing on her kitchen wall, so Maddy would see it when she dropped by for coffee. When Robert died, Jane took it down and threw it in the trash, the way she did with other things didn't work.

In the morning, Jane found a thin layer of white dust on the kitchen floor. She glared at the cracks spreading in the ceiling above her, worse than yesterday.

Grabbing her cell phone, Jane called the number she'd called before. There was a click on the line, then that warm male voice that she recognized.

"Mrs. Westmore. What can I do for you?"

"Those cracks. The ones in my ceiling. They're worse now. They're spreading."

"Are you home right now?"

"Yes. You told me you'd send someone…"

Casper suddenly went stiff and stared wildly at the door, his green eyes flaring wide. Then he exploded into motion, running for the rear of the house, claws scrambling madly on the wooden floor. That's when Jane heard a soft knocking. Realizing it was coming from the front door, she walked over and opened it.

Bradley Smith smiled down at her with his perfect white teeth. Her brain stopped working for a moment.

"Sorry to startle you," he said. "I was actually on your street, just coming up from the site when you called. May I come in?"

"Yes. Yes, of course..." She moved aside to let him enter. She knew she was staring at him but couldn't seem to stop. He stepped carefully over her threshold, looking around appreciatively. Inside her house, he looked even taller. She led him back to the kitchen and pointed to the cracks in the ceiling.

"They've been spreading," she said. She pulled out her cell phone, opened the first photo she'd taken two days ago, and handed it to him. "Look."

He peered at the photo and then at the cracks in the plaster. "Yes, yes, I see." She watched him run his fingers along the thin cracks in the ceiling in a gesture she thought looked oddly tender. "You certainly have a beautiful home, Mrs. Westmore," he said. "I can see why you love it so much."

"So," she said, crossing her arms and making her voice as firm as she could. "What are you going to do about this?"

"Actually," he said, "I was wondering if I could ask you for a favor..."

"What do you mean?" she said uncertainly.

"I've been doing this job for a long time. And one thing I've learned is that people tend not to trust strangers. They're afraid of new things. But people here know you.

They trust you. They respect you. So, I was hoping that you might be willing to help with that. Be my eyes and ears in this community. Find out what people are thinking, what they're saying. Any questions or concerns they might have—"

"It sounds like you're asking me to spy on people."

He threw back his head and laughed. "I guess it does sound like that, doesn't it? Technically, it won't be spying because they'll know you're talking to me. You'll be their voice. The voice of the community. And I'm sure that the people I work for will be willing to offer you... certain valuable considerations."

Jane looked again at the cracks in her ceiling. She had always been good at finding the right people. Building relationships, forging connections. It was how things got done.

"Alright," she said.

Bradley Smith's grin grew even wider. "Thank you, Mrs. Westmore," he said. "I'm very grateful. You won't be sorry."

THAT EVENING, AFTER she'd fed Casper, Jane poured herself a glass of wine, stepped out into her back yard, and listened. There was no infernal pounding noise, only the screaming of the tree frogs. She stood there awhile, watching the light drain from the sky. She felt the pang in her heart briefly before recognizing what it was. Happy hour. The hour she'd always shared with Robert was when they'd both stood outside like this with their first glasses of wine, listening to the frogs, watching the night come on.

A hand touched her arm, and she nearly dropped her drink. She turned and saw Maddy's eyes, wide and startled, staring up at her from behind her big glasses.

"Can you hear that?" Maddy said.

"Hear what?"

"That screaming."

Jane listened. "That's just the tree frogs."

"No," Maddy insisted, her hand still on Jane's arm. "Listen..."

Jane listened harder. At first, all she could hear was the tree frogs' usual high-pitched scratchy squeal. Then she heard something behind the noise, or inside of it, a wave of sound, darker and more full-throated, nearly human.

"You know what that is?" Maddy said in her urgent whisper. "It's *people*."

Jane listened. Then she heard it. Many voices, hundreds of them. One long, furious wail of grief and rage.

By 6:30 on Wednesday, her house was filled with people, some of whom she'd never met before, others she'd known for years. Their anxious voices filled the air, sometimes talking over each other so that Jane had to raise her voice and remind them to take their turn.

"Carol Godfrey told me they're going to start tearing down houses," Debra Simpson said.

"They can't do that," another voice spoke up.

"Yes, they can," Eileen Benedict said. "Eminent domain. Look it up. They do it all the time."

"Does anyone even know who these people are?" Debra asked. "Nobody's talked with them."

"I have," Jane said, feeling the warm blood rush to her face. The frantic voices all around her fell silent. Faces turned toward her. It was Eileen Benedict who broke the silence.

"*You* have." Her voice was level and flat and sounded more like an accusation than a question.

"Yes. Community Relations. I got in touch with them two days ago."

A tidal wave of voices rose up, and dozens of questions were hurled at her. Through it all, Jane was aware of Eileen silently glaring at her. When the other voices subsided for a moment, Eileen spoke.

"And just how long did you plan to keep this to yourself?"

"What do you mean?" Jane said icily. "I just told you, didn't I?"

Jane turned to the other faces filling her living room and explained that Universal Builders was building a new bridge and had agreed to pay for any damages related to the project. Another surge of questions rose. She did her best to address them, relishing this new feeling of power, while sensing Eileen's harsh, cold stare.

THIS TIME, A sharp tapping noise woke Jane. As soon as she entered the kitchen, she could hear the sound coming from outside. She peered out the front door and saw a figure kneeling at the edge of the road in front of her house. Pulling her bathrobe closer around her against the chill, Jane walked toward the figure and the steady tapping.

"Maddy," Jane spoke in a harsh whisper, "what are you doing?"

Jane could now see Maddy nailing a roof onto one of those tiny wooden houses, just like the one she'd shown Jane in front of her house. What had she called it? A hokora. A home for the gods.

"Is that…" Jane started, then paused, unsure how to ask what she was wondering. "Is that for me?" Maddy nodded and kept tapping. "Is that… is that supposed to *protect* me or something?"

Maddy leaned back, apparently finished. She turned and looked up. For a moment, Jane could see the moon reflected in her glasses. Maddy spoke so softly that Jane had to strain to hear.

"I'm worried about you, Jane," Maddy said. "You think you know things. You're always so sure of yourself." For a moment, Jane thought she could see tears behind Maddy's thick glasses. "But you can't always know everything. I know you want to. But you just can't."

Jane was still trying to think of what to say when Maddy stood up, wiped her hands on her jeans, and then walked back into her house, closing the door behind her. Jane stood looking down at the little wooden house, wondering what Maddy was trying to protect her from.

BRADLEY SMITH WAS waiting for her in the back of the coffee shop. He sat across from her, fingers folded on top of his chest, looking at her expectantly.

"So," he asked. "How did the meeting go?"

"Well," Jane said, "Some of them were pretty agitated."

"Why?"

"They're afraid you're going to start tearing down houses."

"What did you tell them?"

She studied his face. It was unreadable as a mask. "Are you?"

"Am I what?"

"Are you going to start tearing down people's houses?"

She searched his face for some lurking trace of evil, some hint of deception, but could find none. His smile was as harmless and bland as the smile of a child's doll. Then she remembered Eileen Benedict's hateful stare.

"Something's bothering you," he said.

"Oh, it's just… It's just this woman. Eileen Benedict." Jane couldn't contain a shiver of anger.

"You don't like her," he said.

"Let's just say she can be… difficult."

"In what way?"

"She…" *Why should I be telling him this?* Jane thought. Then it came out, all the anger and frustration. "She keeps questioning every move I make, accusing me of things. It's like I'm always on trial with her."

"And that's very frustrating for you."

"Yes. Yes, it is." She felt embarrassed at how quickly the anger rose up. "She undercuts everything I do. She practically accused me of being a liar. In my own house…" She noticed him staring at her intently. His blue eyes suddenly now looked green, the same color as Casper's eyes.

"I'm sorry to hear that," he said. "She shouldn't be trying to interfere with you like that. Not when you're trying to do something positive for the community…"

A darkness she'd not seen before had fallen over his face—then it was gone, and he was smiling again. "When are you going to be meeting with them again?"

"Tonight. At seven-thirty."

"Good. When you do, I want you to tell them something for me. Tell them they have nothing to be afraid of."

She wanted to ask what he meant by that, what good he thought it would do, but when she looked into his calm, earnest face, she felt her doubts falter.

"Just tell them that," he said. "You can say I told you. They have nothing to be afraid of."


WHEN JANE GOT home, she went around tidying up the house, getting ready for the meeting. As she went into the kitchen to start the coffee, she saw a fresh smear of blood on the tile floor. Casper. Damn it. It was just like him to drag something in when she was trying to clean up. She saw him watching her from on top of the kitchen cabinet, his wide eyes following her every move.

"Alright," she said, "Where is it?" Casper blinked once and kept watching her.

When she found what Casper had brought in, lying halfway under the refrigerator, a strangled sound rose up in her throat. It was a human finger, the nail perfectly manicured and painted bright pink.

The doorbell rang. Jane kicked the ghastly thing under the refrigerator without thinking, and then ran to the sink. She clutched the countertop as she gagged, but nothing came up. The doorbell sounded again. Breathing faster, she ran some water over a paper towel, dropped to her knees, and wiped up the smear of red. She hurried to answer the doorbell after it rang again, only pausing to check herself in front of the hall mirror. Her face looked a ghastly shade of white.

Jane took a deep breath and opened the door. Debra Simpson and Marlene Parsons stared at her, their faces filling with alarm.

"Jane, are you okay?"

"Yes, yes, yes." the words poured out of her mouth. "Just a little... Come in. Come in." She led them into the living room, her mind still reeling.

"Jane," Debra said, "Are you sure you're okay?"

"Yes, yes. It's just... I just have to check on something."

Jane ran to the kitchen, dropped to her knees by the refrigerator, and looked under it. Peering into the haze of dust and cat hair, she saw something. Grabbing a wooden spoon from the counter, she bent down, her stomach twisting, and scraped the thing out into the open. She stared at it, exposed to the kitchen light, trying to understand what she was seeing. It was a carrot, shriveled and dry. She pressed her fists into her eyes, then looked again, but it did not change back to the thing she knew she'd seen a moment before.

The rest of the evening was a blur. Faces filled her living room again; angry, frightened faces. Throughout it all, Jane was aware of one face that wasn't there. Eileen Benedict's. A few times while Jane was speaking in front of the crowd, she thought she saw Eileen in the corner of her eye, watching her with that same silent, judgmental stare, but when she turned to look, it was someone else.

"Jane? Jane..." Someone was calling her name. It was Debra, looking at her with a trace of the same concerned expression that she greeted her with at the door. "Did you speak with him again?"

"Did I... speak with who?"

"That man. The man from Universal Builders. Did you ask him about what's going to happen?"

Jane thought of the thing under her refrigerator and the bright pink fingernail she knew she'd seen.

"Jane," Debra said again, "What did he say?"

"He said..." Jane closed her eyes and swallowed, took another deep breath, then spoke again. "He said we have nothing to be afraid of." She looked at all the disbelieving faces staring up at her, then said it again. "He says we have nothing to be afraid of."


AFTER EVERYONE HAD gone, Jane finished the last of a bottle of white wine, then opened another. She couldn't get the image of what she'd found on the kitchen floor out of her head. Or the empty chair where Eileen Benedict should have been.

Sensing she was being watched, Jane was startled to see a figure standing close by in the dark. "Jesus Christ, Maddy," she said, "Don't sneak up on me like that! I thought you'd gone home."

"I just…" Maddy paused for a moment. "I just wanted to make sure you were alright."

"Yes, I'm alright. Why shouldn't I be?"

"Jane," Maddy said after a long silence. "Are you afraid?"

*Of course, I am,* she thought. *Of course, I'm afraid. Aren't you?* Instead, she said, "No. Why should I be?"

"I don't know… It's just… it's what that man said. That we don't have anything to be afraid of. People don't usually say that unless there really is something to be afraid of, don't they?"

Jane felt fear rise in her throat, quickly turning to anger. "Are you trying to scare me? Is that what you're trying to do? Because if that's what you're trying to do, you can just fuck off right now."

Jane leaped up and left Maddy staring at her with her mouth open, a hurt look on her face.

Inside her house, she picked up the phone and called Eileen's number, wondering how she could possibly explain why she was calling. The phone rang once. There was a strange rhythmic pulsing on the other end and a high-pitched howling that sounded almost human. Jane dropped the phone and stared at it, half-expecting to see it breathe or crawl away. Then she snatched up her car keys and headed out the door. Whatever was going on, she was going to see it for herself.

Jane stumbled over something on her way to the driveway and almost fell. It was the *hokura*, the little wooden house Maddy had made for her. Anger flared inside, and she kicked the stupid thing, knocking it over on its side.

"No!" Maddy called out. "Jane, no!" She saw Maddy staring at her in horror, her hands clasped over her mouth, eyes wide with fright.

*Fuck you,* Jane thought as she kicked the thing at her feet again and again. *Fuck you and your crystals and your prayer wheels and your stupid little shrines.* She raised her foot and stomped on the little house again and again until it lay in little pieces. Then she climbed into the SUV and drove away, tires squealing on the asphalt.

Jane didn't realize how drunk she was until she found herself struggling to keep the vehicle going in a straight line. She knew Eileen Benedict lived just a few blocks away. Squinting her eyes, she rolled down the window, letting the cold air in her face start to wake her up.

When she came to the place where Eileen's house should have been, Jane slowed down and stopped in the middle of the road, trying to understand what she was seeing. There had been holes in her vision after cataract surgery, bright, angular places where the light bent in strange, unexpected ways and hid things from her—that was what she saw now in the place where Eileen's house should have been, a fragmentation of the light. But this time, she knew it wasn't happening inside her eyes; it was happening out there in front of her. A shifting rupture-like absence in the world.

The sun was starting to break over the trees as Jane drove fast toward the river. The pounding and shrieking were louder than ever. When the gray concrete barrier rose in front of her, she slammed on the brakes, pushed the door open, and climbed down. The thing in the road was too high, so she plunged into the trees, looking for a way around it. The thudding noise was deafening now, almost pushing her backward with each concussion, but she kept going. Whatever it was, she was going to see it. She scrambled downhill toward the river, scraping her hands on the rocks and briars while the terrible sound grew closer. When she finally broke through the trees into the open, her eyes strained to take in what she was seeing.

The thing in front of her reared from the shore in a massive arc, as wide as the river itself. But instead of bending toward the other side, it kept reaching higher and higher until it seemed to break through the sky, hiding itself behind the gray cloud layer above. One moment it appeared to be made of metal, then of glass, then of light, then all three, breaking apart and coming together like sun-glare shimmering on the surface of the water. As she looked up, shielding her eyes against the blinding light, she saw that it was alive or that something alive was joining itself to this colossal thing that broke the sky. Hundreds of wraith-like shapes rose like the bacteria she sometimes saw swimming across her eyeballs. They were all screaming, although whether they were screams of agony or screams of joy, she couldn't tell.

Jane closed her eyes to shut out the sight. When she opened them again, she found herself in the coffee shop. All the tables and chairs were empty. No one was behind the counter, but she could hear the machines making their familiar ticking and hissing sounds.

The figure of a man stood in the back, silhouetted by light from the window behind him, waiting patiently for her. She walked closer to him.

"What..." her voice caught in her throat. "What *is* it?"

"I told you," he said, his lean, impassive face half-hidden in shadow. "It's a bridge."

"Those… things. Those things, in the air, screaming. What are they?"

"I like to think of them as travelers," he said. "It might help you to think of them that way too."

The light coming through the window was turning dim and strange. Something was passing in front of the sun. *Don't look*, her mother had warned her. *Whatever you do, don't look.* The thing that was not supposed to happen for a long, long time—it was happening now.

"Please," she said, "Make it stop. Please."

He smiled down at her, a gentle, sad smile. "I'm sorry. I can't do that. I'm afraid it's out of my hands."

Jane felt the tears running down her face. This time, she didn't try to hide them or wipe them away. "Please. Please. Make it stop." She kept saying it long after she knew it was no use.

She looked up into his face, which was neither young nor old, and saw it flicker. For a moment, she could see Robert's face. Then the eyes became a familiar emerald green like Casper's, the long pupils widening to take her in. She heard him say other things, things she'd been told a long time ago. That it was not as bad as it seemed. That it was all perfectly natural. And that there was nothing for her to be afraid of. Nothing at all.

# The Devil Will
# Be at the Door

I ALWAYS WANTED TO believe in ghost stories. It was easy to do, growing up in the church. On my knees every Sunday, I'd close my eyes and reach out to the invisible world. The invisible world never spoke back, but I knew it was there. As Saint Paul said, *We fix our eyes not on what is seen, but on what is unseen.* It was the unseen world that I was drawn to. The stories of ghosts and monsters that I loved were not so different from the stories I heard in church every week—miracles and curses, blood sacrifice, even the dead being raised up. It was all the story of an unseen power and the promise that one day I could become part of that story.

There was one story that my father used to tell that was unlike all the others. He'd tell it on the long bus ride home from church-school trips to the cathedral in Louisville, where we brought our Lent offerings. About an hour into the trip, when the bus was in that dark stretch of two-lane highway about halfway home, my father would rise from his seat, walk to the middle of the bus, and hold onto the luggage rack with one hand to steady himself. Then, he'd begin to tell a story about a group of friends and a haunted house. One by one, the friends would dare each other to enter the haunted house alone. Then the others would go in and find their friend butchered, each time in more explicitly horrible ways. It was, quite simply, the most violent, gory story I'd ever heard. He told the same story every year, and we all came to expect it with an excitement mixed with dread and nausea. At the end of the story, all the friends are butchered like sheep, except for the last one, who knows that he too is doomed. *"I know I have to go back there. There's something there. It's waiting for me..."* Every time, my father would end the story there with a loud shout that always made us jump and scream, even though we knew it was coming.

My father never explained how the house came to be haunted or who or what was doing the killing. Or why would anyone keep returning to that house, knowing what awaited them there? That was not the point of the story. The point was the cold wave of raw-nerve horror and dread that rose and rushed through that dark bus, taking all of us with it. Listening to his warm, familiar voice turn hard and cold as an ice pick; it was hard to believe that the man telling this story was the same man who stood in the pulpit and talked about Easter morning and God's forgiveness. It seemed like someone or something else had taken his place.

About a year before my father retired, he stopped telling this story. A boy from our church had gone crazy and killed four other kids in an abandoned house they'd broken into. The details were so horrible that the police and district attorney tried to keep them out of the news, but they leaked out anyway, rumors of young bodies hacked into pieces and strewn in every room, floors awash with blood. It was horrible, and horribly familiar. The boy who'd done all that killing had been on those church trips with us and had heard my father tell his story many times—enough to memorize it, just as I had.

It was around this time when I started to notice all the mystery leaving the world. Old, abandoned houses were no longer ghostly habitations; they were rusty nails and rotten lumber, empty shells where terrible human mistakes were made. It was no longer the unseen presences they once evoked that terrified me; it was the absence of any such presence, the complete void of anything *felt* or unseen. I think I spent some time in mourning for the unseen world, for that sense of something beyond what the eye can see.

By the time I entered college, I'd decided that if there was any real mystery left in the world, it was inside the human mind. Not in sacred caves or woodland grottos. Not in churches. Certainly not in haunted houses.

Greta was at least twenty-eight when I first met her in the university cafeteria. I knew she was a graduate student from up north, and that she'd taught a few intro psych classes. There were a few white hairs in her kinky halo of black hair. When she peered down at me through her round granny-spectacles, I wondered if she could tell that I was almost ten years younger than she was.

"You like Neruda?" she said, glancing at a fat volume of poetry that I'd placed, perhaps deliberately, next to my food tray.

"Yeah," I said. "I do."

"Have you read him in the original Spanish?" I don't recall how I responded to this challenge—my Spanish was terrible—but it did start a conversation about poetry. The truth was, I was surprised and excited that she was even talking with me. I'd changed my major from English to Psychology only a month ago, and still felt like a pretentious young romantic hiding behind a long beard and a thick book of poetry. But the longer we sat and talked, for every moment that she didn't get up and walk away from me, the more I felt like part of this new and practical world.

The one area where Greta conceded that I may have known more than she did was the spiritual. She seemed very curious about the fact that I'd grown up as the son of a minister, and from time to time I'd catch her looking at me as if she was surprised that I wasn't more strait-laced or completely insane.

Greta once asked if I believed in God. "It depends on what you mean by God," I replied. It wasn't much of an answer, and Greta, typically, was not satisfied with it.

"What do *you* mean by God?"

"Well," I began, "Not an old guy with a white beard sitting on a big throne up in the sky..."

"Alright. Then what?"

"I don't know," I said. "It's just that... sometimes I feel like there's *something*. I can't describe it, but I just feel like it's *there*."

"But if you can't see it," Greta said, "and you can't describe it, how do you know it's God? How do you know it's not something else?"

"What do you mean?"

"I mean... what if it's not good? This thing that you can't see, but you know it's there... what if it's something bad?"

I didn't have an answer for that. I knew Greta didn't believe in God, but what she'd just said seemed even worse. It was one thing to believe that that universe doesn't care about us—to believe that the universe means us harm was something else entirely.

One day Greta asked if I knew Doctor Mandel. Doctor Mandel was the head of the folklore department. He was famous, among other things, for his books of traditional ghost stories he'd collected from old folks in the country. I even had a few of them that my mother had given me for Christmas over the years.

"He has a tape he wants someone in the psych department to listen to."

"What kind of tape?"

"Interviews. He interviews people. You know, collects their stories. He says a man came to him, about a week ago and wanted to talk to him. About a house he says is really haunted."

"What? Are you kidding? Was he like, messing with him or something?"

"No. Mandel says he was serious. He told him he couldn't help him, but the guy wouldn't listen. Mandel said he was kind of desperate. So, he agreed to record him. Now he wants someone from the psychology department to listen to it. He says he's concerned about the guy."

"Have you heard it?"

"Not yet. I thought maybe you might want to come with me." Greta must have known how this sounded, because she looked down for a moment, and I thought I saw her blush. "I mean, I just kind of thought it sounded like something you might be interested in."

*Of course,* I thought. After all, I was probably the only person Greta knew who believed in invisible things. It was an easy connection for her to make.

Doctor Mandel's office was in Cooper Hall, a hundred-year-old limestone building on the opposite side of the campus. The moment we walked in the door, the smell of old wood and furniture polish took my mind back to my father's church. If I'd seen candles flickering at the end of the hallway and heard the mournful rumbling of a pipe organ, I would not have been surprised.

Doctor Mandel received us politely and invited us to sit down. The sun had set, and his office was dark. As if our arrival had made him notice the darkness, he went around and turned on a couple of lamps that failed to push back most of the gloom.

"I appreciate the both of you coming," he said. "I know this is a little unusual. It's just that I wanted to hear..." he searched for the right words. "...a psychological perspective on this."

"So, there's a tape you want us to hear," Greta said, getting right to the point as usual. I'd said nothing so far. Although I was flattered that Greta had invited me to come along, I felt more than a little like an imposter.

"Yes. It's on the machine over there." Dr. Mandel nodded toward an old reel-to-reel. "It's pretty easy to operate. Just turn it off and close the door when you're through."

"You mean you're not going to stay?" Greta asked. Doctor Mandel had picked up his jacket and was moving toward the door.

"No," he said. "I've heard it." He didn't have to say, *and I don't want to hear again.* I could tell by how quickly he left and closed the door behind him.

After a moment, Greta walked over to the tape player and pushed a button. A loud hiss rose up from the speakers, then Doctor Mandel's booming voice stating the date and time of the recording. Greta adjusted the volume and returned to her chair.

The voice of a man came from the speakers. At first it was hard to tell what he was saying, his voice was so low. Greta turned up the volume. I could hear a tremble in the man's voice that he was probably trying to hide, the catch of breath in his throat.

*It was supposed to be a good day,* the man said. *I took my kids for a hike in the woods. We were only out there for about an hour when this big rainstorm hit. It came up out of nowhere.* The man paused, like he was reliving that moment, the surprise of it. *It was supposed to be a good day,* the man said again, like he was fixating on that small sense of wrongness to delay moving on to what happened next.

The rain came down fast and hard, so when they saw an old white house through the trees, they ran toward it. When they got closer, they could tell it was abandoned. There were no vehicles, and whatever driveway had been there was choked with tall grass and weeds. Kudzu vines crawled up the walls, twisting their way under loose boards and shingles, and the glass was long gone from all the windows that gaped open darkly. *We never meant to go inside,* the man said. He said it again and again. *We never meant to go inside.* The plan was to wait out the rain on the dilapidated old porch. They huddled together under the eaves, pressing close to the house to stay dry. The man described how he could feel the house at his back, how it didn't feel right, and how he eventually had to step away from it, even though it meant getting drenched in the rain—anything was better than feeling that old house pressing close against him. His kids got cold and restless. *Why can't we go inside,* his daughter kept complaining. *Because,* his son said, *It's not safe.* The daughter started teasing her brother. She told him he was scared and kept daring him to go inside. *I dare you. Go on, I dare you,* until the boy finally got angry, pulled open the rotten front door and stepped through it. Right away, the man knew something was wrong. *We should have heard something. Some kind of sounds of him walking around in there.* But there was no sound. Just the final dripping of the rain that had suddenly stopped. The daughter got nervous and asked the man why he wasn't going to look for his son.

*I wanted to go in there, but I couldn't. I tried, but it felt like my legs were frozen. She kept asking, 'Why don't you go in and look for him?' It made me angry, so I told her, 'You made him do it. You made him go in there. Go look for him yourself.' I don't know why I said that. It was like something else was talking through me. I said, 'I dare you.' She looked at me like she didn't know who I was. Then she went inside...*

At this point, there was a long silence. I was sure that the tape had run out, until I heard the scratchy sound of the man's breathing. At first, I thought he was crying, until I realized that he was struggling to breathe.

*I thought it was going to be quiet. Like when my boy went in before. But it wasn't. The sounds that came out of that house... it was like animals being skinned alive...*

When the man started talking again, he sounded exhausted, his voice stretched thinner and weaker, like he'd aged years in the telling of his story. *I don't know how I did it, but I made myself go inside. I was afraid of what I was going to see. The second I went through that door, the screaming stopped. I looked for my kids, but they weren't there. There was no blood, no footprints, nothing. It was like they were never even there...*

There was another long pause.

*Now I know... I have to go back. There's something in there. It's waiting for me...*

When the tape was over, I managed to turn my head toward Greta. I was surprised to see her head resting face down in her folded arms on the table. I said her name and she looked up, her face paler than I'd ever seen it. She'd removed her spectacles, and her eyes looked naked and defenseless.

"Are you alright?" I asked.

"I don't know..." she said, rubbing her eyes with one hand. "It's just... I don't think I've ever heard a man sound... so *afraid* before."

The office door swung open slowly. Doctor Mandel stood in the doorway, looking back and forth between the two of us. "So," he said, "It's over? You heard it all?"

I nodded. I was still finding it difficult to speak.

"So," Doctor Mandel continued. "I suppose you can see why I was so concerned."

"What about his children?" Greta asked. "Have the police been called?"

"Yes. That's just it," Doctor Mandel said, sinking wearily into his desk chair. "There aren't any."

"What do you mean?" Greta asked.

"I mean there are none. The police confirmed it," Doctor Mandel said. "He doesn't have any children."

Later over a couple of beers, Greta told me that she wanted to interview the man herself. At first, I thought she was kidding, until I saw the look on her face. She still looked a little pale, but there was a determined set to her lips that was almost grim.

"Why?" was all I could ask.

"Don't you want to?"

The truth was, I did not. Like Doctor Mandel, I'd heard all I wanted to hear. It had been fun at first, a return visit to the mysteries of the world. But the man's voice had left a kind of raw, open place in my mind, and all I wanted now was to leave it alone and let it heal.

"I don't know," I said. "I mean, he's already told his story once. Why would he agree to talk with us?"

"We could say we're following up on his first interview. You know, just a few more questions."

"Shouldn't we tell Doctor Mandel?"

"No," she said, a little too quickly, I thought. She also hadn't answered my question. *Why?* Why did she want to find and talk with this man who was obviously deeply deluded, possibly dangerous?

"How would we even find him?" I asked, still hoping it was not going to happen. Greta reached into her shirt pocket and pulled out a folded scrap of paper with a phone number hastily scrawled on it.

"It was on the tape label," she said with a slight smile that almost looked mischievous.

I don't know what Greta actually said when she made the call. The man, whose name was Bill Carson, agreed to meet us at his apartment. Greta and I arrived there just as the sun was going down. It was one of those prefab one-story brick complexes that looks like a motel, a few beat-up cars and children's bicycles scattered in the cracked asphalt parking lot.

Bill Carson was a tired-looking man who looked older than he probably was. He was still wearing an oil-stained gray jumpsuit with his last name stitched over the breast pocket from whatever job he'd just left. "You're the people who called?" he said, looking at us cautiously. "The ones from the college?"

"Yes," I said, forcing a friendly smile—so far, it wasn't a lie.

"Come in, then," he said.

I expected the inside of the apartment to be a total wreck, the furniture covered with dirty clothes and food containers. But there was no furniture. The carpet, which was a faded ugly green, was bare. The only evidence that someone lived here were a few photographs hanging from the walls in cheap drugstore frames. The curtains were drawn shut and it was already fairly dark inside. Carson made no move to turn on the lights.

"So," he said, looking back and forth between the two of us. "Are you here to help me?" The question broke my heart, and for a moment I thought about leaving.

"We'd just like to ask you a few more questions if you don't mind, Mister Carson," Greta began. "On the recording, you talk about your children—"

"Yes," I interrupted. "Tell us about your children. Please. If that's alright."

I didn't turn to see the surprised look I knew Greta was giving me, but I saw it register in Carson's face as his eyes kept moving back and forth from her to me. Finally, he gave a ragged sigh. "They were good kids. Good kids. Better than me."

I nodded and tried to look sympathetic. The truth was, I wasn't sure how I felt—I just wanted to hear how far he was going to take this.

"You know the hardest thing?" he said. "They trusted me. I led them right to that damn place, and they followed me. All the way. Right up to the door. I guess no matter how scared they were, they figured nothing bad was really gonna happen as long as their daddy was there…"

At this point, Carson stopped talking. I nodded toward the photographs on the walls. "So," I said, hesitantly, "Those are your kids there?"

Carson started like I'd woken him from a dream. He glanced where I was looking, then glared back at me. "Are you serious?" he said. "Are you fucking serious?"

I opened my mouth, but my mind had gone blank. I stood there stupidly while Carson pulled one of the framed photos from the wall, walked up and thrust it at me. When he spoke, his voice was tight with anger. "What does this look like to you?"

I glanced down and confirmed what I thought I'd seen when we entered the room. It was one of those generic, mass-produced photos of model-families that come packaged inside cheap frames.

"You think I don't know what this is?" He shook the framed piece of paper at me. "This is all I've got now. And you come here and talk to me like I'm crazy or something? Get out. Both of you. Get the hell out of here."

I took Greta by the arm and quickly walked her out of the building. I could hear the door slam behind us, but we didn't stop walking until we reached the car. We got inside and locked the doors, then sat there for a moment before I said what I'd been thinking.

"I think he's telling the truth."

"What do you mean? Telling the truth about what?"

"About his kids. When he was talking about them. I could tell. He's telling the truth."

"Well, he *thinks* he is..."

"No. I mean... he's right. It's true."

Greta stared at me like I'd gone insane. We'd both heard what Doctor Marsden said, what the police had said too—there were no children. But it didn't matter. I knew the man was telling the truth. That every word he said was true. I don't know why I was so sure, or how it was even possible. But I knew it.

Here is where you might ask why we didn't just stop at this point. Just drop it and walk away. There was no real reason for us to keep going. But I think that's why we did it. There was no reason for us to keep going, and no reason for us not to keep going. It felt like some kind of big black hole had opened when we weren't looking, and we were already falling into it.

THE ROAD WE took out of town was familiar. It was the kind of road where the new cheap brick homes become fewer and fewer, and the old dark country takes over. I'd been on many roads like it, but there was something about this one that felt familiar in a deep-down way I could feel in my guts. It felt like I was heading toward something I'd been heading toward all my life, something I could not stop from happening.

"Pull over," I said.

Greta saw my face and pulled the car over to the side of the road. I walked into the weeds and vomited.

"Are you okay?" Greta called out to me. She'd gotten out of the car and was standing next to it, looking at me apprehensively as if she was afraid to come too near.

When I could stand upright again, the sky already looked darker. We'd agreed to do what we had to do in the daylight and had started out with plenty of time to not let darkness overtake us. But now the light was almost drained from the sky. "Why is the sky so dark?" I asked. "It shouldn't be this dark."

The countryside grew starker; a few decrepit barns, then nothing but trees and empty fields. Then the shell of a rusted-out car appeared on the left side of the road, a gnarled tree growing up through the hood where the engine used to be. Next to the ruined car, the faint traces of a rutted trail. Greta slowed the car until we'd come to a full stop in the middle of the road. "This is it," she said.

"How do you know?" I asked.

"It's the way the guy described it."

We sat there, still not turning in, the engine vibrating underneath us. I felt cold inside, and wondered if I was going to be sick again.

"So," Greta said, "Are we gonna do this?"

I didn't know what she meant. We'd been acting like this was all some kind of research project, but now I wasn't sure. Why had we come here? I didn't know the answer to that question. I just felt that same heavy sense of inevitability weighing me down, crushing me. I didn't know what was going to happen. But I knew we had to see it through to the end.

Greta turned the wheel and we rolled into the trees, the car bouncing and rocking on the hard ruts in the ground. Sooner than I expected, the house came into view; first a flash of weathered white through the trees, then the empty black mouth of a window gaping at us. As the road curved around to the right, the house seemed to retreat for a moment and almost vanish, then move toward us. Greta stopped the car and we both sat in silence, looking through the windshield at the thing in front of us, neither of us making a move to get out.

And just as quickly as the fear and nausea had come over me, it went away, and I felt a twinge of impatience. It was just a house. An old, empty house with nothing in it. Nothing but rusty nails and rotten wood. I opened the car door first to show Greta that I wasn't afraid, and to prove it to myself.

We walked through the high weeds toward the house, briars scratching our arms, burrs clinging to the cuffs of our jeans. Up close, the house looked in even worse shape. Weeds and small trees reached up through the floorboards of the porch that split and sagged. The lower windows had been boarded up with plywood, but the upper windows gaped open blackly, the glass and frames long gone. As I stared up at the old house, I had the feeling that I'd seen it before, although I knew that couldn't be true. Now that I was closer to it, the familiar feeling of nausea and dread started to return.

Greta and I climbed up onto the rotten porch, the boards sagging and groaning under our feet. We stopped in front of the door that for some reason had not been boarded up. "Look at this," Greta said. "Look how all the windows are boarded-up to keep out trespassers—why would they leave the front door unguarded like that?"

The answer came to me right away, and it terrified me, so I tried to turn it into a joke, and spoke in a spooky voice, *"Maybe it's a trap..."*

"Don't," she said, her voice suddenly sharp, "It's not funny." I looked and saw that Greta was scared too, all the hard, confident light gone from her eyes.

The door gaped open, breathing its cold breath of mildew and raw earth. Neither of us moved to enter.

"Are you scared?" Greta asked. I knew she wasn't trying to accuse or humiliate me—I'd heard the note of anxiety in her voice—but the anger rose up inside of me anyway.

"You're the one who wanted to come here," I said. The rest of what I wanted to say stuck in my throat, but Greta knew what I meant. The reason we were here, and whatever was going to happen to us—it would all be her fault.

I saw a flash of anger in her eyes, then she turned her back on me and disappeared through the doorway. I hesitated, only for a moment, then went in after her.

Inside, the dank, raw smell was even stronger, like we were in a cave miles below the surface of the earth. A sickly gray light filtered from one of the shattered windows above. I half-expected for Greta to have vanished, but I found her standing just inside the doorway with her back to me. She was staring at something on the wall. I stepped closer and saw what she was looking at: big, spray-painted words on the wall, the dried paint drooling down.

GOD WANTS TO KILL US ALL.

I thought I saw Greta tremble. I put one hand on her arm, and she shook it off. "Come on," she said, making her voice sound hard and commanding again, but I knew it was an act. She was becoming less and less like the Greta I knew with every step she took inside that house.

The deeper we went into the house, the colder it got. It wasn't just the temperature—there was something in the air itself that I could feel entering through my skin and reaching my heart, a cold malignant feeing that came from the walls around me.

"Do you feel that?" Greta asked. She felt it too. I felt startled, then a wave of relief; I wasn't crazy—but that also meant it was real.

"Yes... what *is* it?"

I could hear her trying to keep her voice steady. "The power of suggestion. All those stories we've been listening to..."

We turned a corner into an empty room. It was darker because of the boarded windows, and it took a few minutes for my eyes to adjust. When they did, I saw small objects attached to the mildewed walls. I stepped closer and saw what they were: dozens of tiny nooses made of twine, nailed in a row to all four walls, surrounding us. Hanging from some of them were the corpses of small animals.

Greta spoke, her voice grim and tight. "I think we need to go now."

That was when we heard the sound. Somewhere above us, the sound of something heavy dragging itself over the rotting floorboards toward the stairs.

Then we were running, breathing hard and tripping over the trash and rotted leaves under our feet. But the room we came out into was not the one we recognized.

"Where's the door?" I said. "Jesus, where's the fucking door?"

"Wait," Greta gasped. "Wait. Listen..." I tried to quiet my breath and listened. The dragging noise from above had stopped. I looked at Greta. Her face was deathly white, but her voice was firm. "Okay, listen to me. Animals live in abandoned houses like this all the time. That's probably what we heard. An animal."

"Okay," I said. "Why can't we find the door?"

"We just got disoriented," Greta said. "Let's calm down and get our bearings. It's got to be here. Doors don't vanish..."

I watched Greta turn from one direction to another. "This way," she said. I knew it wasn't the same way we came, and she probably knew it too. I don't know how long we circled around in the dark, looking for that door.

"It's not here," I finally said.

"It's got to be."

"Greta, *it's not fucking here.*"

I could hear her breath coming faster in the dark. "Alright," she said. Those windows upstairs are open, right? We'll have to go through them and climb down."

We looked around until we found the staircase. At the stop of the stairs was a blackness thicker and more impenetrable than any I'd ever seen. I looked up into that blackness and felt that familiar cold sensation of dread deep in my guts. *Sick with fear.* I'd heard that phrase before; now I knew what it meant. *Sick with fear.*

A sudden bright flash of light burst through the holes in the ceiling and the cracks in the walls, illuminating the wretched room around us for an instant. But no thunder. Heat lightning, I thought. I was looking up the stairs at the thick blackness gathered there when the flash came again, and I saw that the blackness did not disappear with the lightning. It remained there, heavy and solid, like a living thing.

"I'm going up," Greta said. "Are you coming?" I could only shake my head. My throat had closed, and I couldn't speak. Greta stared at me. "Alright. I'll climb down and try to get the door open from the outside."

*There is no door,* I wanted to tell her. *Not anymore.* But I couldn't make myself say it.

She turned and walked up the stairs, the rotten wood groaning under her feet. The second she passed into the blackness at the top, everything fell silent again. I listened hard for the sound of Greta's feet walking on the floor above, but there was no sound. I was alone. All the cold dread in this place reached right through my skin and into my heart.

The lightning flashed, and I saw them. Silent, motionless figures, standing on the stairs above me. When the lightning flashed again, they were gone. But I could feel them waiting in the dark.

Then the screaming began. Not from just one throat, but many, until it seemed like the whole house itself was screaming. *Like animals being skinned alive.* I clutched my head in my hands and fell to the floor, screaming myself to drown out the terrible noise. When I realized that mine was the only voice still screaming, I stopped and listened.

In the darkness above, I heard something coming down the stairs. I wanted to run but I couldn't move. I lay there, curled up on the floor, hearing the uncertain shuffling steps coming closer, then stop. A voice spoke. It was Greta's voice, but horribly changed; a wet, ragged hissing noise.

*"Look what they did to me!"*

I wouldn't look. I felt a hand on my arm; it was warm and wet. *"Look what they did to me!"* the voice said again, raising in pitch to a kind of shrill hissing cry that tore into my brain. Something hot dripped onto the back of my neck.

That's when I ran. I ran with my eyes closed so I wouldn't have to see the thing that I knew was right behind me. I ran blind, colliding into walls, until I dared to open my eyes and saw an open window in front of me and leapt through it, knowing that dying when I fell to the ground would be better than what was waiting for me inside that house.

But I didn't die. Not yet anyway. Somehow, I survived that fall. Although sometimes I wish I hadn't.

Of course, I went to the police, even though I knew it would do no good. I knew they would tell me that there was no such person as Greta Hartman—I'd heard this story before. There was no use in asking them to search the house, because I knew the house would not be there. Until the next time.

I know what I have to do now. But first, I'm going to take some time and go on a long trip. I'm going to visit all the people who know me and still remember me. I won't tell them why I've come, about the things that happened and the things I've seen. Why should I make them unhappy?

I know I wasn't supposed to go into that house with Greta. One at a time—that's the way it's supposed to happen, the way it's always been. I broke the rules, but I know that doesn't mean I've gotten away with anything. It just means that it's going to be that much worse when it's my turn.

Because I know how this story ends. I've known it all my life.

# Angelmutter

You can't kidnap your own baby, can you? That was the question on Maya's mind as she steered her car through the dark over the serpentine twists and turns of 31-E.

It had all started when Kaitlyn wouldn't stop crying. Maya had tried everything, the bottle, the pacifier, picking her up and carrying her around their cramped little apartment until the muscles in her back ached. The desperation had started to rise, the one she knew would turn into anger, until she remembered the car—Kaitlyn always fell asleep in the car. So, Maya had wrapped her up in a soft blue blanket, gently lifted her into the infant carrier and brought it out to the back seat of the old Camry. She was just going to drive around the block a few times, but there were too many stop-signs, and Kaitlyn had kept squirming and complaining. So, when Maya saw the green exit sign to the highway, she took it. Soon Kaitlyn had stopped complaining, and Maya was flying along in blessed silence, feeling the steady hum of the highway in her bones.

As the lights of the town disappeared behind her, a thick and heavy darkness seemed to swallow the little car, turning the windshield in front of her into a mirror. She could see the bones of her face lit up from below by the green dashboard lights, and suddenly she was back on one of those wild rides from not so long ago, the air filled with sweet smoke, loud music, and the laughter of friends, the silver metallic taste of vodka warm in her throat. Her hand reached out automatically to turn on the radio, then she stopped, remembering Kaitlyn asleep in the back seat.

The glowing numbers on the dashboard said 11:40. She pictured Brad's red, angry face, and the feeling of peace vanished. Ever since Kaitlyn had been born, Brad had treated her like a different person, hovering over her, judging her every move. She knew that all this caution and watchfulness was not for her sake. When he'd made her quit her job at the record store so she could stay home and take care of Kaitlyn, he'd said, *You're a mother now*, and it sounded like a prison sentence.

Still, there were good moments, like those nights when Kaitlyn finally stopped crying and Maya would walk the floor, holding their two heads close together, so close that she believed she could feel Kaitlyn's brain working, feel her young thoughts blinking off and on inside her little skull like fireflies.

When Maya glanced again at the clock and saw the time, 12:00 am, she felt a pang of alarm. Brad's shift was over, and he'd be home soon. Before Kaitlyn, Brad used to stay out till 2 or 3, drinking with his friends. Now he came home early every night to check up on Kaitlyn, and on her. Had the baby been fed? How long had she slept? Why the hell did she let the baby sleep so much during the daytime?

Maya tried to explain that she was exhausted and needed to sleep, which was true. She also told Brad that she slept when the baby slept, which was not true. She meant to, but the moment she saw that soft, steady breathing take over and sweet silence fill the apartment, Maya felt a surge of energy in her veins like the one she used to feel on those nights when she and Brad would share a few lines of blow and stay up all night, talking, listening to loud music, and fucking till dawn. Now whenever she found herself alone in the late hours, awake and alive, she felt a ghost of that same rush, that same kind of trembling on the edge of something incredible just about to happen. Then Kaitlyn would wake up crying again, and that feeling of freedom would vanish.

Maya looked at the clock on the dashboard. 12:45 AM. She pictured Brad pulling into their driveway, wondering why the hell her car wasn't there, then entering the apartment and walking from room to room, calling her name. She remembered the last time he'd come home and found her gone. She'd left Kaitlyn for a few minutes to walk to the Quick Mart for a six pack. Kaitlyn had kept her on her feet all night, crying for hours, and she was damned if she was going to go without a couple of beers after all of that. So, she'd waited till Kaitlyn cried herself to sleep, then slipped out the door and walked fast along the railroad tracks to the Quick Mart. It was only a hundred yards away, not far at all, but there was a crowd at the register, stoned college kids, so it took her longer than she'd thought to pay and get out. By the time she got back to the apartment, there was Brad's old red truck parked in the gravel lot, an hour early home from work. He'd made Maya step inside the bathroom with him and shut the door before he hit her—he said it wasn't something a baby girl should see.

Maya didn't realize how far she'd gone until the sign for Smith's Grove rose up in her headlights and sped away behind her. She was in Barren County, almost seventy miles from home. What would happen if she just kept going? What would Brad do? What *could* he do? They weren't divorced, not yet. Kaitlyn was still her child. She couldn't be charged with a crime, no matter how late she stayed out or how far she drove. She could do whatever she wanted.

*You are the most selfish little bitch in the whole world.*

It was her mother's voice, cold and cutting as the edge of a knife. When Maya was seventeen, her mother had pretended to be her older sister for about a year and made Maya play along. Maya's father had left them, and her mother was afraid that new men would be frightened off by a woman with a teenage daughter. Once when Maya slipped up in public and called her *Mom*, her mother had struck her across the mouth. The man she was with had turned pale and vanished.

*See what you did?* her mother had hissed at her in that terrible voice. *You are the most selfish little bitch.*

A wave of nausea and exhaustion washed through her and the road in front of her went black for a moment. Quickly, Maya pulled the car over to the side of the road and sat there, taking deep, shaky breaths, the engine idling under her. How far from home was she? How many nights since she'd slept? The scene in front of her, the long grey road and the black trees on either side, flickered like a lightbulb that was about to go out. She would never make it back home this way.

Digging deep into her purse, she dragged out the plastic baggie with five or six black capsules rattling inside, took one out and broke it open. She shook the white powder onto the back of her left hand, lifted it to her nose and inhaled it fast, feeling the bitter burn trickle down the back of her throat, then the rush of power that seemed to rise up from the soles of her feet all the way up to her brain. Black beauties. She'd found them in a drawer a few months ago, souvenirs from another life. Everyone else took what they needed. Why shouldn't she? Didn't she deserve that?

A choked cry from the backseat drove her heart into her throat. Maya twisted around and saw Kaitlyn writhing fitfully in the infant car seat, her tiny fists balled up. *"Shit,"* Maya hissed. Why hadn't she brought a pacifier or a bottle of formula?

*You wouldn't need a bottle,* Brad had told her, if she would only do *what comes naturally.* Maya had tried *what comes naturally* and had hated it. That pinching greedy mouth, her nipple cut and bruised between hard bony gums. *Never again,* she'd thought. Now, alone on a dark highway with a crying, hungry infant, she almost regretted her choice.

It was the idea of another creature, another human being *feeding* on her...there was just something inherently disgusting about it to her. More than disgusting, frightening. That was how she'd felt with that small, pinching mouth latched onto her—frightened. She knew it wasn't how a mother was supposed to feel, but she couldn't help it. Her own mother had surely never done that for her.

When Maya was eighteen, her mother had disappeared, taking the money Maya had been saving for college. Maya had fallen apart for a while after that. That was when Brad had found her. She'd sworn to him and to herself that she would never be that kind of mother. Her child deserved better.

A loud scream from the back seat brought Maya back to the present. Her first reaction was fright, followed by irritation, then guilt and a low-burning resentment. *Why can't you just go to sleep?*

Kaitlyn was screaming full throttle now, the shrillness ricocheting off the windows of the car, drilling into her ears. Maya looked at the clock—almost 2 am. She tried to judge the time it would take to get back home, but her mind wasn't working. She peered ahead through the dirty windshield, looking for a road sign or some sign of light. Service station markets sold formula, didn't they? For people like her. Of course they did.

Maya reached around to touch Kaitlyn's head. The skin under her hand was scorching hot.

Twisting around to look at the back seat, Maya felt a jolt of fear. Kaitlyn's face was burning bright red, and between her cries Maya could hear a harsh, rasping sound.

Throwing the car into drive, Maya pulled back out onto the highway, tires spitting dirt and gravel. A hospital. There had to be a hospital somewhere, an emergency room open all night. But she didn't know this part of the country, so she just kept driving deeper and deeper into the night, searching for some kind of light, while Kaitlyn's harsh cries filled her ears.

Her heart, still pounding from the black beauties, felt like it was going to explode. She could see it now, the police finding her car crumpled against a tree, or lost in the middle of a cornfield, flashlights bobbing and weaving through the darkness, stabbing through the driver's window, and finding her body slumped against the steering wheel. Would there still be a faint cry in the back seat? She could see the ruined car door being pried open, strange arms reaching in and pulling Kaitlyn free, lifting her to safety. If it was going to happen, Maya thought, let it happen like that.

When a light rose up out of the darkness ahead of her, a sob of relief burst from her throat. A low cinderblock building came into view with a single light burning at the end of a high wooden pole, two old-fashioned gas pumps rusting at the corner of a cracked asphalt lot. Maya pulled into the lot and saw that one side of the building was open: hubcaps and fenders on the rear wall, coiled rubber hoses hanging from the ceiling like black jungle vines.

Maya got out, ran to the edge of the light, and stopped. There was a man inside, huge, bearded, and shirtless, working on a large tire that he held between his knees.

"Please..." Maya said, "Is there a hospital around here? My baby... she's sick..."

The man's eyes flickered up at her face for a second, then back down at his work. Maya watched him take a swab at the end of a long wooden dowel, dip it into a bucket of thick black liquid, then rub it slowly over the inside of the tire.

"Please," Maya spoke louder, wondering if the man was deaf. "My baby is sick. She's really sick..."

Putting the tire down, the man glared at her, stood up and disappeared without a word through a small door in the back wall. A moment later, a woman with a gaunt, weathered face appeared in the doorway. She stared cautiously at Maya, unsmiling. "Where's the baby?" she asked in a flat, hard-sounding voice.

"She's in the car..." Maya said, then looked away, afraid to face the judgement in the woman's eyes. *What kind of mother leaves her sick child in the back seat of a car?*The woman said nothing but followed Maya out to her car. Maya unsnapped the car seat straps and picked Kaitlyn up. Her eyes were glazed and half-closed, and her breaths were now coming in harsh, irregular rasps.

"Please," Maya said, "Is there a doctor here? Anybody...?"

The woman stared down at Kaitlyn in Maya's arms. "Wait here," she said in the same flat voice. Then she turned and walked back through the door in the rear wall and closed it behind her.

The garage was full of the stink of oil and gasoline, so Maya stepped outside to wait in the open air. The woman was going to call somebody. A doctor, or maybe someone who knew where to find one. She wouldn't just leave her here like this. She was going to help her. She had to.

Kaitlyn was almost completely silent now, still burning hot in Maya's arms. Maya lifted her head and stared into the single light burning high above her, at the halo of bugs whirling and pinging around the white-hot bulb. How did she get here? Why was this happening to her? Her back was aching, and her arms had started to tremble. She knew she was being tested. She'd failed every test till now. She was not going to fail this one.

The light above her shrank smaller and smaller to a pinpoint and began to wink off and on. A heaviness seemed to rise from the ground through the soles of her feet and through her whole body, threatening to pull her down. She had to stay awake now. She had to.

Putting Kaitlyn back in the car seat, she dug the plastic bag out of her purse again, broke open another black capsule and sniffed the bitter white powder from the back of her hand. She held her breath and shut her eyes tight against the frightening galloping of her heart.

The sound of gravel popping and crunching under four wheels made her open her eyes to the glare of two headlights swinging toward her. When the car stopped, the driver left the headlights on, so Maya had to lift one hand over her eyes to see the small figure getting out and walking toward her out of the blinding glare. When the figure came closer, Maya could see a small woman with close-cropped gray hair. The woman wore faded blue jeans and a white cotton shirt, and peered at Maya intently through large, thick lenses.

"You the one with the baby?" the small woman said.

"Yes," Maya said, "Yes... are you a doctor?"

The small woman scowled and shook her head. "Registered nurse. Where's your baby?"

Maya led the woman to the car where Kaitlyn lay quiet in the back seat. The woman scowled disapprovingly, reached down, and touched Kaitlyn's head, and her scowl softened to a look of concern. "How long's she been like this?"

"I don't know," Maya said, "A few hours. She was fine before..."

The woman knelt beside the car, touched Kaitlyn's chest and stomach, leaned closer and put her face against Kaitlyn's to feel her breath, laid her head against her small chest for a long while. Maya stood and watched, feeling stupid and useless.

When the woman finally stood up, she sighed, then looked Maya in the eye.

"What's your name, sweetheart?"

"Maya."

"Maya, my name's Cora. Maya, your daughter has an infection. It's serious. Where's your home?"

"Owensboro..." Maya could barely get the name out.

"Owensboro..." the woman scowled, glancing back down at Kaitlyn lying still in the back seat.

"There's a hospital in Franklin..." Maya said. Cora shook her head slowly.

"That's too far. It'll take too long to get there."

Maya listened hard, trying to understand. When she realized what the woman was telling her, her whole body began to tremble. "No! Please...you've got to help her!"

The woman sighed again, her lips set grimly. "I can try to make her comfortable..."

"No!" Maya cried out, "She was fine this morning... she was fine..." Maya said it over and over again, as if the words could change what the woman was telling her, change what was happening. Then the light was growing smaller again, dwindling down to a tiny point that dimmed and flickered out.

WHEN MAYA COULD see again, she was looking up into Cora's face, so close that she could see her own face reflected and distorted in the woman's thick glasses.

"You better lie still a while," Cora said. "How long since you slept?"

"My baby... where's my baby?"

"She's right here."

Maya reached out and held onto the woman's wrist. "Please. Don't let my baby die. Please... Don't let her die."

Maya watched the older woman slowly remove her glasses and rub her eyes. She looked weary, as weary as Maya felt. She looked away into the darkness for a long time, as if she was trying to decide something. When she put her glasses back on and looked at Maya again, there was something different about her, something softer and more open.

"Do you think you can come with me somewhere right now?" the woman asked. "Do you feel strong enough to do that?"

A few minutes later, Maya was sitting in the passenger seat of Cora's car, holding Kaitlyn tightly in her lap. They drove past a few old, weathered houses that quickly disappeared behind them, and soon they were in the old, dark country again. Maya didn't ask where she was being taken; she knew somehow that she was not supposed to ask.

It was Cora who broke the silence. "How did you come here? I mean, how was it you came to be here tonight?"

"I don't know. My baby wouldn't sleep. She wouldn't stop crying. So, I just put her in the car and started driving..."

"And you ended up here." The older woman nodded to herself as if Maya had just explained something important.

Maya looked down at Kaitlyn's face. In the dim light from the dashboard, it looked drained of color, ghostly. When Maya realized she couldn't feel Kaitlyn breathing, she almost cried out, then she saw Kaitlyn's mouth twitch and saw a tremor run through her small body. When Maya could speak again, she asked, "Where are we going? I thought you said there was no hospital near here."

The older woman said nothing. They rode in silence for a while. Finally, she nodded at something outside the window.

"Here we are."

Maya looked outside and saw what looked like a huge barn door made of old gray wood and rusty metal. When they drove closer, Maya could see that the door was built right into the side of a hill, like one of those old-fashioned icehouses, although she'd never seen one this large before. There was a huge metal bolt across the door, holding it shut.

The woman turned the ignition off but didn't get out. They sat there in the terrible silence for a long time before Cora spoke.

"Maya... I have to ask you some questions. First, I need you to promise me something. You need to promise me that you'll answer them truthfully." Cora turned her gaze away from the giant door outside and looked at Maya. "Because I think maybe that's something you've had some trouble with. I mean, it's been hard for you sometimes. Am I right?"

Maya couldn't speak. She nodded once. Cora continued.

"So, it's really important for you to be honest with me now. Can you do that?"

Maya nodded again.

"Alright then," Cora said, "Do you have any people out there? I mean, people who depend on you?"

Maya thought of Brad sitting alone in their apartment, watching the clock, and getting drunker, and the hell that was waiting for her there.

"No," she said.

"No father? Or mother?"

*I don't know,* was what Maya almost said. But instead, she shook her head again.

"No."

Cora continued to study her face. Then she sighed again. "Well... come on, then." Cora got out of the car and walked around to open the passenger door. Maya got out carefully, still holding Kaitlyn in her arms.

She could see now that they were standing in a kind of circular clearing. The sky was a black bowl of stars over her head. Walls of rough-hewn rock surrounded them—a quarry. She knew then that whatever was behind that giant door hadn't been dug out of the earth, but out of solid rock.

When they were closer to the big door, Cora stopped and turned to face Maya. She laid her hand again on Kaitlyn's head, then her chest. She looked back at the big door behind them, then turned and looked into Maya's eyes.

"Maya... How strong a woman are you? Because you're going to need that now."

Maya didn't know how to answer. The older woman studied her face for a while. Then, seeming to have found whatever she was looking for, she walked over to the big door and dragged back the thick metal bolt. Maya felt a damp, chill breeze as the big door swung open. Clutching Kaitlyn closer to her chest, she followed Cora into the dark.

For a long time, Maya could see nothing. She didn't understand how the older woman could see where she was going, but she stayed close to her, following the sound of her footsteps on the rough rock floor.

Before long, the chill seemed to fade, and the air around them became warmer. A heavy animal smell she couldn't identify filled her nostrils, along with a sweet cloying scent that reminded her of funeral flowers.

Maya could hear other noises, soft shuffling and sliding sounds in the dark, and what sounded like faint, guttural animal noises echoing around her. The sounds were closer now and were coming from directly in front of her. She felt Cora's hand on her arm.

"Stop. Just stand right here."

There was a quick scratching noise, then a small bright flame sputtering to life. Maya could see Cora holding an old kerosene lantern, adjusting the flame, then holding it out in front of her where the noises were coming from.

At first Maya didn't understand what she was seeing. It came to her piece by piece—pale flesh, arms and legs, hundreds of bodies entwined and moving separately and together, twisting, and heaving gently like flotsam on the surface of the ocean, but vertical, reaching up into the darkness. It was their limbs rubbing and sliding together that made the rustling, slippery sound of skin on skin. The low animal noises she'd head before were coming from them too. Maya thought of animals feeding in a barnyard.

Cora lifted the lantern higher. Maya followed the light with her eyes. Once again, she couldn't understand what she was seeing. A large round orb the size of a boulder, glistening wet and black with a cold glint of light at its center. The orb blinked.

Maya screamed, a short, dry scream that caught in her throat. She could see the other eye now, equally huge, a jagged mouth like the entrance to a dark, wet pit. A face.

Maya felt a gush of warm liquid soaking her jeans, running down her leg. Her mouth moved to make a word she couldn't say. Cora's hand was on her shoulder now, squeezing firmly, holding her down. "It's alright," she whispered, "It's alright. She won't hurt you."

*What is it,* were the words Maya was trying to say, but all that came out was a choking sound. Cora seemed to understand and spoke in a hushed, calming voice.

"She came here a long time ago. My grandmother told me her grandmother remembered it. Said she fell from the sky. People here were all German back then... they called her Angelmutter."

A wet, ripping sound came from above, and Maya saw what looked like sheets of wet, wrinkled membrane unfolding from behind the immense thing in front of her. It took her a moment to realize that what she was seeing were wings.

"She was hurt. She came in here to die. Some people tried to help her. They brought her things, but none of them helped. Then they finally figured out what she needed..."

The hundreds of bodies clinging to the front of the thing stirred and shifted, and Maya realized why she couldn't see their faces; they were all turned inward toward the huge thing. That was when Maya recognized the wet, animal noises she couldn't identify before. They were the sound of sucking.

"She doesn't want anything from us," the older woman continued, reverently, "She's not like you and me. All she wants is to give. It's what she was made for. It's what keeps her alive."

Maya stared at the mass of naked white bodies shifting and churning like a whole colony of larvae devouring a dead bird, swarming over its breast between outspread, motionless wings.

"Who are they?" Maya finally managed to say.

"They're all the ones who need her. The sick, the dying. She won't let them die. They know that. As long as they stay here with her like this, they'll never die. That's why they're here. That's why you're here too."

Maya tore her eyes away from the sight in front of her and looked at Cora. The older woman's face was illuminated by the soft kerosene light.

"I knew it the minute I saw you," Cora said. "You need something. Something you can't find anyplace else. That's right, isn't it?"

Maya looked up at the wall of pale naked bodies in front of her. A ripple seemed to pass through them like grass moving in the wind. Maya felt her whole body begin to tremble again.

"Don't be afraid, sweetheart, just do it. Do it now."

Maya looked down at Kaitlyn's face, all the color drained from it in the dim lamplight. Then she stepped closer to the thing in front of her, the trembling in her body growing. By the time she held Kaitlyn out in front of her, lifting her up, she was shaking so hard she was afraid she might drop her. She watched, transfixed, as Kaitlyn was taken in and joined with the rest, like a single drop taken in by a deep body of water. Far above in the dark, Maya heard a long, sibilant hiss that sounded like a sigh.

From the darkness behind her, Cora spoke again. "Now you."

At first Maya didn't understand what she'd heard.

"You know it's true, don't you, sweetheart?" Cora said. "I knew it the minute I saw your face. It's your heart. You won't make it home."

Maya stood there, trying to understand what the older woman was telling her. When she did, she felt the earth fall away beneath her feet. It was true. She would never make it. She'd always known this, ever since she was born. There was a weakness inside of her that no earthly thing could repair. Not her mother, not Brad. Not even Kaitlyn. She tried to look inside herself, but the only thing there was an emptiness waiting to be filled.

Tears running down her face, Maya turned to face the wall of writhing white bodies and began to unbutton her shirt and jeans. Then she was stepping out of her clothes and climbing upward into that living tangle of arms and legs and beating hearts, trying to find her place among them, searching for what she needed to stay alive.

# That the Sea Shall Be Calm

*Our fevered nights were hung with strange new stars.*
— Spanish Mariners' Ballad

*Tell us, we pray thee, for whose cause this evil is upon us? What is thine occupation? Whence comest thou? What is thy country? And of what people art thou?*
— The Book of Jonah

**5TH MARCH.**

Our sixth day in harbor. The outbreak of cholera on shipboard has been contained, but not without the loss of five crew members, as well as the captain of our vessel. The harbor master has lifted the quarantine so that we may take on provisions and begin the search for new crew as well as a new captain.

Since it is the policy of the sponsors of our voyage that the ship's captain and chief scientist should be of equal status on shipboard, the task of securing a new captain for the remainder of our voyage falls to me. I confess that I do not feel equal to this task. Still, if we are to complete our mission on schedule, it is one that I must take on.

### 9TH MARCH.

AFTER A DIFFICULT search, I believe we have at last found a man to take command of our vessel. Captain Daniel Hawkins, like Captain Howard before him, was a member of the Royal Navy, now retired. Twice decorated for his service during the Crimean War, he is, by all accounts, a highly skilled ship's captain and a man of great bravery.

Unlike his predecessor, Captain Hawkins has no prior experience with scientific voyages such as ours, and in fact appears to have little patience with them. He has made no secret of his disapproval of the removal of all the ship's guns save one to make room for the scientific equipment necessary for our endeavor. Our vessel, like Captain Hawkins himself, once served in the Royal Navy, and I believe he regards this to be an act of wanton vandalism and a waste of a good warship.

Captain Hawkins' greatest impatience appears to be reserved for me. My quarters, for example, have been moved to the lower deck, a sure sign of his lack of respect for me. Thankfully, the mate, Mister Wilkins, acts as a go-between to convey messages between myself and our new captain, so there is little need for actual contact between us. I confess that I am glad of it.

### 12TH MARCH.

Left Port Moresby this morning after twelve days in port. Fair weather.

In addition to Captain Hawkins, we have taken aboard six new men, Germans from the colony at Port Moresby, only two of whom speak English. Sailors in general are a superstitious lot, and these men are quickly proving themselves to be no exception. They watch with great interest the flocks of birds that follow our ship, which some of them take to be the souls of dead sailors, though whether these souls of the dead are here to protect or harm us is a matter of some debate among them.

### 14TH MARCH.

Gloomy weather today, though calm seas. Signs of a storm to the southwest.

Today is the birthday of my youngest son. He will be four years old today. I was at sea when he was born and have yet to lay eyes upon him. For these four years, I have not seen any of my five children, nor my wife. I miss them greatly and am impatient for our eventual reunion.

I have but one picture of my family that I keep in my cabin. The salt and sea air have stolen in through a crack in the glass, and ghostly fingers of white mold have crept across the faces of my loved ones like the mark of some dreadful disease, so they are now almost unrecognizable to me. This, I am loathe to admit, is a kind of reflection of my own mind, where I find it difficult at times to recall the features of all five of my children or find myself unknowingly exchanging the features of one child for another.

It is in my dreams that my children are most vivid to me. It is not an entire picture that appears to me there, but fragments, small things that take on the quality of a whole life. A childish laugh, the tug of a small hand at my sleeve. The sweet scent of familiar hair and skin. These are the seeds from which a whole world grows, and when I wake in my small and musty cabin to the harsh clanging of the bell and the creak of ship's timbers all around me, it is that other world of dreams that I wish with all my heart to return to.

## 15TH MARCH.

At one o'clock we reached our next sounding station where we took a sounding of 2,800 fathoms. The trawler was lowered and recovered with a great deal of silt and undersea life which was brought to the laboratory, cleaned, and preserved. Among these were several species of Molluscoidea and Arthropoda, as well as much plant life, including Mastogloia apiculata with unusual striae.

One particularly noteworthy object we recovered from the sea floor was a small hammer with an iron head and wooden handle, remarkably well-preserved, free of barnacles and corrosion. From its condition, it is obviously some ship's tool that has lately fallen overboard and would have been lost to the depths had we not happened upon this precise spot. The odds against such a thing seem very great. I have cleaned the hammer and brought it to my cabin where it now sits on the shelf above me where I write.

## 19TH MARCH.

We have taken a stranger aboard the ship.

This morning around half-past nine o'clock, the lookout cried that he had sighted a longboat off the starboard bow, about a half a league distant. Captain Hawkins ordered Mister Wilkins to bring the ship around and make toward it. When we had trimmed the sails and come alongside the open boat, we could see there was a man inside, laying face down, no doubt in an effort to prevent the sun's rays from burning him. In this position, he had either perished or fallen unconscious. The captain sent two men down to see about him, and when they had reached the little boat, they called up that the man was indeed alive.

Two more men went down to assist, and the man was brought up onto the main deck. The stranger was dressed in a long raincoat of yellow color which I heard several of the German sailors whispering about nervously, although the cause of their excitement was unknown to me. The man's hair was long and tangled and hid his face, the matted locks so encrusted with salt that it was impossible to discern their true color. The captain ordered the man to be taken below to the medical quarters where the ship's surgeon could examine and attempt to revive him.

Around one o'clock, Mr. Wilkins reported that the man had been revived but was behaving in a strange and inexplicable manner and refusing to speak. Captain Hawkins requested that I accompany him below to question the man we had taken aboard. When we arrived, the ship's surgeon, Mister Phillips, admitted us with a drawn and distracted look.

Once inside the darkened cabin, I was startled to find the man huddled on the floor in a corner, his arms clasped around his knees which were drawn close to his chest. Although his eyes were closed, it was evident that he was awake, for every inch of his body communicated a fierce, animal alertness.

The captain approached and addressed the man who gave no reply, but I saw a slight tremor pass through his body, after which he drew his knees closer to his chest and closed his eyes even tighter. It was clear that he had indeed heard the captain. Moreover, it appeared that he was making a great effort *not* to hear. That suspicion was confirmed when the captain addressed him a second time, asking for the name of his ship, and the stranger promptly covered both ears with his hands. After several more attempts, all equally ineffective, we left the man to the care of Dr. Phillips and returned to our duties.

This man we have taken aboard is obviously suffering from some kind of madness, though whether this madness is temporary or permanent remains to be seen. Captain Hawkins said that we should change course and hand our nameless passenger over to the hospital at Manilla. But because we have lost so much valuable time in quarantine, I have requested that the captain set a course northward for Japan and the British colony at Yokohama. Captain Hawkins was reluctant, but finally agreed, on the condition that I take personal responsibility for this stranger on board our vessel.

I have also persuaded the captain to refrain from ordering the poor wretch to be kept in irons since he has done nothing thus far to prove himself a danger to the crew or to himself.

With the ship at anchor, I took the opportunity to sound for depth measurement and take samples from the ocean floor. The depth taken was 3,011 fathoms, much greater than any taken previously. We recovered with the trawler a good amount of sediment including samples of Cymbella and Amphora, as well as unusual plant life such as I had never seen before.

I must confess that when I stand alone surrounded by these many specimen jars containing the remains of things from thousands of fathoms below us, I am sometimes struck with a feeling that is very close to awe. The source of this feeling is the realization that these things would still be dwelling in their world of cold and darkness, away from sunlight and the eyes of man, were it not for my own actions. There is a kind of pride in this, but there is also another feeling that is more uncomfortable and difficult to name.

## 21ST MARCH.

Last night Captain Hawkins sent word through the mate that I was to come to his quarters at eight o'clock. Upon entering the captain's cabin, I was surprised to find a table set with a good supper of herring and potatoes which the captain encouraged me to join him in. We also shared a bottle of wine, a good Madeira from his own private stock. We spoke of small things for a while, of the weather, of ports we had visited prior to his signing on with our voyage, and the ones we had yet to visit.

At one point the captain asked what had compelled me to become a scientist, a question which startled me, since I had no notion that he had any interest in such things. I replied that the natural world had always been a source of great interest to me, since childhood, and that I wished to do my small part to add to the great store of human knowledge of the world.

The captain remarked that I spoke of knowledge as if it was a good in itself, something to be valued for its own sake. I agreed that it was indeed. It was then that the captain expressed his opinion that an excess of knowledge can be dangerous—not knowledge itself, he said, but the desire for it, an insatiable hunger for the reasons behind things, especially when no reasons can be found. The confusion upon my face must have been evident, for he then went on to provide me with an example from his own experience:

The incident Captain Hawkins related took place six years earlier when he was captain of a merchant ship bound for the Azores. On the night he described to me, he had been on the quarterdeck during the Middle Watch in calm seas, when he spied a great light on the eastern horizon. At first, he took it to be the lights of some other vessel, until it drew nearer, and he could see without doubt that this great light was coming from *beneath* the water. The look-out, who had seen it as well, began to cry out. It was only then, Hawkins said, that he was sure it was not the kind of waking dream that befalls men at sea. There was no time to turn about, and before he could give the order, the great light passed directly beneath the ship and emerged on the starboard side, then kept moving away from them toward the west until it vanished completely on the far horizon.

I received Captain Hawkins story, I must admit, with much amazement. When I asked him what he believed he had seen, he explained that he would not allow his mind to linger on the question of what the source of that mysterious light had been, its purpose or its meaning. To do so, he said, would distract his mind from its true purpose, which was the safe delivery of his vessel, its crew and cargo. To dwell overmuch on what he had seen or to seek an explanation for it would endanger both his crew and his voyage.

Had he recorded this incident in his ship's log? Certainly, that too was part of his duty. He'd made sure to record clearly and plainly what he had seen, no more and no less. The fantastical tales that the sailors told afterwards in an effort to explain what they had all witnessed, he did not see fit to include in his account, nor did he see fit to dwell much on them in his own mind. But to omit such an occurrence from the ship's log was unthinkable, and would be to him, I believe, a small act of cowardice.

"I saw what I saw," the captain said, drawing our conversation to a close, "And that, as far as I was concerned, was the end of it."

### 22ND MARCH.

This afternoon at nearly two o'clock, the ship's surgeon sent word that the man we had taken aboard had begun to speak, and that I should come to his quarters as soon as possible. I found the man in the same position as the previous day, still clutching his knees in a corner of the cabin. He still wore his bright yellow raincoat which appeared to shed its own light in the darkness of the cabin. The man's eyes were tightly shut, but the firm set of his lips and the rigidity of his posture communicated the same fierce alertness as before.

I addressed the man, introducing myself and inquired of his name. The tremor that passed through the muscles of his face told me he had heard me, so I addressed him once again. It was then that he finally spoke two words that I did not understand but recognized as German.

I asked the mate to fetch one of the German sailors to serve as translator. He explained that he had already done so, but they had refused to come. I then demanded that the mate go and compel one of the Germans to come and translate for us. A few minutes later, he brought forth one of the sailors who appeared very nervous, wringing his cap in his hands while keeping his eyes cast down. Again, I asked our mysterious passenger to tell me his name. Again, I received no reply. When I asked again, he said the same words in a louder voice. *"Halt bitte..."* I heard the sailor whispering to the mate, who informed me, "He says to you, Shut up... please."

I began to instruct the sailor as to what to say next, but before I had spoken three words, the stranger shouted in

a terrible, agitated voice, *"Halte den Mund!"* Despite the
unfamiliar word, his meaning was clear. I turned to address
the German sailor again and was startled to see that he
had completely turned his back and was standing stiffly
in the corner of the cabin like an errant child awaiting
punishment, with his face pressed against the wall.

At this point, the surgeon said he thought it best for us
to discontinue the interrogation and leave the man at peace,
at least for a brief while. As much as I was in sympathy
with the surgeon's viewpoint, I wanted to continue with
the questioning. It was my duty as a leader of the voyage.
The safety of the ship might even be at stake. These were
the arguments foremost in my mind, but in truth my brain
was ablaze with curiosity about our nameless passenger. It
was a pure and fundamental *need to know* that drove me.

I addressed the German sailor, demanding that he ask
the stranger his name, his ship, and how he came to be
alone in the water. I then turned and discovered to my
great surprise that the sailor who was still facing the wall
had begun to weep.

It was at that point, having little choice, that I agreed
to discontinue the interrogation, and left the stranger to
the surgeon's care.

### 23RD MARCH.

I HAVE CEASED TO be able to dream of my children.

It is not that I dream of other things. In truth, I dream
of the same places where they have always appeared to
me before in dreams, the same rooms at home, the same
green parks and sun-warmed beaches. But now instead of
their beautiful familiar faces, all I sense is their absence.
It is a feeling of absence so powerful and real, it is almost
a solid thing, a vacuum longing to be filled.

Last night I woke in the dark before dawn with a feeling of great pressure in my chest, and a burning desire to see the faces of my children. I struck a light and went straight to the photograph of my family, but I saw in the lamplight that the white discoloration had spread even further across their faces, obliterating them. I blew out the light and returned to my bunk and lay there sleepless till dawn.

### 29TH MARCH.

Captain Hawkins has been told of our failure to get answers from the man we have taken aboard, and that the stranger speaks only German. The captain, it seems, is fluent in that language, which is fortunate since none of the German sailors aboard will go near the man.

It was the captain who explained to me the cause of the German sailors' strange dread of our new passenger.

"Have you heard of Klabauterrmann?" he asked. I confessed that I had not. "It is a kind of spirit," the captain said, "One who hides on shipboard, unseen by the crew. His job is to protect the ship, to make repairs, ward off danger. They say he carries a hammer and wears a bright yellow raincoat. Now you know why the Germans were so frightened by this man's appearance."

"But if the task of this spirit is to protect the ship from danger," I asked, "Why were they frightened?"

"The Klabauterrmann works in secret, unseen by the crew and captain. When he is seen by a crew member..." here the captain smiled a faint and troubling kind of smile, "it means that the ship is doomed." I immediately recalled the sailor who stood weeping silently in the corner of the surgeon's cabin.

When Captain Hawkins and I entered the surgeon's quarters, we found our nameless passenger in the same attitude we had left him in, hunched in a corner of the cabin and clutching his knees to his chest. His eyes were now open and fixed on the wall opposite him, although it was obvious that he was aware of our presence.

The captain spoke a few words to the man in German, asking for his name and for the name of his ship. Again, the man gave no reply.

I asked the captain why he believed the man would not speak with us. The captain posed this question to the man in German. Again, receiving no reply, he asked again. This time the man replied in a low voice through gritted teeth.

*"Du bist nicht echt..."*

The captain frowned and appeared to ponder what the man had said. When he began to address our passenger again, the man spoke slowly and emphatically in a louder voice, biting off each word. *"Du...existierst... nicht."* At this, the man wrapped both arms around his head as if to shut out all sight and sound of us. It was clear that this interview was over.

When we had left the surgeon's quarters, I asked the captain what the man had said. "He says that we are not real," the captain informed me. "He says we do not exist."

I offered my opinion that the poor man was surely mad, the type of madness that seizes men lost at sea for long periods of time and forces them to see things that exist only in their imagination. I offered a story I had heard of a man who spent six weeks adrift, believing that his dead mother and father were in the boat with him the entire time.

The captain shook his head impatiently. "This man... he is different. He must have realized that the things he was seeing were not real. He must have understood what was happening to his own mind and decided to fight it. He is still trying to fight it now."

"He does not understand that we are real?" I asked, "or that he has been saved?"

The captain shook his head gravely. "For all he knows, he is still alone at sea, and we are phantoms that his mind has sent to torment him."

As I stood taking in the meaning of the captain's words, I saw a group of German sailors gathered on the main deck, muttering in their guttural language and casting dark glances toward us. "The story you told me, of the invisible spirit," I said, "Surely not every sailor on board believes this superstition."

"Perhaps not," the captain said. "But even among those who do not believe such a story, it still may have a strong effect. I have seen it happen before. It distracts the crew from their work. It causes mistakes, injuries, and worse. The sailors are right. The man is a danger to this ship. Not in the way they believe he is. But a danger nonetheless."

I asked the captain what he proposed. For a moment he looked as though he was about to speak, then I saw him swallow the words before they could rise through his mouth. He shook his head, peered to the northern horizon, and simply said. "We will be in Yokohama in twelve days. And that will be the end of it."

### 28TH MARCH.

Last night I was kept awake until the early hours by a strange knocking sound. It seemed at first to come from the ceiling above my bunk. It fell silent for a while. When it began again, it seemed to come from the cabin next to mine, and later from below the floor. After what must have been an hour or more of this, I became so desperate for sleep that I rose from my bunk and exited my cabin to see if I could locate the source of this sound. Standing outside on the lower deck, the sound now seemed to be coming from above, so I took it to be the sound of the rigging knocking in the wind. But this knocking was so steady and even in its rhythm, it was impossible to believe that it was not made by a human hand. I peered above me into the darkness but could only barely discern the shapes of mast and spar against the night sky. After a time, I went back to my cabin and spent a fitful night.

*10TH APRIL.*

Today is the day we expected to reach Yokohama. It is now midday, and no land is in sight.

Weather is fine and clear and visibility good, still no land can be seen in any direction. A failure of navigation is the only explanation, but an error of this severity and magnitude does not seem possible.

I would like to ask the captain what he believes is the reason for this anomaly, but he remains intent upon setting a new course and has not come down from his quarters. I believe it is best for me to leave Captain Hawkins to his task and not disturb him. God willing, we will reach Yokohama soon.

*13TH APRIL.*

The ship is now becalmed, and we have made no progress since early yesterday. The captain assures us that the wind will pick up again.

*14TH APRIL.*

This morning, with the ship still becalmed, I took the opportunity to sound for depth. I had a sounding lead lowered from the dredging platform, attached to a line of solid Indian hemp with flags marked at 25 fathom intervals, the same apparatus we have used during the entire voyage. The greatest depth we had measured previously was 3,011 fathoms. Today I watched the hemp continue to vanish beneath the water past that depth, farther and farther than I believed possible, until we had come to the full length of the hemp, 181 miles, 158,000 fathoms.

This, of course, is not possible. One explanation is that the sounding lead may be caught in some kind of powerful deep-sea current and carried laterally for many miles, thus accounting for the extraordinary measurement. Tomorrow I will sound for depth again using a heavier weight.

THIS MORNING, WE took depth measurements again as planned, attaching a much heavier weight to prevent the line from being dragged by undersea currents. Once again, we came to the full length of the hemp, 158,000 fathoms. I ordered more line to be attached and continued lowering the weight until the line had reached nearly 200,000 fathoms.

After several minutes during which I attempted to gather my thoughts, I was faced with the question of how to record this incredible finding in the logbook. Indeed, I found myself questioning whether or not I should record it at all. I then recalled the words of Captain Hawkins, *I saw what I saw,* took up the pen and wrote down the number.

### 15TH APRIL.

This morning the mate came with a grave face and informed me that all of our remaining barrels of salt pork and herring have leaked and spoiled. With the ship still becalmed, this is the most unfortunate news. The captain has been forced to reduce the crew's rations even further.

Their distress upon receiving this news was severe, and I can only imagine how it may worsen as the days pass and hunger takes hold.

### 19TH APRIL.

The lack of good meat aboard has led some men to try their hand at fishing, but with no success. So, they have taken to casting their nets into the sky rather than the sea and have managed to capture and kill four of the birds that have been following us since we left port. The report is that their meat is tough and gamey, but I will not partake of it. There is something about the cries of these birds that prevents me, although that is a reason, I will keep to myself. They are not the mewling cries of gulls, but a more harsh and doleful sound that seems at times to take on the semblance of a human voice, a semblance that has not escaped the notice of my crew. At times, it almost seems as if the creatures are attempting to force from their inhuman throats a human word, one that is unrecognizable and beyond their power to produce.

### 20TH APRIL.

Last night at two o'clock I was awakened by the same knocking sound that has plagued me for these past many nights. I could tell by the roll and pitch of the ship beneath me that the calm had finally broken and that we were now in rough waters. The knocking was louder than ever, rhythmic, steady, and insistent.

I stepped out of my cabin, determined to find the source of this sound, and was struck full in the face by rain and a wind such as we have not seen or felt for many days. The sound seemed to come from above. I looked up and was startled to see what looked like a bright yellow banner flying high above on the main mast, fluttering and snapping in the gale. A flash of lightning revealed that it was a man, our nameless passenger, now somehow two hundred feet above deck, his yellow raincoat billowing loose around him like the wings of some gigantic bird. Even from that height, I could see his arm moving in rhythm to the knocking sound and knew at once that the sound I heard now and had been hearing for days was that of a hammer. The thought that the man was out to do some damage to the ship occurred to me, along with the urge to wake and warn someone. I then saw the man pause for a moment. I could see the pale oval of his face turn down toward me. I was thankful that I could not from this distance discern his expression.

I awoke at dawn in my bunk with no memory of having returned to my cabin. I could have easily believed that the entire incident had been a dream, were it not for my nightshirt, still damp with rain.

### 21ST APRIL.

With the ship no longer becalmed, the mood among the crew is much improved. Captain Hawkins and Mr. Wilkins have again carefully plotted a course for Yokohama, having first taken care to ensure that all navigational instruments are in good working order. We should, God willing, arrive at our destination by midday tomorrow.

### 22ND APRIL.

Today at midday we reached the place where, according to the best calculations of our captain and first mate, Yokohama should have come into view. Instead, we were greeted with the sight of an empty ocean, a vast and empty expanse in all directions with no land in sight.

This time, there were no voices raised in confusion, no loud and angry debates about how such a thing could happen. Only a terrible silence that fell over the crew until it seemed that not a man on board was breathing. The only audible sounds were the creak of the ship's timbers and the snap of sails. And, of course, the strange and awkward cries of the flocks of birds that still follow us.

This peculiar silence was short-lived, for in no time at all, a contingent of the crew began to demand in loud and passionate voices that the stranger be put off the ship. The fact that there was no land in sight, as well as the man's debilitated condition meant that such an act would be tantamount to murder, which Captain Hawkins made plain in his refusal. Still, the group continued to cry out for the stranger to be brought up from the surgeon's quarters and delivered into their hands. One by one, Mr. Wilkins and two other sailors fell silently into place beside our captain, firearms and cudgels visible, and for a moment it appeared as though this confrontation would end in bloodshed.

At that moment, a great shadow fell over the entire ship, causing every man to fall silent and look upward. All eyes were focused on the strange lights that flickered and danced inside the dark belly of the massive cloud that had formed without warning over our heads.

There is only one way to report what happened next, and that is to say it as quickly and plainly as possible. Fish fell from the sky. They rained down by the hundreds in a great flashing of silver, thundering down on our deck with a sound like the beating of drums that went on for some time. The men stood by, stunned by this strange spectacle, then fell upon the fish like ravening beasts, tearing into them with their teeth while the creatures still writhed and twisted in their hands. The deck was soon covered with blood and entrails, as were the faces and hands of the men, a sight that so repelled me that I was forced to retreat to my cabin where I sit now, writing this. Still, I cannot escape the sounds of that awful feast, sounds that are more like wild dogs than men.

### 23RD APRIL.

This man we have taken from the sea believes that we are inside his mind. If this is true, could it also be that he is inside our minds as well? That he knows our thoughts, our hungers, our dreams and desires, since to him there is no boundary between his thoughts and ours? If this is true, it would mean that he has to power to destroy us, or to save us. It would mean that everything is possible.

### 24TH APRIL.

Tonight, I entered the surgeon's quarters after dark. I approached the man where he sat in the corner and withdrew from my coat pocket the object I had brought with me from my cabin, the hammer we had recovered from the ocean floor. I set the hammer down carefully on the floor in front of him. The man's eyes opened slowly, and he glanced down at the object I had set before him. Instantly his posture became straighter, and a bright light seemed to enter his eyes.

I then brought forth the second object I had brought with me, the photograph of my beloved children, obscured by the hateful fingers of white mold. Kneeling in front of the man, I held the photograph outward toward him so he could see it. My hand trembled so that I had to grasp the frame tightly in both hands to hold it steady. I then spoke the German words that I had taught myself.

*"Bitte... Denken Sie an meine Kinder... Träume von meinen Kinder."* "Please. Think about my children. Dream about my children."

The man's cold, grey eyes flickered between the photograph and my face. I set the little frame down on the floor in front of him where he could see it, and slowly backed away, repeating the words I'd learned. *"Denken Sie an meine Kinder... Träume von meinen Kinder."*

I fear that I may have done a terribly foolish thing. All that remains now is for me to wait and see what the results may be of this thing I have done.

**26TH APRIL.**

No land in sight. This is not possible. But there is no denying it.

The mood among the crew now is now very bad. I fear for what will happen when they finally get their hands on the man we have brought aboard. *You do not understand,* I wanted to tell them. *He is not here to destroy us. He is here to save us. He is the only thing that is holding us together—* though how these things are true, I cannot hope to explain.

**27TH APRIL.**

At five o'clock this morning, they came for him. I watched them drag our silent passenger up to the main deck where he stood blinking in the sunlight. The crew formed a circle around him but did not move closer, as if they were afraid to touch him. First, one broke out of the circle and moved toward the man. Then they were all upon him. I cried out for them to stop but was struck upon the head from behind and fell to my knees.

When I could look up, I saw the man standing on the rail, not looking at his attackers, but gazing over their heads as if at something only he could see. Before they could put their hands upon him, he closed his eyes, and with an expression I can only describe as beatific, spread his arms out at his sides, and fell backward, his yellow raincoat billowing around him in the wind. It seemed to take longer for him to fall than it should have. Indeed, he almost seemed to hover, and for that moment I believed that I might see him fly. But he did not fly. He did not turn into an angel or a god. He did not explain the great secrets of life and death to us. He simply fell. And where he fell, he made no sound and left no mark upon the surface of the water. It was like he had never been with us at all.

A great roar went up from the mob. It was not the sound of men rejoicing. It was the noise of animals who have tasted blood and now want more. It was then that I saw the captain standing on the quarterdeck. From his angry and disheveled appearance, I knew he had broken free from his cabin where the crew must have tried to confine him. As they began to surge toward him, the captain brought out his pistol, raised it into the air and fired a single warning shot.

The men froze where they were, their faces white with terror. But it was not terror of the captain that had halted them in their steps, for I could see their faces lifted upward in the direction where the pistol had been fired. I looked up and saw what every man on board was seeing. A great hole was opening in the sky. Like a sail with a weak spot slowly torn in two, I saw a great split opening, traveling from high above all the way down to the horizon. And behind that rift in the sky was neither heaven or hell or any other world at all. There was nothing. A kind of color that was not like any color on earth, but an absence of color, the absence of everything we recognize.

It was then that I heard the screaming of the birds, louder and more shrill than before. Their sound filled the air and seemed to be pouring through that split in the sky. I shut my eyes and covered my ears but could not shut out those terrible sounds that were mingled with the screams of the men, screams of grief and terror. I did not look up. Instead, I fled to my cabin and locked the door.

HERE I HAVE remained for what I believe may be a period of seven days and nights. I cannot be sure since there are now no more days and no more nights, only this one strange light that seems without color, without warmth or cold.

The cries of the birds, always half-human, are now fully and horribly recognizable to me—they are the screams of my own children. I knew their voices as surely as I know my own. Still, I cannot force myself to leave this cabin. I cannot bear to see what is making those terrible sounds, although I know that, in my mind, I will never stop seeing them—terrible winged things with half-finished faces, once familiar, now scarred beyond recognition by water, salt, and time.

# The Man Outside

HE SEES THE man when he goes outside to bring in the firewood. The winter air is sharp and burns when he breathes it, so he tries to hold his breath until he can make it back inside, a full load of firewood in his arms. Just a few steps from the front door, he sucks in a deep breath that sears his lungs, and now he's coughing, sucking in more icy, burning air with every breath until the edges of his vision start to turn black, and he thinks, This is what drowning must feel like.

As he struggles to open the door with one hand, he notices something moving out of the corner of his eye, some kind of dark figure far across the field, but it's too cold and he has to get inside. He manages to get the door open, a furnace-blast of light and heat, stumbles inside and drops the load of firewood that goes clattering to the floor.

Walking toward the wall to hang up his coat, he glances out the window, and that's when he sees the man walking toward the cottage over the snow. There's something strange about the man, his shape and the way he moves, a sort of lumbering hulk. For a moment he wonders if what he's seeing might not be a man at all, but some kind of animal, maybe a bear, and fear rises in his throat. The big windows and latticed glass doors that he's always loved now make him feel vulnerable. He wishes for thick stone walls and tiny windows big enough to see out, but too small to let anything in.

Now he can see that the thing moving toward him across the snow is carrying something in its arms, so it can't be an animal, but must be a man or a woman. He leans closer to the window for a better look, but his breath fogs the glass, and when he wipes it away with his sleeve, the figure is gone.

He quickly scans the dark treeline that surrounds the snow-covered field, thinking that the figure must have simply changed course and stepped into the trees. He stands watching for someone or something to emerge into the clearing, but nothing does. As he watches, it begins to snow, white flakes so large he can see their crystalline patterns. He decides that the figure he saw must be some local man, a farmhand out working late, just passing by on his way home.

Noticing the firewood scattered on the floor, he bends down and picks up one log, then another, and carries them over to the hearth. He imagines what his wife would say if she was here; that he has no business stumbling around in single-digit weather with a full load of firewood, that he is no longer a young man, that he needs to recognize that there are limits. He understands all of this, but he does not believe it.

When he feels how cold the room has become, he crumples three sheets of newspaper into balls and places them together in the hearth, then starts building a teepee-shaped structure of sticks around the newspaper. He thinks of how much he loves the complete absorption in this task, how it focuses his thoughts like a camera lens focuses sunlight down to a single point. That is why he came here, to be focused. And to be haunted.

He wonders, can you be haunted by someone who isn't dead? He hopes so. That's why he's come here to this cottage at the edge of the woods where the two of them have come so many times before. How many times? He's not sure. He's never sure when it comes to numbers, but she always is. He thinks, *she is,* not *she was,* and this is how he knows she's still alive. Little things like that, the mind choosing one word over another.

She is missing but not gone—this is what he tells himself. Between *missing* and *gone*, there is a whole world of difference. After fifty years together, he can't imagine any other kind of life now. The universe, he believes, will not allow it.

He strikes a match and gently touches the flame to the crumpled paper, careful not to topple what he's built, and watches the fire spread with a satisfying, crackling sound. It makes him feel strong and capable, like a man who can do things. The man he wishes his son could still see in him.

*Dad, why don't you let me hire someone to come in and help you? Take some of the burden off of you?*

*She's not a burden,* he wanted to say. *She's your mother.* Instead, he'd told his son not to worry, that he would take care of her, that they would take care of each other, the way they'd always done.

He thinks of how it started. A moment of forgetfulness. Searching for a misplaced word or a name. How it had taken her longer and longer to retrieve it, until she'd finally abandon the search. Then the little flashes of irritation and anger that couldn't cover the fear in her eyes.

One night when he was reading, he'd looked up and saw her standing over him. Her blank expression told him she'd lost whatever she'd come into the room to tell him. The panic in her eyes brought him to his feet, then he was holding her as tightly as he could, because he didn't know what else to do for her. "What's wrong?" he heard her say.

"Nothing," he'd said, holding her even tighter. "Nothing's wrong."

Lately, he's started dropping things. Like her favorite teapot. A beautiful antique hand-painted thing, it had belonged to her mother and to her mother's mother before that. One day when he was making tea for her, it had somehow slipped from his hands and fallen to the kitchen floor where it shattered into a dozen pieces. He fell to his knees, gathered up all the pieces and brought them to the attic where he tried to glue them all back together. It was the best he could do for her. He was halfway finished when she noticed it missing and asked where it was. He promised to look for it, but when she didn't ask again, he knew that she'd already forgotten. That was when he'd stopped trying to fix it. Every time he had to go into the attic, it seemed to stare at him accusingly from the shelf, a jagged, half-finished thing.

He realized that he no longer had to hide things from her. She hid them from herself. Or, rather, the thing that was happening inside her brain was hiding them from her. *At least she's not suffering.* That's what people said about the dead, wasn't it? *How do they know,* he wondered.

He saw her world getting smaller around her and wondered if she could feel it. He tried to give her things that might make her world feel larger, letting her cook for herself, letting her work in the garden. And when she wanted something from the store, he began letting her go out on her own. He had faith that she would return safely. Every time she reappeared at the door, holding tightly to the item she'd gone out for, he felt sure that it was his faith that had brought her home to him.

On that night when she didn't come home, he'd watched the clock as one hour went by, then another, then another, all the voices in his head clamoring louder and louder for attention. When it finally became too much for him, he'd turned the clock around to face the wall so he wouldn't have to see it.

*The first twenty-four hours are the most important.* That was what the police had said when his son finally called them. He could still hear the horror and outrage in his son's voice when he'd found out. *Oh my God, Dad, why didn't you call somebody?* His son meant well, but he didn't understand. How could he explain? If he'd called someone, especially the police, that would have made it real. It would have been exactly the same as killing her.

The room has suddenly grown cold again, and he notices that the fire has gone out. He pushes more newspaper and sticks under the blackened log, then strikes a match and eases the small white flame into the kindling, careful not to topple what he's built.

He believes that there are two different worlds, one in which something terrible has happened to her, and another in which she is fine and nothing terrible has happened. He knows that one wrong move or thought can cause him to slip from one world into the other. This is why he has come here to this quiet, faraway place, to keep his mind from slipping in the wrong direction.

He stands up, his knees aching from where they've been pressing into the brick hearth. As he turns to go into the kitchen, he glances out the window, and that is when he sees the man again, walking across the snow-covered field, closer than before. He can see now that it is definitely a man, not an animal, because of the dark winter coat with the hood. Because of the hood and the distance, he can't make out the man's face. He sees again that the man is carrying some kind of heavy bundle, but from this distance he can't tell what it is.

He checks the lock on the sliding glass door. He thinks about turning the lights out but thinks that might draw more attention. He doesn't like the thought of drawing the attention of the man outside. Or worse, waiting alone in the dark while he gets closer.

There is something familiar about the way the man outside is moving, about the way he holds himself. His coat, dark charcoal-gray and heavy with its wide, deep hood, is so much like his own that he turns to make sure it's still hanging on the wall where he left it.

When he turns back around, the man is closer, closer than he should have been in the time it took to look away and look back again. He can just make out the lower half of the man's face under the hood, a pale suggestion of a jaw. With the sharpness and clarity of a blow to the face, he knows that he will soon see these things, the man's face inside the hood and the dark burden he is carrying, because the man outside is coming here to show them to him.

He starts going around the cabin, picking things up and putting them away, as if he was preparing to receive a guest. A half-full mug of cold coffee slips from his fingers and falls clattering to the floor. Lately, he has begun dropping things. More and more, he's been startled to find things slipping from his fingers and falling to the floor. Strangely, they always seem to be objects on which he thought he had the firmest grip.

The glass door, he knows, will not keep the man out. He looks around for something and picks up one of the logs from the floor. It's still freezing cold in his hands. He grips the log as tightly as he can and makes a promise, that whatever happens, he will hold on and not let it fall.

He thinks of his wife and wonders what he would do if she was here now. He's done the best he could for her, hasn't he? And if one day, in some other world, he has to stand before her and say those same words, *I did the best I could for you*, she will say, *Yes. I know you did. I know.*

The man outside is closer than ever now, plodding steadily through the deep snow, still carrying his burden. He thinks he sees something move in the man's arms, something drifting and curling in the wind like a trace of smoke. He realizes what he's seeing is hair. Long pale hair, like hers. That's when he understands why the man has come here, across the miles, across this snowy field. To bring her to him. All his longing, all his patience, all his faith, will be rewarded here tonight.

He sees the figure stumble and struggle to stay upright in the thick snow. His heart freezes, and he sends a silent message, *Don't let her fall.*

The man has reached the back porch and is now standing right outside the sliding glass door. Fingers trembling, he unlocks the door and slides it open to the cold wind and whirling snow to receive what the man has brought him.

The man outside opens his arms and all the pieces of her fall to the floor with a sound like muted drums. They bounce and roll away as he tries to stop them, falling to his knees and trying to gather the pieces of her into his arms while a smell like rank river water fills his throat. A loud howling sound is coming from inside the man's hood. The hood falls away, and the upper half of the man's face is missing like a broken mask. Where his nose and eyes and forehead should be, there is only a jagged emptiness where the howling sound is pouring through, like a cold wind howling through a broken window, the same sound coming from deep in his own throat and through his empty mouth, while he keeps trying to gather all the pieces of her that are somehow still falling. Like the night and the snow, and all the things he can no longer hold onto, they will not stop falling.                                       .

# Where the Monsters Are Lonely

TODAY, COURTNEY'S FOURTH-GRADE teacher is taking the class on a "nature hike". I don't like school trips, but I go along anyway to be with Courtney. The teacher always tells you to pay attention to all the kids in your group, not just your own. I put on a good show of it, but after a while you end up gravitating toward your own kid, or they gravitate toward you. It's only natural.

I watch Courtney shuffling around, up to her knees in the fallen leaves, trying to keep up with the rest of the group. The teacher is pointing out all the trees and rocks and bushes, calling them by their fancy scientific names. I watch Courtney dutifully writing down all those big words, and I wonder—how many times in her life will she have the opportunity to use those words? How long will she remember them?

I hear some kids up ahead talking in excited voices. Suddenly there's a stampede of small bodies scrambling up the hill and through the trees. I follow them as best I can, grabbing onto the smaller trees to pull myself up the ridge to where the kids have all stopped and are staring down at something on the other side. I finally reach the top and see what they're all looking at. At first, I think it's a mass of tangled vines that's grown over a boulder or a fallen tree—then I realize it's manmade, hundreds of long sticks all bent and woven into a twisted, fantastical shape.

The kids start skittering down the slope, fast at first, then slower, edging closer and closer to this strange thing. Courtney is out in front, as usual, leading the pack. Then I remember.

"Stop!" I shout. "Get away from there!"

"Why?" one of the kids turns and asks.

"Because. Somebody lives in there."

Courtney doesn't stop or turn around. She just keeps walking toward the dark opening in that towering shape like there's nothing else in the world but it and her.

She's about ten feet away when a man appears. I don't see him move outward into the light. One moment the opening is dark and empty, the next moment he's there, filling it. Everything about him is unexpected. He wears a bright green suit, threadbare and faded with a white shirt under it. His hair is coarse and wild, his cheeks hollow. His eyes are green like his suit, and they blaze at me. Then at her.

"Courtney!" I shout. As soon as I do, I feel a rush of searing regret, because now he knows her name.

I rush toward Courtney to grab her and pull her away, rushing toward him too, and I find myself thinking that if he's going to take her, let him try it now while I can put my hands around his throat and stop him, stop this whole thing that I know has started. But he doesn't move. He just stands there and watches me grab her by the arm and pull her away, back up the trail and away from him, and even while I'm saving her, I can't help but think, *I'm showing him how to do it. I'm showing him how easy it is.*

On our way out of the woods, all the other kids are chattering wildly about what just happened, but Courtney is silent. She looks like she's thinking about something, trying to figure it out. Later, on the drive home, she finally asks.

"Daddy, who was that man?"

I keep my eyes on the road and try to think of what to say. All the possibilities crowd my mind and freeze in a tangled mess.

"He's just some man who lives there," I say, hoping this will be enough.

"Do you know him?"

A trapped feeling rises inside my chest. I don't want to lie to her, but what good is telling her the truth? That will only open the door to the past and a lot of things she's not old enough to understand yet.

"No," I say, trying to ignore the stab of guilt. "Why do you say that?"

"I don't know. It just looked like you knew him or something." The trapped feeling in my chest grows. She's seen far more than I realized.

"No, sweetheart," I say again. "I don't know him."

It's true. I don't know him. Not anymore. Any part of him that I might have come close to knowing years ago is gone. But his name comes back to me like someone speaking directly into my ear.

*Warren.*

I'd heard about the house made of sticks in the woods long before I saw it. Warren had always been good at making things with his hands. I remembered that from art class, strange paintings and sculptures that looked like they'd grown from the earth, graceful and twisted.

Like me, Warren had been born and raised here. We even went to the same high school. But that person is gone—I knew it the second I looked into his eyes. So, I'd pulled Courtney away from him like he was some kind of rabid animal. He's sick, I know. But it's the sick and wounded animals who do the most damage. It's only in the movies where the monsters are lonely and all they need is friendship and understanding to blossom into something beautiful.

A PICTURE RISES IN my mind, of Warren's green eyes in the rear-view mirror of my car. That was the night back in high school when we let him ride along with us because we wanted to see if what people said was true.

The story was that if you went driving with Warren, you never had to stop for any red lights because he made them all turn green. Warren was a witch, people said. *Warlock* was the right word, but most people said *witch* because it was easier to remember.

I don't remember who invited him to ride along with us that night. I think it was Rick. Girls were starting to like Warren, to say he was cute, including Rick's girlfriend, so I think Rick wanted to humiliate him and put an end to it. Everyone else was just curious to see what would happen.

To me, it seemed that Warren knew something mysterious and powerful that the rest of us didn't know. If Warren really was a witch, I wanted to be one too.

When I was eleven years old, I'd found a book about black magic in the local library. A fat, black, dusty tome, it was filled with old woodcuts of medieval witches and horned devils and pentagrams. Unlike the harmless Halloween decorations I was used to, it felt dangerous as a gun.

One illustration, a woodcut from a three-hundred-year-old book, showed a woman on her knees, pressing her lips between the cheeks of the devil's ass. That should have been funny, but it wasn't. That book scared the hell out of some of the kids in my class, including one bully who used to torment me on the playground. All I had to do was bring out that big black book and stare at him while flipping through the pages, and he'd grow pale and leave me alone. That was when I first understood how magic works—by making people believe in it.

We picked the road with the most stoplights, the one through town that was full of fast-food joints and gas stations. We counted the green lights, laughing and howling as we went through them. After the seventh or eighth one, it started to get quiet inside the car. As we kept flying through green light after green light, I looked up and saw Warren's cold green eyes in my rear-view mirror, their corners twisting into a slow smile, and I thought, *He's doing it. Jesus Christ, he's really doing it.*

We were coming up to another light—I'd lost count of how many we'd blown past—when Rick told me to stop the car. The light was green, like all the others, but Rick shouted at me to stop. When I hesitated, he reached over and stomped down on the brake himself. I cursed at him, but he wasn't listening to me—he was just staring at that green light above us. Cars were honking angrily and flying past us, but I knew Rick was going to make us sit there until that light turned red. When it finally did, he turned and sneered at Warren, "Alright, witch boy... make *that* one turn green!"

Warren said nothing. I don't think his expression even changed. When the light turned green again, some of the guys in the car started to cheer but Rick yelled at them to shut up. Then he told me to take a left and drive out to Old Frankfort Road. When I asked him where we were going, he told me to just keep driving.

Pretty soon, the lights from the stores and gas stations were far behind us. When we were about three or four miles outside of town, Rick told me to pull over. I looked out the window and saw nothing but darkness out there. I had a bad feeling, but I pulled over and left the car running.

That was when Rick told Warren to get out of the car. At first, I thought Rick was going to give Warren a beating. Warren didn't move for a couple of seconds. I saw him staring silently at Rick. Then at me. Then he slowly and deliberately opened the car door. As soon as Warren was standing on the side of the road, Rick turned to me and shouted, "Go!"

I didn't want to leave Warren in the middle of nowhere, but I was so relieved that Rick wasn't going to hurt him that I just took off. I looked in my rear-view mirror and caught a glimpse of a lone figure standing in the dark, growing smaller and smaller as it faded behind us until I couldn't see it anymore.

Someone asked how Warren was going to get back. "He's a witch, ain't he?" Rick said. "He can *fly* home."

Everyone in the car started laughing, but not me. For them, Warren was an oddity, a joke, something to laugh at. But in that moment when his eyes had met mine in the mirror, he'd seen that I believed. And because I believed, I was his. I belonged to him.

The louder the laughter and jokes became, the angrier I felt. Part of me wanted to see Warren come flying down in front of the windshield like a great dark bird with blazing green eyes to strike terror into their small, ugly hearts. I concentrated hard and imagined it, *willing* it to happen. But it didn't. The only thing I could see were the plain white lines in the middle of the road appearing in the headlights and disappearing under my wheels.

COURTNEY WANTS TO stop and get ice cream. I agree—anything to take her mind off of what just happened. We pull into the Minit Mart near our house. As soon as I open the door, the smell of gasoline fills the car. I don't know why, but the smell of gasoline always makes me feel sick. Not just nauseous, but anxious, like something bad is about to happen.

I glance down at the gas gauge and see it's almost empty. I insert my debit card and enter the code, put the nozzle in the tank, take a deep breath and squeeze the handle. As usual, I can't hold my breath long enough; when it's a quarter full, I throw the nozzle back in its place, get in the car fast and drive away. I don't notice till we pull into our driveway that I forgot to put the gas cap back on, and the smell has followed me home.

TONIGHT, I HAVE that dream again, the one where it's night and I'm running across dry grass. I can hear someone else running ahead of me in the dark, their feet pounding and scraping on the same dirt I'm running on, their breath rasping along with mine. I know I need to catch up with this person; I have to stop them. But no matter how fast I run, they stay just ahead of me in the dark, out of sight, out of reach.

I wake up with my heart pounding, and a feeling of urgency, like there's something I need to do. Something important. But I don't know what it is.

I try to get out of bed, but something is wrong—it takes me a moment to realize, I'm huddled at the foot of the bed, curled up in the fetal position, the sheets twisted around me. I untangle myself, get up and go to the kitchen to start the coffee.

While I'm waiting for the water to heat up, I think of Warren, about that night when we'd left him standing on the side of the road in the middle of nowhere. That was when I'd realized it was all bullshit. There was no magic. Warren was no wizard pulling lightning bolts down from the sky or summoning demons from the darkness. He was just some weird guy in the backseat of an old car, pretending to make stoplights turn green.

WARREN DISAPPEARED AFTER that. There were rumors that he'd transferred to another school, or that his family had moved to another town, although some doubted that Warren even had a family, and claimed that he lived under a bridge somewhere like a troll.

It wasn't until senior year that we found out where Warren was. He was living in an old ramshackle white house near the railroad tracks. I drove by it one night with Rick. The sagging front porch roof was propped up with wooden boards, and the downstairs windows were boarded over with plywood. Rick said that Warren had covered the windows so that nobody could see inside.

You'd think that Rick would have been satisfied after what he'd done to Warren, but he wasn't. For Rick, Warren's humiliation would not be complete until he'd walked back through those school doors and suffered the laughter and jeers of the crowd. Warren had cheated Rick by disappearing, and Rick could not forgive him for that.

I remember sitting parked across the street, passing a pint of Jack Daniels back and forth, and staring at that old white house.

"You know what kind of shit goes on in there?" Rick said, glaring at the boarded-up windows.

"No. What." The whiskey was working on me, and my brain could only make one-word sentences.

"Evil shit. Some seriously evil shit..."

I'd heard the rumors. A whole coven of young girls. Runaways. Warren's disciples or slaves. Some as young as eight years old. I wasn't sure where the rumors were coming from until I watched Rick getting all worked up, rolling out a long list of Warren's evil deeds. I wasn't sure if I believed them. Not all of them, anyway.

"Makes me sick..." Rick muttered, "Just thinking about what's going on in there right now..." Rick took another pull from the pint and handed it back to me. It was almost empty. "What if that was your girl in there? Or your sister? Or your daughter?"

A picture came into my mind—the illustration from that old library book, of the woman on her knees in front of the Devil.

I saw Rick bring the back of his hand up to his face and sniff loudly. His head snapped back like someone had hit him. Then he handed me half a black capsule broken open and filled with white powder, and a plastic straw cut in half. I hesitated for a moment, then shook a tiny pile of white powder onto the back of my left hand. I brought the straw to my nose and inhaled. A bright light exploded behind my eyes, then I was flying forward, riding the wave of blood rushing fast in my veins. The bitter medicine-taste of the speed hit the back of my throat. I took another drink of whiskey to wash it away.

Whatever happened after that is gone.

TODAY COURTNEY IS sad. It's one of those weekends when all of her friends are doing things with other kids or are out of town with their parents. I watch her sulking around the house, angry that her weekend has turned into a giant disappointment.

"Don't worry, sweetheart," I tell her. "We can still have lots of fun."

"It's not the same," she says bitterly, and I feel a stab right in my heart. *Am I not enough for you anymore?* That's what I want to say, but I don't. I don't want her to feel any worse than she already does. The truth is that I'm happiest when it's just the two of us. That was true before Annie left, and it's even more true now.

Of course, I'm glad that Courtney has friends—except sometimes, when it takes her away from me. I know how that sounds, but there's nothing wrong with a father wanting to spend time with his own daughter. Sometimes you have to fight for that.

I order Chinese food, Courtney's favorite. I've got a couple of old animated movies on DVD from the library, one that Courtney loves and another that I've been wanting to show her. After what happened in the woods, I want to fill her mind with something else.

We're making popcorn on the stove when my phone buzzes. It's a text from the father of one of Courtney's best friends, Sarah, inviting Courtney to go to their house on the lake for the weekend. *Sorry for the short notice,* he writes.

*Sarah would love it, and I'm sure Courtney would too.*

I stare at the words on the screen, panic and resentment rising in my chest. I glance at Courtney watching over our popcorn. *No,* I think. *You can't have her.*

I type a quick reply. '*Thanks. I'm afraid Courtney can't make it.*' I pause for a moment, then type, '*She's not feeling well. Maybe next time.*' I turn the phone off and put it in my pocket.

"Who was that, Daddy?" Courtney asks.

"Nobody, honey," I say. A wave of guilt washes through me, but I do my best to push it back. It *was* short notice. Besides, what do I know about this guy? I've never even met him. He's probably fine. But how do I know that?

Later, after the movie, a big thunderstorm rolls in, with loud ear-splitting crashes that rattle the windows. Courtney's still afraid of thunder and hides her face in my shoulder. My heart swells in my chest and I pull her close.

"Don't worry, honey," I say. "I've got you. I've got you."

After Courtney's in bed, I walk around the house, unable to settle in one place. Now that I've seen Warren, I can't shake the feeling that something has been set into motion, something necessary and inevitable.

I think of those days when I used to want what Warren had, or what I thought he had, back when he seemed mysterious and powerful. Now Warren is just the crazy man in the woods. I've never been able to cast spells or keep stoplights from turning red, but I've had a home and a family. And that's better than anything he's ever had.

ON MONDAY MORNING when Courtney is about to leave the house to meet the school bus, I quickly pull on my shoes and go with her. I catch her looking at me curiously.

She's been walking on her own for over a year and must wonder what I'm doing. That afternoon, when she steps off the school bus and sees me there waiting for her, she looks surprised at first, then I'm glad to see her smile. But the next day when I turn up to walk her home again, I see her smile wilt into a look of annoyance and embarrassment.

"Daddy," she whispers, "What are you doing?"

"Gee," I say, "Can't a guy walk his little girl home?" At the words *little girl,* I think I see her flinch. I see her cut her eyes nervously toward a small group of girls who look like they're waiting for her. She looks down at the ground, her face turning red. I'm not sure if she's angry or if she's going to cry. "What's the matter, sweetheart?" I ask.

"I want to walk home with my friends." She says it softly, but I can hear it. A surge of resentment rises inside me, but I swallow it back.

"You promise to walk with them the whole way?" I ask. She nods. "And be home by four?" She nods again. "Okay then." Like someone's fired a starter pistol, she runs to join the little group of girls on the corner. I watch them laughing and chattering and feel the same surge of anxiety and resentment. I turn away before she can see it in my face, but of course, she's not looking.


EVERY SCHOOL-DAY, STARTING at three o'clock, I think, *She's leaving school now...she's walking out of the building and getting on the bus... she's getting off the bus and walking home with her friends... now she's on our street... she's walking up the driveway... she's at the door...* Then the door opens and Courtney steps through it as if she's been waiting for her cue. Part of me believes that by picturing every step of her journey home in my mind, I've somehow actually made it happen.

It's the same thing I used to do before Annie disappeared. Whenever she walked out on me after one of our terrible fights, I used to think, *She's out there walking it off. Now the anger is fading, little by little. Now she's turning around. Now she's walking back home to me.* And it seemed to work, every time. Until it didn't.

After Courtney leaves for school, I walk around the house, checking all the doors and windows, making sure the locks are in working order. One lock on the hallway window is old and broken, so I go to the hardware store to buy a new one, then find myself buying all new locks. It takes me all day to install them. I work quickly and steadily, not stopping to eat or rest, my hands sore and my shirt damp with sweat.

After dinner, I go out to take one more tour around the house, checking the new locks I've just put in. It's dark now, and when I walk around back, away from the streetlights, I realize how dark it is, how anyone or anything could be hiding back here. I walk with my hand stretched out in front of my face, careful not to run into anything, trying to sense what's in front of me, and suddenly I'm back in my dream. I hear footsteps running ahead of me, someone breathing hard, ragged and heavy, the way I am. There's the sound of liquid sloshing to the rhythm of those running feet. Then the smell that enters my nose and cuts straight to my heart, making it clench and freeze. The smell of gasoline.

TONIGHT, WHEN COURTNEY comes through the door, I'm ready to scold her for being late. Then I see the look on her face. I've seen her look angry, but there's a hard light in her eyes I've never seen before, and it stops me cold.

"Why did you tell Sarah's father I was sick?" she says. My brain freezes for a moment, like a small animal caught in a bright light.

"What do you mean?" I hear the ridiculousness in my own words. Courtney hears it too.

"I wanted to go to the lake with her! But you told her I couldn't! Why did you *do* that?"

I try to speak but I can't. I feel all the blood drain from my brain, and for a moment I think I might black out. I take a deep breath and push the words out.

"Sweetheart, I didn't say that. That's not what I said..."

"You're a liar!" Courtney shouts at me. I can see Annie's face, the same angry accusatory stare, and the hurt behind it. *You're a liar.* Then the sound of the door slamming, just like before. The same paralysis flooding my veins. By the time I make myself walk to the door and open it, it's too late. She's gone.

I spend the next hour pacing around inside the house, my heart beating fast. *She'll be back,* I tell myself. *She's angry, but she'll get over it. She'll be back.*

I go back to Courtney's room and look around, not sure of what I'm looking for. One piece of paper on her wall catches my attention. A drawing, one of hers, a geometric tangle of thin lines, a wild and twisted shape that I recognize immediately. It's Warren's den in the woods. His *lair.*

I stare at the ugly thing, imagining Courtney's hand drawing it. I think of storybook illustrations of beautiful treehouses and underground grottos lit by torchlight and fairy dust—maybe that's what Courtney saw when she ran toward that ramshackle shelter, believing it would be like the ones in the storybooks. Then Warren had appeared, and I'd pulled her away, stopping her from entering, so that whatever was inside is still a mystery. That means it still has a hold on her. And even though I managed to pull her away, he is pulling her back.

I PARK THE CAR and walk deeper into the trees, fallen branches and dead leaves snapping and rustling under my feet. The tire iron feels heavy and solid in my hand, and it makes me feel bigger, stronger than I am, which is what I need to keep going and do what I've come here for.

When I see the stick-house, it looks taller than before, a cyclone shape of dead branches and vines woven together and unraveling. In the fading light, it almost seems alive, like something twisted and malignant seen under a microscope.

I move closer to the thing, into its shadow. I think about what I'm going to say. Any words I'd tried to assemble ahead of time seemed ridiculous. *Stay away from her. She's not yours. She's mine.* I hear how pathetic those words sound, the fear behind them. My legs feel weak, and I stumble. *Please,* I think, *Please,* and suddenly I'm in bed, curled up like a child in the dark, hiding from the light.

That's when it all comes back. Not in pieces, but all at once. Those footsteps I'm chasing in the dark. I know whose they are. I'm running across the dry grass, trying to keep up with Rick, my heart hammering in my ears from the amphetamine, the sound of gasoline sloshing in the can in Rick's hand. Some small part of my brain that hasn't been extinguished yet knows I'm supposed to stop him. Then the darkness closes over that thought like water snuffing out an ember, and from then on, I'm no longer running after him, I'm running *with* him, carried along by the current of this thing we're doing. Breathing the smell of gasoline, then the smell of smoke. Watching the flames rise over the rooftops and trees, like watching a movie. *It's not real. It's not real.*

When I open my eyes, I bend over and vomit into the grass, trying to get rid of this thing inside of me, but it's still there. The memories keep coming. The wild rumors and accusations. Warren's arrest. The charges of arson. His trial and sentencing—six years in county jail. Worst of all, the memory of lying in bed with the shades pulled down, how I lay there for days, curled up like a baby in the womb, trying to shut out the sunlight and that small, terrible voice in my head. *Say something. Do something.* Knowing I could free Warren anytime and take his place with just one word. But I couldn't. I couldn't do it. Warren was the kind of person these things were supposed to happen to, I told myself. *Not me. Not me.* Still, the urge to say something and save him kept rising inside me again and again, while I lay there in the dark and struggled to crush it, to kill it. Until finally, I did.

I look up again. The dark twisted thing is still there, looking down at me. I try to stand up, but my legs won't work. It feels like I might never stand again. I could die right here.

Then I think of Courtney.

The sun is already setting as I struggle to my feet and move toward that crooked, gaping hole. I enter and the darkness closes around me. While my eyes adjust, all the things I've been trying so hard not to see, the things I've been keeping at the back of my brain come crowding forward, flashing behind my eyelids at rapid-fire speed, until the light moves in and they fade, and I see that there is no blood-soiled dress, no bruised and broken limbs, no malevolent figure waiting in the shadows. I look around and notice there's no torn and muddy sleeping bag, no old plastic bottles filled with water, no sign at all that anything human lives here.

Then I see him. Sitting in the darkest corner, legs crossed beneath him. His green eyes fixed on mine like a wolf's, and for a moment I'm sixteen years old again, looking at his eyes in my rear view mirror. Watching him watch me.

"Where is she?" The words burst out too quickly. He stares at me. No answer. Nothing. Green eyes looking into mine. They're unreadable, like an animal's eyes. For a moment, I think he doesn't know me.

"Do you remember me?" I ask. Again, no answer. He wants to make me wait. Finally, he speaks in a low, dark voice.

"I know who you are."

Suddenly I want to weep. There are too many things going on inside of me. "Where is she?" I ask again. "Please."

He rises to his feet. I've forgotten how tall he is. He takes a step toward me. The heavy thing I've been holding slips from my hand and falls to the ground.

"I know what you want," he says. He moves around me and stands in the opening, looking back at me. "Wait here." It's a command, and a promise. Then he's gone.

I keep looking at the opening where he was a moment ago, at the trees outside and the pale light already fading. He'll be back, I know. The sun will set, the air will turn colder, and he'll need to return to this place, like any animal. I'll be here waiting for him. This thing that began so many years ago. It's going to end here.

Finally, I hear them coming. First, the sound of children's voices, raised in excitement. Then the rustle of leaves and the snapping of twigs. My body feels strange, somehow both lighter and heavier than before, but I manage to push myself up, rise to my feet and shuffle to the opening where those sounds are coming from.

That's when I see her, running down the hill toward me with several other children, her face flushed from running. When she sees me, she slows down, her eyes grow wider and lock with mine. *Don't be afraid,* I think. *I won't hurt you.*

I hear a man's voice call out, *"Courtney!"* I feel her name enter my brain and start to take root there. Then I see him come running up from behind and take her by the arm and turn her around, taking her away from me. *You can't have her. She's mine.* Those words rise in my head and then fade—I look into his eyes and see those same words aimed back at me. He smiles. That's when I understand what has just happened.

His eye's aren't green anymore—they're brown.

Like mine.

# When the Circus

DANNY HAD BEEN warned that New York would eat him alive. On his first day in the city, he'd seen pigeons eating another pigeon on the street, pulling it apart with their beaks while making those muttering, cooing sounds. He didn't want to watch but found that he couldn't look away. How hungry do you have to be, he wondered, to eat one of your own kind?

Danny's friends said he was crazy when he told them he was moving to New York. They didn't understand. *Crazy* was what he needed.

It had all started last Christmas Eve. He was driving down the two-lane highway that ran through town, past the same stores and signs he'd known all twenty-three years of his life, when a cop car came out of nowhere and ran the red light, blasting right in front of him at ninety miles an hour. If Danny had hit the brakes a second later, he'd be dead. It would be like that film he'd seen in drivers' ed class—the shattered glass, the crumpled metal, the mangled bodies. That would be him.

*Don't look,* a quiet voice had whispered next to him in that dark classroom when the film had started. Danny could see other students putting their heads down on their desks, hiding their faces, closing their eyes. But Danny looked. He looked because he was afraid of appearing weak, and he wanted to prove he could take it. The things he saw on the screen burned into his brain but gave him a rush of adrenaline like he'd never felt before. His nerves were on fire for days, until reality closed in around him again.

Danny needed something big. Bigger than he was, bigger than any place he'd ever been. Something strong enough to rip him open and let everything that was small and weak and frightened pour out of him. Like one of those cartoon characters he used to watch on TV, he was going to step off a cliff into space—like them, all he had to do was not fall.

On his second day in the city, Danny spotted the doorway to a bar hidden under some construction scaffolding. The old-fashioned stained-glass window looked cool, and he wanted a drink, so he stepped under the shadow of the scaffolding and went inside.

It was what he'd always imagined a real New York bar would look like. He loved the old tile floors, the sour perfume of stale beer, cheap cleanser, and furniture polish. There were old wood booths that creaked when you sat in them, and plenty of dark corners to get lost in.

Danny ordered a pint of Killians, took a spot in a corner booth, and looked around. He'd half-expected to see grizzled old men huddled over their drinks. He was surprised to see piercings and tattoos, young faces engaged in earnest conversation. Here were the young and the almost-young who'd been drawn to the city like he was. Artists, actors, rockers, and writers who'd come chasing dreams that had not quite died but had been put on hold, placed in limbo for later. While they were waiting, they could wait here. Here there was no pressure, no judgement, and pleasure and relief were as reliable as a cold Rolling Rock and a dollar shot.

It was after dark when Danny first saw Lenny. He was sitting on his personal bar stool, holding a whiskey glass full of milk from a half-gallon that the bartender kept behind the bar exclusively for him. With his long black leather coat and long graying hair, he looked like a wizard in exile, holding court for a small throng of listeners.

Lenny had the best stories, different stories for different hours of the night. Stories about his drinking days. Tales from his life on the road with a famous punk rock band.

One night after three or four rounds, Danny reached into his back pocket for his wallet and realized it was gone. Panic rising in his chest, he'd looked around the dirty floor under his stool, but it wasn't there.

"You looking for this?" He turned and saw Lenny holding his wallet in two fingers.

"Yeah, thanks," Danny said. He reached for the wallet, but Lenny pulled it back out of his reach and Danny's fingers closed on empty air.

"Never put your wallet in your back pocket," Lenny said. "That's just like throwing it away. Understand?"

Danny swallowed the lump of frustration and resentment rising in his throat. Lenny kept holding the wallet out of Danny's reach, waiting for an answer.

"Yeah. Got it..."

Lenny studied Danny's face a moment longer, then passed the wallet back to him.

"Okay," Lenny said. "Don't fucking do it again."

For the rest of that night, and ever since, Lenny told him things. Things he needed to know. What streets not to walk down after dark. What to do when a taxi driver tries to cheat you. How to tell when the guy asking for directions is about to mug you. Danny listened and tried to absorb it all. With his long black coat and narrow watchful eyes, Lenny reminded Danny of a retired gunslinger teaching a young apprentice how to know when the other guy is about to draw.

"Lenny's great," Kara said. "He can be a little scary sometimes, but he's a good guy. He looks out for everyone."

Kara was a fixture at the bar, with her loud laugh and copper-colored curls that spilled down her back. Danny had been looking at Kara's big smile for weeks but hadn't worked up the nerve to talk to her until tonight.

"What about you?" Danny asked. "Does Lenny look after you too?"

"I can look after myself," she smiled, downing the last of her vodka and lime. *I'm sure you can,* Danny thought. "I'm an actress," she said, giving her curls a flip with one hand. "So... what do you do?"

"I'm a musician. And a writer."

"Oh yeah? When did you get here?" She grinned when she saw his puzzled look. "It's that accent of yours, honey," she said in a bad imitation Southern drawl. Danny felt the heat rise to his face. "Aww, look. I made the country boy blush!" she laughed, then touched his arm. "Oh, don't worry about it. We're all from somewhere else here. Fuck, I'm from Indiana. Lenny's the only real New Yorker in the bunch. Hey!" she said, leaning forward excitedly, "Want me to tell your future? I can tell futures, you know. Give me your hands..."

Danny thought she was going to read his palm, but she clasped both of his hands in hers and gazed intently into his eyes. He felt how small her fingers were, like a child's, how warm and dry her skin was against his. He looked into her eyes that were a sort of golden brown, and noticed how huge her pupils were, like deep black wells.

"You know what I see?" she said. "I see you're going to have a great life. A beautiful, beautiful life. With lots of friends, and lots of success." She held onto his hands a moment longer. Then her serious expression melted, she let go of his hands and laughed.

"See?" she said. "What did I tell you? Nothing to worry about! What are you drinking?" She called out to the bartender for another round. When the drinks arrived, she raised her vodka and lime and flashed her blinding grin at him. "Okay... Here's to our beautiful, beautiful lives!"

THE NEXT DAY, Danny went down into the subway to catch the C train when he noticed a man acting strangely on the opposite platform. The man was pacing up and down like a caged tiger, pausing every few moments to snarl and shout at someone only he could see.

The sound of an approaching train began to fill the tunnel, growing from a distant rumble into a loud roar. Danny watched in amazement as the man took off the dirty green raincoat and began to remove his clothes until he was completely naked. Before Danny could react, the man climbed down onto the tracks and started running toward the oncoming train. The next moments were a blur—the piercing shriek of the train's brakes, the terrible sound the man's body made when the train hit it. Then the excited babbling of the crowd, the urgent static crackling of announcements on the P.A.

Danny had left the subway and walked in a daze all the way to the bar where he sat drinking shots to stop the shaking in his body. He told Lenny all about what he'd just seen. Lenny sat with his whiskey glass of milk, listening quietly.

"Let me ask you something," Lenny said, "Why did you watch that?"

"What do you mean?"

"I mean why did you fucking watch that? You didn't have to look at that. But you did."

While Danny struggled for an answer, Lenny put his glass down on the bar and learned closer.

"Listen. You're from some kind of small town, right? There's a lot of things you've never seen before. And you're gonna wanna see all of them. But some things you don't need to see. Maybe later, after you've been here a while. And some things... some things you don't *ever* need to see."

After Lenny left, Danny stayed at the bar, drinking more, still trying to erase what he'd seen.

"Hey, country boy. You okay?"

Danny turned and saw Kara looking at him, a concerned expression on her face.

"Yeah..." Danny said, "Maybe... I don't know..."

"Lenny told me," she said. She peered at him closely for a moment. "You know what? Let's get you out of here."

Danny didn't realize how drunk he was until he tried to stand up and the floor moved underneath him. He felt Kara wrap one arm around him and help him out to the street. Before he knew it, she'd waved down a cab and was helping him into the back seat. "Forty-two Ludlow Street," he heard her tell the driver. He felt her arm drawing him close, then they were flying through the streets of Manhattan, his head resting on Kara's shoulder.

"You smell like honeysuckle..." he mumbled.

"And you smell like a fucking distillery," she laughed.

The cab stopped. Kara paid the driver and helped Danny get out. Kara fumbled with the keys, then they were inside, the smell of cold curry and skunk weed following them up the crooked stairs as they climbed upward.

They stopped at a one of the thick black doors, scratched and tagged with graffiti. Kara fumbled with the keys again. "It's not fancy," she said, "Just so you know..."

It was dark inside Kara's apartment. Danny heard the pop of a light switch and was blinded for a moment. When he could see again, he noticed a bare lightbulb with some kind of purple batik scarf draped over it, casting colored light across a cracked linoleum floor. Dozens of pictures covered the walls. Danny looked closer and saw they were all of the same woman. He knew the long, firm jaw and cat-like eyes, but it took him a moment to find the right name.

"So... you like Katharine Hepburn...?"

"I don't *like* Katharine Hepburn," Kara said. "I fucking *adore* her. Katharine Hepburn is the greatest fucking woman who ever lived."

*No,* he thought, *You're the greatest fucking woman who ever lived.* He wanted to say it, but he didn't, because he knew how ridiculous he would sound.

She led him to an old white futon, yellow with age, rummaged in a tiny closet and came back with a pillow and blanket. The moment he laid down, he felt all the muscles in his body loosen, his thoughts drifting out of his head like smoke, rising toward the ceiling and disappearing. He forced his eyes open and saw Kara standing in the doorway, all her red curls lit from behind by the hallway light.

"Thank you," he said. "You're a very nice lady."

"Yeah, right," she laughed. She stood there for a moment, watching him, and he felt hope rise inside of him for a moment. Then she said, "Good night. I'm right down the hall if you need me."

*I need you now,* he wanted to say, but before he could, he was asleep.

In the morning, Danny woke with a splitting headache. He shuffled to the tiny bathroom and found the biggest bottle of Advil he'd ever seen. He took five, went back to the futon and waited for them to take effect. When the hangover had loosened its vice-like grip on his skull, he got up again and found a note on the tiny Formica table. BAGELS ON THE FRIDGE. It was a disappointing note. What did he expect? Flirty terms of endearment? Hearts and smiley faces? He found the bagels and ate one, then started looking around for coffee to make, but it felt too strange and lonely being in this place alone without her, so he found his coat and left.

Danny went back to the bar that night, hoping to talk with Kara again. He spotted her sitting at the bar with a big, tough-looking guy in a green army jacket. There was something about the way they looked together, a kind of tension, not friendly or relaxed, that made him keep his distance. They disappeared together for a few minutes, then Kara came back to the bar alone, and the guy in the army jacket had disappeared. Danny figured some kind of deal had gone down—it happened here all the time.

Feeling curiosity and a sense of dread, Danny went over to where Kara was sitting. When she turned to look at him, her eyes were dead. No more golden brown. They were all black like marbles in a doll's head.

"Hey, country boy," she said. "How's that beautiful life treating ya?"

"Good," he said, forcing his face into what he hoped was a smile. "Real good..."

There was something missing from her smile; some kind of bright light deep inside her had been turned off. It made something go cold inside of him, so he kept walking past her until he found an empty corner-booth to settle in.

Later, Danny heard Kara yelling. He looked around and saw her at the bar, shouting at Lenny, her face pale and haggard looking. Lenny tried to put a hand on Kara's arm, but she pushed it away. When she started crying, Lenny helped Kara to her feet, wrapped one arm around her shoulder and walked her out onto the street. Through the window, Danny could see Lenny load Kara into the back seat of a cab and put some money into the driver's hand.

IN THE MORNING, Danny stopped by a bodega and bought two coffees and a couple of bagels, then walked to Ludlow Street. He'd thought about going to check on Kara the night before but didn't. She'd looked like she was in a bad way. Maybe she just needed some time to straighten out.

Danny was imagining handing her the bag, saying, *I wasn't sure how you like your coffee,* then her big sleepy smile, when he turned the corner and saw the small crowd gathered in front of her building. He stopped and tried to take it all in: the police car, the white van. As he stood there watching, the door opened, and two paramedics came out carrying a stretcher with something covered with a blanket.

What happened after that, Danny wasn't sure. He remembered dropping the bagels and coffee into a trash can, then walking and walking, the sound and motion of the city around him muffled like it was coming through heavy wool. *Kara wasn't the only person in that building,* he thought. *It could have been anyone under there. Anyone at all.*

It was almost dark when he found himself in front of the bar. Danny walked inside and found Lenny hunched over his glass, his face more pale than usual. Lenny looked up at Danny, studying his face.

"You know, right?" Lenny said.

Danny's throat felt strangled, and he didn't trust himself to speak.

"Sit down," Lenny said. Danny obeyed, sinking down onto the stool next to him. He glanced over at Lenny who was staring down into his glass. He'd never seen Lenny look so bad.

"What happened?" Danny asked. When Lenny spoke, his voice was hoarse and weary sounding.

"You think I should've gone home with her and watched her, right? You know how many times I had to take her home like that? How many times I woke up and found her on the floor and had to call the fucking ambulance? Listen, she was going to do it, sooner or later. No matter what I fucking did. And I didn't want to see that, understand? Why should I have to fucking look at that?"

Lenny turned away and stared at the window like there was something out there that only he could see.

"She thought she was gonna be this big fucking actress or something. You know something about actresses? They're always like *look at me, look at me.* But they don't look at themselves. 'Cause they're afraid of what they're gonna see." Lenny drained the last of the milk from his glass and set it back down on the bar. "That's what happened to her. She looked."

DANNY KEPT GOING to the bar every night, but something was different now. After a few drinks, he'd look around the place and see it mostly empty, except for Lenny and his little group of listeners, and he'd wonder—why was this dirty old bar still here when so many others like it had vanished, gutted and forgotten? Sometimes after midnight when the streets looked strange and vacant, the answer was obvious—it was a ghost bar. A ghost bar, filled with ghosts, it appeared when he needed it and vanished into nothingness when he wasn't looking. Like the Flying Dutchman, a phantom ship taking on lost sailors who then became part of its ghostly crew forever. When he left the bar and turned the corner, how did he know it didn't just blink out of existence like someone turning out a light?

He thought about Kara. She'd seemed like the brightest light in the whole place. Now her light was turned out. If someone like her couldn't make it, what chance did he have?

He thought about what Lenny had said. *That's what happened. She looked.*

What happens, Danny wondered, when you really look inside yourself? What was it that she saw?

Danny put the bottle to his lips, tilted it up and felt the last swallow of beer run into his mouth, warm and bitter. He wanted to order another, but Lenny was right in the middle of one of his stories, and Danny didn't want interrupt.

"The circus used to come to the Garden every summer," Lenny said. "They'd walk the elephants down 34th Street late at night. The cops used to block off the street. People would come out of the bars to watch. Right out there…"

Lenny pointed toward the window. Danny tried to picture it. Throngs of late-night bystanders on the sidewalks, men, women and children. Huge grey bodies passing by, the lights of a hundred skyscrapers looking down on them.

"They kept the elephants chained up when they were walking them," Lenny said. "You could hear the chains rattling and dragging on the street before you even saw them. You could always smell them first. That's how you knew they were coming..."

"Did you ever see them?" Danny asked.

"Yeah, sure," Lenny said, taking a sip of his milk. "Not anymore. They stopped doing it."

"Why?"

"There was a fire," Lenny said, "Happened twenty years ago tonight. It started in the train cars, where the elephants were. All that straw. Went up like *that*." Lenny snapped his long fingers, and the sound made Danny jump. "By the time they broke open the railcars to get the elephants out, they were all on fire."

"Jesus..." Danny exclaimed. "How?"

"Someone doused the elephants with coal oil. Circus said it was some kind of accident, but it wasn't. People said it was for the insurance, that they didn't mean to burn the elephants. Other people said it was just one crazy guy who did it. Nobody knows."

"What about the elephants?"

"They broke out of the railcars and headed straight down 34th Street. That was the way they always went, so that's what they did. They were burned up pretty bad. Most of them were still on fire. Bad thing was, they were all running. That made the fire worse..."

Danny tried to picture it. The big grey bodies blackened and covered in flames, stampeding past in the dark.

"All those people," Lenny continued, "The ones who came out to watch. Some of them brought their kids. They all saw it. It did something to them. After that, a lot of them went crazy and killed themselves. Like they couldn't live with what they saw or something..."

Danny felt his mind recoil from what Lenny was saying. He looked around at the others listening, their faces slack and empty in the dim bar-light. He noticed one of them glancing down nervously to check his watch.

"Then, a year later," Lenny said, "On that same night, some guy here stepped outside to have a smoke, when he started smelling this burnt smell. He was here the year before, the night it happened, so he knew what it was. He said nothing else in the world smells like that. Then he heard them coming. First the chains rattling. Then the sidewalk rumbling and shaking like when a subway's coming. That's when he said he saw them, running right down the middle of the street, just like before. All of 'em on fire and screaming..."

A loud metallic rumbling made Danny's heart stop for a second. He looked around and saw one of the waitresses dragging down a metal shutter over one of the windows.

"The guy came back in here and cut his wrists in the bathroom," Lenny nodded toward the bathroom hallway, "Right back there."

"How do you know all this stuff?" Danny couldn't stop himself from asking.

"Because. I was here that night," Lenny said, "The EMT, the one who worked on the guy. He told me everything the guy said. Right before they lost him."

Danny felt a surge of resentment. Lenny had an answer for everything. He thought of something he'd once heard. *When someone knows everything, they're making half of it up.*

Another loud rumbling noise startled Danny again. He looked around and saw the same waitress pulling down the metal shutter over the last window, blocking out the view of the street outside. What was she doing? Closing time wasn't until one AM. Danny watched her pull a heavy-looking padlock from her pocket and snap it into place before walking away.

"Then a few years later," Lenny continued, "There was this woman. A tourist, from South Dakota or something like that. Never heard about the fire or the elephants or the whole story. She went outside for a smoke, then came back in and told people there was something burning out there. She went back out by herself to check it out. They found her curled up on the sidewalk, crying and screaming. They took her home and put her in a psychiatric hospital. About a year later, they let her out. And she threw herself in front of a bus."

Danny felt a rush of anger. Why the hell was Lenny going on about people killing themselves? Why did he think anyone wanted to hear this? Especially so soon after Kara? Who the fuck did he think he was?

"Bullshit."

Lenny stopped and looked at Danny. "Yeah? You think so?"

"Yeah. I mean, how do you know all this shit?" Danny felt he was stepping out on a dangerous ledge but couldn't stop himself. "I mean, the first guy. That happened here, right? But that girl. Throwing herself in front of a bus. You said that happened after she left. In South Dakota or something, right? How are you supposed to know about that?"

"How do I know?" Lenny said. "What do *you* know? You got here, what, six months ago? *Six fucking months?*"

The air in the room turned dangerous and electric. Danny didn't look away or back down. He'd needed Lenny for a while, he told himself. Not anymore. He was tired of playing the ignorant apprentice, giving his attention and respect to a burnt-out loser whose best moments had been over with twenty years ago.

One of the listeners was getting off his barstool and reaching cautiously for his jacket. Lenny's head swiveled around to follow him.

"Where are you going?" Lenny barked at him. "You see what time it is?"

The guy's eyes darted around nervously. "Yeah..." he muttered. "Eleven fifty-six..."

"That's right. So, *sit the fuck down!*"

The guy flinched at the sound of Lenny's voice raised at him. Slowly, he replaced his jacket across his barstool and reluctantly slid back onto his seat.

Danny heard the sounds of a struggle across the room. He turned and saw a young woman with bleach blond hair and a Ramones T-shirt trying to leave through the front door. One of Lenny's friends was blocking her way, the other was pulling her away from the door by one arm. She looked drunk and angry and swung at them once, then seemed to give in and let them lead her away, sobbing while they guided her to a seat at the far end of the bar.

"What's the matter with her?" Danny asked.

"Nothing," Lenny said. "She's new here. It's her first time, that's all."

Before Danny could ask what that meant, Lenny got up and walked to the front door. Danny watched him pull a set of keys from his coat pocket, slip one into the lock and turn it. It made a loud metallic *click* sound that seemed to echo off the walls.

Danny turned to the guy sitting closest to him. "What the fuck is going on?" he whispered.

"Nothing," the guy whispered, not meeting Danny's

eyes. "Just do what he says."

Lenny returned to his barstool, glanced up at the clock on the wall and announced in a low, grim voice, "Eleven fifty-nine."

A heavy silence seemed to fall over the bar, weighing everything down. Danny looked at the gated, lightless windows padlocked shut, at the pale, serious faces that seemed to grow more pale and haggard by the minute. The bleach-blond girl who'd tried to get out was hiding her face in her folded arms. At other tables, he saw more people putting their faces down in their arms and covering their eyes.

*Jesus, they're crazy*, Danny thought. *They're all crazy.* He'd always thought that he was safe in here, that it was the outside world that was dangerous. Now he knew. The real danger was in here with him. A raw, animal panic started to rise inside his chest.

Danny stood up unsteadily and grabbed his jacket from his barstool.

"Where do you think you're going?" Lenny said.

"I'm leaving."

"You *can't* leave."

There was an EXIT sign glowing at the back of the bar. The guys in Lenny's crew eyed him suspiciously. When two of them got off their barstools and started moving toward him, Danny ran straight toward the glowing red EXIT sign.

"*Stop,*" Lenny shouted. Danny heard chairs and tables clattering and falling to the floor as his pursuers pushed them out of the way, trying to get to him. Danny flung himself at the metal door, hoping it wasn't locked, that he wouldn't have to turn and fight.

The door flew open, and he stumbled out into a dark alley. He ran toward a light in the distance that he knew must be 34th Street, hearing other footsteps closing in on him from behind. He could hear other sounds, a metallic clanking and scraping, and a kind of rhythmic rumbling that sounded like the subway, but it wasn't coming from under the street. It was coming from the West Side, from the direction of the river, growing closer and louder. Danny went toward the sound and the light that seemed to flicker and pulse at the end of the alley that was obscured by some kind of thick haze or smoke. An acrid burning smell choked him, but he was drawn toward that flickering glow. Whatever it was, he wanted to see it.

In the next moment, something slammed into him from behind, shoving him to the street. He felt the full weight of a body pressing down on him, caught the familiar smell of leather and the sour tang of milk on someone's breath.

The street beneath them rumbled and shook. Danny tried to lift his head, but Lenny held his face down to the concrete while the great flood of smoke and fire and agonized animal sounds like souls dying thundered past. Heat from unseen flames raked his skin. It felt like the world had cracked open and was about to swallow them. The only thing left to hold onto was the sound of Lenny's voice in his ear.

*"Don't look,"* Lenny said. *"Don't fucking look."*

# Eyes Like
# Small Black Stones

THERE USED TO be swans at Castle Hill. In summer, they flocked from the south and turned the whole surface of the lake white. Wide, shifting fields of snow-white feathers, breaking apart and swirling together again. Cassie would watch the birds on their way to the water, black shapes crossing a ragged red sky. Father taught her to identify the various birds as they passed overhead. Mallards flying in loose groups. Smaller bunches of teals flashing by. Canvasbacks in wavering lines that would form a temporary V-shape and then break apart and reform again. When Father recognized the outline of a swan, his face would turn dark and his voice angry.

To Father, the swans were a pestilence, a plague upon the land. Cassie would listen silently as he enumerated their many evils—the valuable plants they devoured, the other birds they attacked and drove away. The swans were also a threat to humans. Males could weigh forty pounds and reach five feet from wingtip to wingtip. Father told tales of boaters being attacked, of children's arms and legs being broken, and forbade Cassie from going down to the lake by herself. So, she would sit and count the dark shapes passing overhead, imagining the lake full of them, a shifting, surging field of white, tinted red by the evening sun. She wondered how something so beautiful could be so dangerous. *Invasive species.* That's what Father called them. She asked what that meant. *It means,* he said, *they don't belong here.*

Castle Hill had been Cassie's home until she was eighteen, when she'd met and married Brad and, over Father's objections, had moved back to the city where she was born. It seemed so different from the one she remembered. There was no place to hide from the blistering Southern sun, or from the mobs of tourists who crowded the streets and parks, gaping up at the marble monuments and statues of great men. *Where are the statues of great women,* she'd asked, and Brad had laughed like it was the funniest joke he'd ever heard.

On the night they were married, Brad, a little drunk, had stood underneath the statue of Thomas Jefferson and struck the same proud, erect pose. She'd laughed but suspected that he was also trying to make a point, or at least plant the suggestion in her mind, that he too could be a great man one day.

Father, who'd fought and been a hero in the Great War, had certain ideas about what a great man should be. *You need a strong man to take care of you,* he'd said. His meaning was clear—she needed a strong man, and Brad was not one. She'd tried to tell Father that his ideas were old fashioned, that they were a modern couple and would take care of each other. That was before Brad's drinking became worse. Before the long silences and terrible arguments. Before their son Jack was born.

Cassie's world was not the only one that was changing. She could feel it in the city streets, in the crowds of people who seemed to move a little faster as if trying to make it home before a storm. Something was coming, something that could not be stopped. In the evening, she would find Brad sitting close to the big wooden radio with its glowing dial, leaning close to catch the urgent voice stabbing the air in harsh static bursts.

It was springtime when the letter came, a bright yellow envelope with official-looking writing. She'd found Brad staring at it, his face a blank white mask. At first, she was sure that someone had died. A month later, Brad was gone to some place called Fort Leonard Wood in Missouri. After that, to Germany where the war was.

*COME HOME NOW.*

The first two words of Father's telegram were an invitation; the third, Cassie knew, was an order. At first, she'd tried to resist. She could make it on her own, she'd told Father—she and Jack, with the money Brad had left. That was before she found out that there was no money, that Brad had drunk and gambled it away.

Other women she knew, wives whose husbands were gone, had turned back the clock to survive and gone home to their families. But the thought of running home to Father, of proving him right, made something inside her rebel. She tried secretarial work, but when the piles of paper in front of her grew higher and higher until she couldn't breathe, she left early for lunch one day and never came back. In a factory at the shipyard, where the noise was one endless train wreck that tore at her nerves, she'd lasted only one day.

*Come home now.*

Father's words that had sounded like an invasion now began to feel like an opportunity. A summer at Castle Hill. A chance to rest and recover. Maybe that was what she needed.

JACK WATCHED HIS mother struggle with their heavy suitcases as they made their way through the crowds at Union Station. The great white granite hall was full of soldiers. Jack had never seen so many in one place before. They moved in large groups, shouting in loud rough voices, others silent and grim, their stiff green uniforms a little too big for their youthful bodies. The air was heavy with the smell of cologne, sweat, and cigarettes.

Jack saw his mother holding her chin up high, a trickle of sweat running down her forehead. She paused to set the suitcases down and wiped her eye, causing a flood of other people to swarm around them.

"Mommy, can I help?"

"No, thank you, darling. It's alright. We're almost there." She picked up the bags, her lips set firm, and started walking again. Jack didn't offer to help this time but stayed close to his mother's side. He looked up in wonder at the giant beams of sunlight that shot down from the big high windows, cutting through the gloom.

One sign on the wall caught his eye. It was a picture of a giant spider with the head of a man. The man's face had a nose like a vulture's beak and dead white eyes. Jack read the words on the sign.

*DON'T TALK.*

Jack pulled on his mother's sleeve. She turned and looked down at him, her face flushed and distracted.

"What is it, Jackie?"

Jack pointed at the sign. "Mommy. Who is that?" He could see her eyes darting about, straining to find what he was pointing at. "The spider," he said. "The spider with the man's face." He saw her eyes find what he was talking about. A strange look passed across her face.

"Nobody."

Jack knew his mother was lying. He could always tell when there was something she didn't want him to know. There were more words on the sign. He looked closer, trying to read them.

*THE WEB IS SPUN FOR YOU WITH INVISIBLE THREADS. STAY OUT OF IT. HELP TO DESTROY IT.*

JACK FELT A vibration deep inside. HELP TO DESTROY IT. The sign was talking to him. It was asking for his help. There is a monster out there, the sign was saying. Help us. Destroy it.

Jack was about to tell his mother about what the sign said—then he read the rest…

*STOP. THINK. ASK YOURSELF IF WHAT YOU ARE ABOUT TO SAY MIGHT HELP THE ENEMY. SPIES ARE LISTENING.*

Jack looked at the people around them. The tall man with a thin mustache and wide-brimmed hat reading a newspaper. The old woman with angry eyes, clutching a large package. An older child standing in line with his father just a few feet ahead of them. As Jack watched, the boy turned and looked right into his face, his eyes narrowing distrustfully. Jack felt the words he was about to say freeze and die in his throat.

*I will not talk,* Jack thought. *I will not help the enemy. Spies are listening. I will destroy them.*

THE TRAIN LURCHED and clacked. Cassie glanced out the window at the last traces of the white marble city falling away. She glanced down at Jack sleeping next to her, lulled by the rocking motion of the train. He'd been so young the last time he was at Castle Hill. She wondered how much he remembered.

When Jack stirred in his sleep, Cassie wrapped one arm around his small shoulders and drew him close. This trip would do him good. God knows she hadn't been much of a mother to him for these past few weeks since Brad had been gone. Or for all the ugly months before that. She wished she could protect Jack from all the ugliness. The way that Father had protected her. The last time she was at Castle Hill, Father had seen the bruises Cassie tried to hide. The next day, Father took his shotgun down from the wall and told her that he and Brad were going hunting. They were gone all day. Brad never told her what happened, but he never laid a hand on Cassie again.

Protection. Protection and a man's influence. That's what Jack needed now. She owed him that much.

As the taxi climbed the steep, familiar hill, Cassie saw the house emerge from the leaves, the dark, rocky bulk of it rising against the sky, like pictures she'd seen of medieval castles perched above tiny villages. The house had been built with stones carried in horse-drawn carts from the moraine to the top of the hill. Every stone was a different size, a different shape, even a different color, so the house had a rough-hewn, primitive look like something built a thousand years ago.

Father had bought the house in 1924 and had moved the family there when the city had become "too dangerous". Mother, who'd come unwillingly, filled the dark and stony rooms with her expensive, delicate furniture shipped from the city, so the house looked—as Brad once described it—*like a dollhouse inside a dungeon.* Brad hated Castle Hill. He hated its thick stone walls, tiny windows, and airless rooms. *It's like a prison,* he'd complained. *Why do we have to go there every summer?*

"Look, Jack," Cassie said, pointing toward the great house. Jack peered through the car window and squinted suspiciously.

Before she'd even had a chance to knock, the thick wooden door swung open and there was Father, standing tall above her in his grey wool suit and bright wide grin. He gathered her into his arms and rocked her back and forth like a child, whispering, "Welcome home. Welcome home." Cassie closed her eyes and breathed in his familiar scent of old wool and crisp linen, witch hazel and the faint trace of tobacco smoke.

Father finally loosened his grip on her and grinned down at Jack. "Well, well, hello there, Jackie boy!" Jack stared up at Father, not smiling.

"Jack," Cassie said, "Say hello to your grandfather." Jack kept staring and said nothing.

"That's okay," Father said, "He's just feeling a little shy. We'll have plenty of time to talk later, won't we, Jackie?"

Father ushered them inside, and there was Delia standing at a distance in her crisp white uniform, waiting to be noticed. Cassie nearly ran to her, and Delia opened her arms, taking Cassie in. "Delia..." Cassie said, then could speak no more. Delia held onto her, patting her back gently, saying, "Miss Cassie... Miss Cassie," again and again.

"Supper's at seven," Father announced in a firm voice. Cassie felt Delia's arms loosen around her and slip away.

"It sure is good to see you, Miss Cassie," Delia smiled. Cassie noticed the gray that had crept into Delia's hair since the last time, and it made her sad. "And there's Mister Jack," Delia said, smiling down at him. Jack took one step behind his mother, holding onto her leg, and glared up at Delia suspiciously.

"Jack!" Cassie said, "It's Delia. You remember her."

Jack kept glaring and said nothing. Father made an impatient sound and Delia turned and went quickly back toward the kitchen.

"It's really good to see Delia again," Cassie said to Father. "It feels...it feels like everything's the same."

Father, who'd been watching Delia go with a stern expression, turned back to Cassie and broke into his broad grin again.

"Oh, you know. Nothing ever changes here."


CASSIE WAS AMAZED at how easily everything fell back into place. In the evenings, Delia would prepare dinner for them. After dinner, they would all go out and sit on the hillside to watch the sunset like they used to when she was younger. Father sat on the ground in the same freshly pressed gray wool suit and tie he wore to dinner every night. Cassie sat by his side on the tablecloth spread on the grass, her bare legs stretched out immodestly in front of her like a little girl's. She sipped the sweet bourbon highball her father had poured for her, feeling the warmth hit her chest and spread outward, melting the years away while Jack ran and tumbled on the hill below them like she'd once done. It was good to see him start to come out of his shell.

"Jack loves it here," she said.

"Of course he does," Father said. "Children are like horses. They need to be run."

"I know," she sighed. "He'll probably never want to leave."

"The city's no place to raise a child."

"You raised me there."

"I got you out. Soon as I could."

"We'll do alright," she said, hearing the lack of conviction in her own voice.

"Cassie... A woman alone? In that awful place? Besides. What about Jack? You have to think about him." When he spoke again, his voice was still quiet and firm. "You're not going back there."

And there it was. She'd known this was coming. Before they'd even arrived, when they'd boarded the train and watched the city flash past and fall away behind them.

"Our things..." she began.

"I'll send for them."

Cassie felt the urge to object rise briefly inside her and then fade away like a trace of cloud evaporating in the sky. She'd known this was going to happen. And somewhere inside of her, she'd wanted it. Why would she have come here, knowing this would happen, if she didn't want it?

A breeze moved up the hill and a kind of calm settled over her. It was strange how easy it felt. She'd thought that returning here would feel like a defeat, but it didn't. The familiar trees overhead, the ground beneath her; it all felt comforting and natural. It was her life with Brad that had been unnatural. Their apartment on Connecticut Avenue and everything in it, the clothes she'd worn, even the way she wore her hair, had all been an act. *This* was not an act. This was who she was.

ON THE STEEP green hill, Jack ran and fell, ran and fell again, charging the invisible enemy on the hill. Bang. Fall. Get up. Run again. The glare of the late afternoon sun blinding his eyes. This was war. Fight and die. Get up. Fight again. This was what men did. What he had to learn how to do.

Someone was calling him. Jack squinted into the sun and saw a lone figure standing against the sky at the top of the hill above him. It was Mother, calling him in for dinner. She'd been calling him for a long time—he could tell by the annoyance in her voice. Jack brushed the grass and dirt from his knees and started climbing the hill, his heart still hammering in his chest.

Inside, the house was full of the smell of cooking, and that strange old musty odor the place always had. Mother had gone into the kitchen with Delia. Granddad stood looking down at him from high above. "Follow me, Jackie," Granddad smiled and winked. "We don't want *them* listening, do we?"

Jack stared up in surprise. Granddad knew. *Spies are listening.*

Jack followed Granddad out onto the porch that looked over the wooded hills below. He felt Granddad's large warm hand rest itself on his right shoulder, while the other hand pointed out over the miles of green trees turning blue in the dusk.

"Look out there, Jack," Granddad said. "See that?" Jack nodded. "Other people look out there and think it's beautiful. Know what I see? I see *cover*. Under every one of those trees, an enemy soldier could be hiding."

Jack looked out across the wooded hills below, imagining an enemy hiding behind every tree. He pictured the trees crawling toward them through the dimming light, slowly, silently.

"That's why it's important to hold the high ground," Granddad said. "The point where the defender has the greatest arc of observation and an unobstructed line of fire."

Jack tried to understand the words that Granddad was saying to him. Other grownups leaned down and cooed in his face, talking in ridiculous high voices. Even Mother did that. But Granddad wasn't talking to him like a child. He wasn't taking about childish things. He was telling him important things. Things that mattered.

"I need your help, Jack. I need you to help keep watch. Cover the terrain. It's a big job. I can't do it alone. Can you do that for me?"

Jack nodded. He felt Granddad's large, warm hand tighten its grip on his shoulder. "Good boy. I knew I could count on you."

CASSIE'S HEAD HURT from the bourbon she drank the night before. Rising slowly, she moved to the window and looked out across the green trees that sloped down to where the lake was hidden.

*Don't go down to the lake.* Father's words came back to her every time she looked in the direction of the lake, or even thought about it.

When Cassie was four years old, she'd been attacked by a swan. The memory was both vivid and vague, a few sharp fragments surrounded by a haze of forgetting. She could remember the strange sight of the creature on land, haltingly lumbering toward her, its eyes like small black stones fixed on her, the great wings lifting higher and higher, feathers spreading apart like the fingers of a hand, making her think of pictures of angels. For a moment, it was almost beautiful—then the long neck stabbing at her, the sound of hissing and the muffled thunder of wings beating the air all around her in a terrible flurry of white.

She could never remember how long the attack had lasted, or how it ended. Here at Castle Hill, those thoughts came to her when she slept, and in the moments between sleeping and waking. Quick flashes of white and red. Red and white.

Father was already in his seat at the head of the table, reading the newspaper from New York, a scowl of disapproval on his face. Cassie settled into her chair and breathed in the good smell of hot coffee, feeling it open the tight spaces behind her eyes. All the while, she could feel Delia moving around them, the familiar warmth of her body leaning close from behind to place a platter of warm biscuits on the table.

"Thank you, Delia," Cassie said, turning to smile up at her. Delia's smile flickered like a lightbulb, then went out. She said nothing, finished setting the table and disappeared into the kitchen.

Cassie watched Delia go and felt uneasy. Throughout her life, Delia had been a constant presence, providing a kind of balance against her mother's fragility and otherworldliness. Questions that had been too delicate for Mother, Cassie knew she could ask Delia. It was Delia who'd first told her about sex, saying the kind of words Cassie could not imagine coming from her mother's mouth.

Lately, though, Delia had begun to keep her distance, to establish a degree of formality like the one she displayed toward Father. Cassie preferred the old Delia, the one who baked cinnamon bread for her in the kitchen when she was young, told her stories and made her laugh. Not this distant, silent presence who rarely met her eyes and slipped in and out of rooms like a shadow.

When Delia came to clear away the dishes from breakfast, Cassie rose and started to take her plate to the kitchen.

"What are you doing?" Father asked. She saw him watching her with a stern look on his face.

"I'm just..."

"Leave it."

Cassie stood uncertainly for a moment, the plate still in her hand. Her old resistance at being told what to do rose up inside of her. "Excuse me," she said, then turned and walked back into the kitchen.

She found Delia at the sink, scraping leftovers into the slop pail. "Here," Cassie said, holding out the plate to her. Delia glanced at the plate quickly as if she didn't know what to do. Then she reached out and took it.

"Thank you," Delia said under her breath.

Cassie picked up a plate and began to dry it with a dishtowel, watching Delia bending over the sink, busily scrubbing a dirty pan.

"Delia," Cassie said. "Is everything... okay?"

Delia replied without looking up from her work. "Not sure what you mean, Miss Cassie."

"I don't know. You seem... you seemed happy to see me. Jack and me. But..." *But now you don't.*

"You're a grown woman, Miss Cassie. You can do whatever you want to do. It's none of my business."

Delia had rolled up her sleeves to wash the dishes; Cassie looked down and saw four blue-black marks on Delia's forearm, each one roughly the size of a finger. She felt a cold shock wash through her, followed by the first stirring of rage. She wanted to say something, but the words caught in her throat, so she turned and walked back out to the dining room where Father was still sitting, still staring at her disapprovingly.

"Cassie," he said, "You are not to clear the dishes from the table again. It's what I pay that woman for. If you do her work for her, it's exactly like stealing from me."

Cassie stood trying to absorb this, then remembered what she'd come back to ask.

"Have you seen the bruises on Delia's arm?

Father's scowl relaxed, and he shook his head gently as he spoke. "Cassie, I'm afraid that's just part of the world she comes from. It's sad, but it's true. It's none of our business."

"But...I'm worried about her," Cassie said. "Shouldn't we...*say* something?"

"Cassie, I told you," Father said, a cold and steely edge in his voice. "It's not our business." He must have seen the look of alarm on her face, because he flashed a quick and patient smile. "Don't worry about Delia. She'll be fine."

Cassie reprimanded herself. Of course, Father cared about Delia. How could he not? After all these years together, she was like part of the family. The gruffness he displayed, calling Delia "that woman", was just an act, like so much of what he said and did. Father loved her. Father loved Jack. Father loved Delia too. She'd forgotten that for a moment. She promised herself to never forget it again.

\*

After breakfast, while Jack was playing in the garden, Cassie went out for a walk. She needed some fresh air and sunshine to clear her head. The large meadow behind the house that sloped down toward the trees moved and whispered invitingly, and Cassie plunged right in. The tall grasses with their milky tops rose all around her, waving and speaking in their hushed voices. For a brief moment, she couldn't tell where she was, which direction the house was in or how to get back.

That was when she remembered the babies. The swan babies. What were they called? Chicks? Goslings? It was a moment before the right word came. *Cygnets.* She had stumbled upon the cygnets in the high reeds by the shore. Little white balls of fluff with open mouths. She could hold one in her hands if she wanted to. She'd held out her hands as if one of the cygnets might leap into her open palms, but they scattered away from her. That was when she turned and saw the mother swan charging, wings spread wide enough to blot out the sun, open black mouth wide enough to swallow the world.

Later, the sound of a gunshot echoing off the lake and entering her own chest. Father returning with the shotgun cradled in the crook of his arm, the charred smell of gunpowder clinging to his clothes. *It was just protecting its babies,* she'd cried. Father told her it didn't matter, that just because swans have babies, eat, drink, and breathe air, that didn't mean they were the same. *They're just animals,* he'd told her. *You are not. Remember that.*

Jack opened his eyes and saw a bar of sunlight stabbing through the darkness of the bedroom like something solid. He turned and saw his mother curled on her side next to him. Her hair wild in sleep, her mouth open, a spot on the pillow under her face dark with spit.

Jack slipped through the bedroom door, down the hallway to the kitchen where the single pane of glass in the kitchen door glowed in the dark like a beacon. Before he pushed the door open, he felt in the dark for the nail in the wall where his weapon hung waiting for him, patient, faithful. He lifted the flyswatter down from the nail, feeling the power in his hand, pushed the door open and stepped over the stone threshold into the garden.

The morning air slipped around his skin, cool and fragrant with the breath of a hundred plants and flowers. He stopped for a moment to peel his shirt off over his head so he could feel the cool air on his naked belly and chest. *Like a pirate,* he thought. He'd seen pictures of pirates with their shirts wide open or missing entirely. Bare skin against bullets and swords. Braver than knights with their armor and shields. Braver even than soldiers with their iron helmets, hiding behind sandbags.

Not like Granddad. Granddad never hid from anything. On that hill in France, he'd stood up to face the enemy while bullets flew right past him, taller than the other soldiers, taller than anything, daring them to take aim and kill him. Tall and indestructible like a statue. Like a giant.

Jack walked further down the path to the garden wall, to the shed and the bags of soil and mulch where he knew the enemy was waiting. There they were, smaller than the bees, black and ugly, making their angry little circles in the air. There were a lot of them. They carried diseases that could make you sick, Mother said. They eat shit and then land on your food, on your arm or your face. They were disgusting and needed killing. Who else would do it? Who else if not him?

He would kill them, he decided. It might take a long time, but he would do it. He would kill them all.

He slashed the air with his weapon, testing it, hearing the satisfying *whoosh*, feeling the power rise up his arm and into the rest of his body. Then he stepped in and started killing.

*Whoosh. Crack.* Tiny black bodies crushed and sticking to red plastic, a few tiny legs still struggling.

*Crack.* No more struggling. That was death. He made it happen. Again and again, *Crack, crack, crack*, until the bodies were piled around him at his feet.

CASSIE WAS COMING up the stairs when she heard a sound she recognized, one she remembered from childhood, a loud *whomp*, like a sail cracking in the wind—Delia shaking out the bedsheets. She followed that sound down the hall to her bedroom. When she entered the room, Delia glanced up at her, then quickly looked away. "Scuse me, Miss Cassie…" Delia muttered and started to leave.

"No," Cassie said, "Don't stop. It's okay."

Delia paused for a moment as if she was still unsure whether to leave or stay. Then she turned back to the bed and started smoothing and tucking the sheet. Cassie moved around to the far corner of the bed to help.

"You don't need to do that, Miss Cassie," Delia said.

"No, it's okay," Cassie said, trying to smile. "I feel like I haven't done any work all day." Cassie busied herself, working next to Delia in silence, trying to think of what to say next. "How are your boys?" Cassie didn't say their names. She'd forgotten them. Jackson? She thought that might be one, but she didn't want to risk it.

She thought she saw Delia sigh. "Rodney's in Germany."

"Does he…do you hear from him often?"

Delia shook another pillow down into its pillowcase and shrugged. "He writes. Sometimes…"

"How…" Cassie started, not knowing what to say. "Does he tell you…what it's like?"

"A little. They don't let them do that, mostly. Some of his letters, almo st half of them are blacked out. You know how they do."

Cassie looked away. She did not know. Six months, and Brad had sent only one postcard from Fort Dix, nothing since he'd left for Germany. For a moment, she'd felt that she and Delia were the same, two women joined by a common bond. But they were not the same. Suddenly, Delia turned to face her.

"Why did you come back here?"

Cassie felt the breath pulled right out of her lungs. "You… you know why."

"Because your husband's gone? Lots of women whose husbands are gone."

"Delia… this is my home."

"You *had* a home. You had your *own* home." Delia looked away and went back to work, pulling at the sheets a little harder. "Why did you bring that little boy back here?"

"He loves his Granddad."

"'Course he loves his Granddad. He's a *child*." Cassie saw Delia start to say more, then close her eyes and shake her head. "I'm sorry. I said too much. I got no right to talk to you like that."

"No, it's alright…" Cassie said, but she felt resentment rising inside her. Who was Delia to tell her she shouldn't be in her own home? After all that she and Father had done for her, giving her a good job and a beautiful place to live. And that terrible summer when the sounds of shouting, police sirens and gunshots rang out for five days and nights, when tanks had rolled through the streets of Washington, Father had kept Delia safe inside their house in Chevy Chase. *A black face on Connecticut Avenue?* Father had said. *She wouldn't last five minutes out there.*

Father had kept her safe. He'd kept them all safe. Delia had a lot to be grateful for.


THEY WERE CLOSER now. Jack could feel it in the dark shapes that passed overhead at sunset. He could feel it in the looks that passed between Mother and Delia, between Mother and Granddad. He could feel it in the spaces between the words they said to each other, and in the way that the trees thrashed and nodded outside his window while the wind was moaning a word it kept trying to say.

In the morning while Mother was still asleep, Jack patrolled the house to see if anyone or anything had gotten in during the night. He'd brought the flyswatter for protection, clutching it tightly in his fist. He had killed with it, had made death happen, and that gave him a power he hoped would protect him.

At the end of the hallway, the front door stood open. Clutching his weapon, he stepped through the half-open door out into the morning light. A movement caught his eye. Jack turned and had only a second to see the man standing with both arms raised, a gun in his hands. Before Jack could cry out, there was a loud crack, then the smell of gunpowder. The man lowered the gun and Jack saw his Granddad's face, a wide grin spreading across it.

"Gotcha!" Granddad's voice was booming with laughter. Then he was walking toward Jack, holding the gun out to him in one hand, the handle pointed toward him now.

"Wanna try it?"

Up close, Jack could see it was a toy, but more real-looking than any toy gun he'd seen before. Shiny silver metal, heavy in his hand, like he believed a real gun would be. The gunpowder smell rose from it and entered Jack's nose.

"Go on," Granddad said. "Try it."

Jack looked around for something to shoot at. A movement above caught his eye. Geese crossing the sky on their way to the lake below. Jack raised the pistol in both hands, the way he'd seen Granddad do, pointed the pistol at the birds and squeezed the trigger. It was harder to do than he'd thought, and for a moment nothing happened. Then he felt the *click* under his straining finger and at the same time a loud crack. Jack saw a trace of smoke come from the pistol before the wind carried it away.

"Good shot," Granddad said. Jack frowned. Granddad was lying. The bird he'd aimed at was still flying.

"I missed," Jack said.

"Try again."

Jack searched the sky for another target, but birds were hard; they were far away and moved too fast. High above, he heard them calling in their awkward, mocking voices. Mocking him.

Jack turned and pointed the gun at Granddad, still holding it in both hands. He was about to say *Freeze* or *Hold it right there,* things he'd heard the cowboys say on the radio. The next thing Jack knew, the pistol was clattering across the pavement and his hands were empty, his wrist throbbing. He looked up in shock at a twisted, blood-red face he didn't recognize.

*"Don't ever do that!"* the thing roared at him. *"Don't you ever point a gun at someone like that!"*

Jack couldn't move or speak. Everything inside him, including the urge to cry, had been blown out of him and lay scattered on the ground.

Jack saw the thing raise one hand and pass it over his face like he was trying to rub something away. Then it was Granddad's face again. He nodded toward the toy gun that lay on the pavement where it had landed.

"Pick that up." It was Granddad's voice, weak and hoarse. "It's yours."

JACK SAW DELIA enter Grandma's room. The room was always locked, and Delia had the only key. He waited for a moment, then followed her inside. The gun that Granddad had given him felt heavy and hard in his pocket.

Delia was dusting a small table with a white cloth. She looked up at him for a moment and then went right back to work. Jack had never been in this room before, and he looked around, trying to take it all in.

He could not remember Grandma's face. The one that Mother had showed him in photographs, the pale-looking woman with heavy dark eyebrows and the serious expression, was a stranger to him. But inside this room, the scent of mothballs, lavender, and something else he couldn't name opened a door somewhere in his mind, and for a moment he was in the presence of something warm and living.

"Why does Granddad keep Grandma's room locked?" Jack asked.

"That's his business," Delia said. Jack immediately felt small and foolish again, shut out. Then, as if Delia sensed that, she added in a softer voice, "I guess he doesn't want anyone messing with your Grandma's things."

"But *you're* in here messing with them." Jack knew there must be something wrong with what he'd said, because he could see Delia stiffen and pause for a moment before she continued with her work. When she spoke again, her voice was not as soft.

"I do what your Granddad pays me to do. That's all."

Jack felt a door shut in his face. And it made him angry. The soft, fragrant, invisible presence he felt in this room belonged to him. Not to her. This was his place, not hers. Everything here belonged to him.

"Why don't you go play outside?" Delia said. Jack didn't want to play outside. He was tired of killing flies. Tired of being told what to do.

When Delia left the room for a moment, Jack looked around, not knowing what he was looking for. His eye fell on a small box on the dresser table. It was made of black, shiny wood and the lid was painted with what looked like Japanese women in long flowing robes dancing under spidery-looking trees full of white flowers.

He tried to open the box but couldn't. Then he found the small golden clasp, undid it and lifted the painted lid. Inside was a necklace made of what looked to him like pearls, and a gold ring that held what he knew must be a diamond. The soft, fragrant presence that he'd always felt in this room—this was where it was coming from. This was its beating heart.

Jack scooped the necklace and the ring up into his hand and shoved them deep into his pocket. He snapped the lid shut, then turned and walked out the door, passing Delia in the hallway.

"Don't you be late to supper this time," he heard her say behind him, but he was busy thinking about what he'd just done, and the new soft weight in his pocket.

*Treasure.* He had treasure. It was his now. No one else's.

Walking down the stairs, Jack suddenly knew what to do next.

Everybody knows what you do with treasure, he thought. You bury it.


FATHER WAS SITTING alone at the table when Cassie came in for lunch. It wasn't unusual to find him here alone reading the newspaper or going through his mail. Today he was sitting with nothing in front of him, his hands out of sight beneath the table, his face set in a stony expression that made something in her gut feel tight.

"Cassie. Tell Delia to come in here."

*Why?* That was the question she wanted to ask, but something in Father's voice and expression told her not to.

Cassie found Delia at the kitchen counter preparing lunch for the family. "Delia, Father wants to see you." Cassie saw an expression she couldn't read flicker across Delia's face, a kind of tenseness that she immediately smoothed over. Delia set the plate she was filling down on the countertop, wiped her hands with a dishtowel, then followed Cassie out into the dining room.

"Sit down," Father said. Cassie saw Delia hesitate, her eyes moving around as if she was trying to decide on the proper place. She finally chose a chair across from Father, pulled it out carefully as if she was afraid of hurting it, then sat down, her hands folded in her lap, her eyes focused on the bare table in front of her.

For a while, Father did not speak. When he finally did, it was in a voice that was so low and measured that Cassie recognized he was exerting a great deal of effort to control himself.

"You remember Jeb." It was not a question, but Delia answered anyway.

"Yes sir."

"You were here when we bought him. How many years did we have him?"

Delia didn't answer for a moment. Cassie tried to imagine why Father was asking about a dog who'd been dead for fifteen years.

"How many years did we have him?" Father asked again.

"Ten," Cassie answered.

"Ten," Father nodded. "Ten years. During all those years, you think I treated that dog well?"

"Yes sir."

"When he got sick, I took care of him. Sat up with him all night. You remember?"

"Yes sir."

"And that time he ran off and I went looking for him. Found him stuck in a briar patch, all cut up. I carried him all the way back home myself. You remember that?"

Delia nodded.

"And that day he turned on me. Bit my hand clean down to the bone, and I shot him. Do you know why? I shot him because I couldn't trust him anymore. I never imagined he would do something like that to me. Never even thought of it. And then he did. Because something changed. There was something inside of him all those years that stopped him from doing something like that to me. Then it was gone."

Cassie saw Father bring his hands up from his lap and set something down on the table. It took her a moment to recognize what she was looking at. A small, shiny black lacquer box with a painted lid. Delia was now holding herself so still, Cassie was no longer sure if she was even breathing.

Father pushed the box across the table toward Delia. It made a harsh sliding sound that seemed louder than it should have been.

"Open it."

Cassie saw Delia's eyes dart back and forth and come to rest on Cassie's face, only for a second, a look of pure fear and pleading. Then Delia looked away again, back down at the small black box on the table in front of her.

"Open it." Father's voice was louder now, with a harsher edge to it. Delia took a deep, shuddering sigh, then moved her hand closer to the box.

*Don't,* Cassie thought. *Don't do it,* she wanted to say, but the words stuck in her throat. Cassie opened the metal clasp and lifted the lid that came open with a soft sucking sound.

"What's inside?" Father asked. Delia held herself very still. Cassie thought she could see the light dimming in her eyes. Father asked again, "What's inside?"

"Nothing." Delia's voice sounded both very clear and very far away.

"Nothing," Father repeated. "Put your fingers in the box."

Cassie saw a flash of fear in Delia's eyes. "Father..." she started to say.

*"Shut your mouth!"* Father roared. It was the first sign of anger he'd showed so far, and it stabbed her through the heart like a sword, pinning her to the wall. Father turned back to Delia and repeated in the same quiet, steely voice, "Put your fingers in the box."

Cassie could see Delia trembling now. She wanted to run over and gather Delia up in her arms, take her away from here, but the sword Father had put through her heart still held her. Frozen, like in a nightmare, she watched Delia close her eyes, reach over slowly, and put her fingers inside the black lacquer box.

In an instant, Father was on his feet, snapping the lid shut on Delia's fingers and smashing down hard with both hands while Delia screamed and struggled. Cassie saw her slide from the chair and onto her knees, shrieking and begging, her hands still held fast by the box while Father stood over her, pressing down on the lid with his full weight, the muscles and veins in his neck bulging with effort.

Then he was pulling Delia up from the floor by one arm and dragging her toward the door. Opening it with one hand, he flung Delia outside, roaring, *"Never come back here, do you hear me? Never!"* Cassie caught one final glimpse of Delia sobbing and rocking on her knees, clutching her hands to her chest, before Father slammed the door shut.

Cassie felt as though the trembling she'd seen in Delia's body had somehow passed into hers. She couldn't move or speak. She could hear Father breathing heavily, and saw him reach up and undo the top button on his starched white shirt. "Take that thing away," he said, glancing irritably at the box on the table. Then he was gone.

Cassie waited until she trusted her legs to support her. Then she walked slowly over to the dining room table where the lacquer box had fallen over onto its side. Hands trembling, she reached over and turned it right side up. Inside, the faded velvet lining was wet with blood.

A few minutes later, she heard Jack laughing outside. He and Father were in the garden, playing. She could see them through the window, Father holding a red rubber ball high above his head, teasing Jack like he was a dog, then tossing the ball into the high grass at the edge of the lawn. Jack eagerly ran after it, plunging into the tall reeds; she could see them moving even after Jack had disappeared, the tops of the reeds lashing back and forth.

*

CASSIE WAS IN her bedroom packing clothes into her suitcase when Father found her.

"What do you think you're doing?"

Cassie froze for a moment, feeling she'd been caught doing something wrong. But she wasn't. She was doing what she had to do. She kept packing, not looking at Father.

"I'm sorry you had to see that," Father said, his voice low, almost gentle. "Things like that... I've always tried to keep you away from them."

"Things like that? *Things like that?* Jesus Christ, Father... Thirty years. She's been with our family for *thirty years.*"

"I know. That's what makes it so terrible."

Cassie stared at Father standing in the doorway of her room and saw that he didn't quite fill the doorframe the way she remembered. He was growing smaller. When had he started growing smaller?

"You feel sorry for her," he said. "You think she's been hurt."

"Jesus, Father, her hands..."

"The woman lives under my roof for thirty years. Takes the money I pay her. Eats the food I provide. And she steals. From your mother. From a dead woman. And you think *she's* the one who's been hurt."

"I can't... I just can't believe..."

"What? You can't believe she'd do it? Why? Because you grew up with her? Because she helped raise you? She was *paid* to do that. You think she loves you? For God's sake, Cassie, grow up. She's not your family. She's a thief and an opportunist. You think this is the first time she's done something like this? It's just the first time she's been caught, that's all."

The more Father talked, the weaker Cassie felt. All she wanted was to sink down into the darkness somewhere and sleep. Then the sound of Delia's screams came back to her, and she shook off the dullness fogging her brain and kept packing, shoving things into her suitcase without even looking at them. She had to get out. She had to take whatever was hers and get out of here now.

"Where do you think you're going to go?" Father's voice pursued her. "You have no money. No home. What do you think is going to happen to you out there? And what about Jack? You're going to take a child out into the world with nothing? You don't know anything about life. About how people live. About how they really are."

As Cassie watched, the scowl on Father's face faded and transformed into a friendly-looking smile that was even more horrible to look at. Cassie knew without turning around that he was no longer looking at her. *"Hey* there, Jackie boy..."

Casie turned and saw Jack standing in the hallway outside, looking in through the open door. The expression on his face was unreadable, but Cassie could see a glint of fear in his eyes, although whether it was fear of her or of Father, she couldn't tell.

"Jack, come here," she said. She could hear how ragged and strange her voice sounded and knew how strange she must have sounded to Jack too, because he stayed where he was in the hallway, not moving. She held out her right hand toward him, grateful to see that it wasn't trembling. "Jack... please..."

Before she could finish, Jack ran past her and buried himself in his Grandfather's arms. Father beamed and reached down to run his big hand through Jack's hair. "That's right, Jackie, that's right," he said. "Your mother isn't feeling very well right now. Let's you and me go outside and give her a little time to rest. Okay?"

Cassie stood by the bed and the pile of unfolded clothes, watching the two of them go through the door and down the hallway. She could almost swear that she saw their solid bodies dissolving in the afternoon light, their backs turned to her, holding hands.

THE FEEL OF dried breadcrumbs in her pockets, rough against her fingers. She could still feel them. Why were her pockets filled with breadcrumbs? For the cygnets. She had filled her pockets with breadcrumbs for the cygnets. She had to find them. She had to find them and feed them the breadcrumbs so they wouldn't starve. They were starving now because of her. Their mother was dead. Because of her. It was all because of her, and now she had to find them. Into the high reeds she went, nearer and nearer to the water, the ground turning soft and wet under her shoes that came loose with a soft sucking sound. Then she felt something else beneath her feet and looked down.

Red and white. Downy white feathers trembling in the wind, rising out of deep smears of red, something like crushed eggshells and the huge footprint that had smashed and ground them all into the mud. All of them. All of them.

There was vomit down the front of her dress when she got back to the house. Delia had brought her inside and helped clean her off.

THE PHONE RANG and cut through the fog of Cassie's dream like a knife. Delia had always taken Father's messages; now, every time the phone rang, it was a reminder of her absence and of what had happened. The guilty ache that Cassie had managed to dull with bourbon pierced her chest again and again with every ring, and she snatched the receiver off the cradle to stop it.

"Hello…" Cassie slurred, alarmed by the drunken sound of her own voice. There was silence on the other end of the line, then a slow and tense-sounding intake of breath. The voice on the other end of the line was familiar but grim.

"Miss Cassie…"

At the sound of her name, Cassie began sobbing. "Oh God, Delia, I'm sorry. I'm so sorry…"

Silence on the other end again, longer this time. Cassie was sure that Delia had hung up. Then she heard that same weary drawing in of breath. When the voice began to speak again, it was even slower and more deliberate. Deliberate and cold, cutting into Cassie's flesh.

"There's some clothes and pictures in my room there. I want them. I'll come for them tonight."

Terror pushed its way up into Cassie's throat so fast, she almost couldn't speak. "No! No, don't! It's not safe…"

Another pause. "Come to the back door at eleven. Bring my things down. I won't come inside. I'll just take my things and go."

"No, Delia, please. I just… I just don't want anything bad to happen…"

"Something bad *already* happened. You ought to know—you were there."

"I know. God, Delia, I'm so sorry. It just happened so fast…"

"I don't mean *that*," Delia spit out the word. "Thirty years. Thirty years, you were there watching. You didn't say anything. And *now* you're worried about it."

The silence now was vibrant with rage and pain—better,

much better, Cassie thought, than the coldness from before. Better to be attacked than shut out.

"Eleven o'clock," the voice on the other end finally said. "I'll be at the back door for my things. You can do that?"

"Yes," Cassie said. At that moment, she felt sure that she would do anything for her.

Cassie heard the line go dead in her hand, and that was when she remembered what she'd been dreaming. She saw the cygnets huddled together in the tall reeds by the shore, crying for food, crying for their mother. She was one of them, the reeds tall as trees around her, bending back and forth in the cold wind. She could hear the sound of something coming closer, something large and powerful moving through the reeds. She tried to call out for help, but her voice was nothing more than a strange mewling cry in her throat.

Red and white. When Cassie closed her eyes, that's what she saw. Red and white and a feeling like wanting to vomit and scream rising in her throat.

*They're animals. You are not. Remember that.*


WHEN JACK WOKE up in the dark, he knew instantly that he was alone in the big bed. Mother was gone. He sat up in bed and listened. No sounds in the dark room. No sounds in the hallway outside.

Moonlight poured in through a window ahead of him like a spotlight on the cold stone floor. Jack stepped into it and looked through the glass at the dark shapes of trees gathered on the other side. The trees were thrashing back and forth like something enormous and invisible was moving through them.

They were coming now. He'd felt it for a long time, ever since he and Mommy had come to this place. Now it was real. Now it was all about to happen. He had to stop them. It was his duty. It was what he had come here for.

Jack reached up and dragged the heavy iron bolt back, then pulled the big front door open. Wind and the smell of pine trees rushed in over him. He stood there for a moment, safe on the inside. Then he stepped over the threshold onto the front porch where the wind was louder. Below him was the lake, hidden in the trees. Words Granddad had used, *high ground, line of fire, arc of observation,* came and went through his head like the leaves scattering in the wind across the lawn. Then he stepped off the porch and started making his way around the big house, holding his toy gun out in front of him.

Voices came toward him around the corner. Loud, angry voices, but the wind tore the words into pieces and scattered them. His arm started to tremble, but he kept holding it straight out in front of him as he stepped around the corner.

Granddad was standing in the backyard, pointing his shotgun down at someone who lay huddled on the ground. It was Granddad's voice he'd heard, raised in anger, but the wind was mixing his words up and Jack could only hear a few of them that blew in his direction. They were ugly words, words he knew no one should ever say.

At first, he thought the body on the ground was dead, but then it moved, a face lifted up, broken and twisted. He knew that face. A few shreds of wailing blew past him, lost in the wind. He saw Granddad lift the shotgun higher, taking aim.

Jack raised his toy gun toward Granddad. He tried to shout *No* but what came out was a wordless noise that the wind carried away. Jack aimed, closed his eyes and squeezed the trigger.

There was a loud noise, a sharp *crack.* Jack opened his eyes and saw Granddad drop the shotgun and stumble backward until his back hit the trunk of a tree. Mouthing more words that Jack couldn't hear, Granddad clawed angrily at the front of his shirt where a dark stain was growing. He sat down on the ground, slowly, awkwardly. Something black came out of his mouth, and he stopped moving.

Jack saw Mother standing inside the back door, holding one of Granddad's pistols in front of her with both hands. The person on the ground got up and ran, but Mother stayed in the doorway, not moving. It was Mother's face, but it was not her face. There was something gone from it now.

Jack turned and ran away from the house and down the hill in the dark, down the long sloping road through the trees toward the lake. Flashes of bright white light came to him in the spaces between the trees.

When Jack reached the shore, the lake was on fire, its whole surface a sea of blinding, surging white. Hundreds of strong wings and long graceful necks stretching and uncurling themselves like sleepers waking. The sound was deafening and terrible; Jack covered his ears to keep it out, but it would not be kept out. He shut his eyes against it and when he opened them, the white had turned to red and white.

As he watched, both colors rose into the air and broke apart, a whole sky of strong wings and beaks and black eyes that saw him and were coming for him now. Jack raised his toy gun again and held it straight out in front of him. But in the moment before they reached him, he knew he could not stop them. He knew that whatever power he had or thought he had was not enough and could never be enough to stop what was coming now.

# Lost River Boys

I DON'T KNOW WHO brought the first gift down to the cave. I'd heard about it but didn't want to believe it. One lonely, gift-wrapped present sitting on the cold ground outside that deep, dark hole—it was too sad, too terrible to think about. But it was impossible not to think about.

That first Christmas was the hardest. No one could bring themselves to put up a tree or lights, except for Mary Davis. Her boy Jordan had loved Christmas. *What if he comes back*, she said, *and there's no tree, no lights? How will he know he's home?* No one had the heart to argue with that.

That's how it started. You spend so many years doing things for your kids, it's hard to stop. Besides, once one of us had done it, how could the rest of us just stand by and *not* do it?

There were a couple of video games that I'd bought for Billy a few months ago and hidden in the closet. I took them down and wrapped them in Christmas paper. Then I put on my winter coat and drove down to the cave.

There were a lot of cars parked along the road when I got there. I climbed down that steep trail and saw candles flickering in the darkness ahead of me. They were all there—Mary and Bill Davis, Betty and Randall Corwin, Elly and Robert Carver, and all the rest of us.

Today we keep the mouth of the cave clear and open as it was ten thousand years ago. No wire fence, no KEEP OUT signs—because there's no one left to keep out. We're a small town, barely a town at all, and when Billy went down into the cave that night, he took every boy in town with him. Every one.

The pile of presents was bigger than I'd expected. They weren't inside the mouth of the cave, but on the wide, flat shelf of limestone rock that led down into it. Big presents and little presents wrapped in bright, colorful wrapping paper covered with candy canes, Christmas trees, laughing Santa faces, and angels blowing long golden trumpets.

My legs felt heavy like I was walking through something thick and unyielding, but I pushed my way through it and walked over to that big, shiny pile and laid my gift down alongside the rest. I was just going to drive home and drink the pint of bourbon I'd bought this morning. Then I noticed that no one else was going anywhere. They were all standing around the presents like people gathered around a bonfire, waiting for something to happen.

Someone handed me a candle, the flame trembling in the cool breeze blowing from the mouth of the cave. We all stood there in the dark with our little candles, not speaking. I thought of pictures I'd seen in the news of men and women doing the same thing in New York City, in Israel, and other places. Always the same faces, always the same candles.

Then Mary Davis started to sing *Silent Night*. That thin, quavering voice stung me like an electrical shock. I could feel the candle in my hand, a drop of hot wax landing on my index finger and turning cool and hard while Mary sang. By the time she got halfway through, a few more voices had joined in. I sang too. How could I not?

When we were done, no one spoke. The air had turned cold, bitter cold, and I could see a few flakes drifting down from the darkness into the weak circle of light we made. Randall Carver put his hand on his wife's arm, turned her around, then they left first. Then the Bakers. Finally, we all turned around and started climbing the steep trail back up the ridge and away from the cave.

I didn't want to look back, but I couldn't help it. I'd thought that a whole pile of Christmas presents somehow wouldn't look as sad as one or two, but I was wrong. It was the saddest thing I'd ever seen in my life.

BOYS LOVE FORBIDDEN places. Put a sign over the gates of Hell that says KEEP OUT and boys will run right into the fire, every time. A few warning signs and some chicken wire might keep out chickens, but it won't keep out young boys.

The first time Billy came home with that red clay all over his knees and elbows, I knew where he'd been. I was all set to punish him, then he started telling me about the things he'd seen down there. Rooms big as cathedrals. Snow-white fish with no eyes. Crickets big as dogs. I listened and knew he was making it up, but the longer he went on, the more I started to believe it. Not because I thought it was true, but because it made him happy, and that made me happy too.

That first Christmas when we all sang and left our presents at the cave, I went home and had a dream. In my dream I saw snow falling from the sky, each flake so perfect it looked like they were cut out of paper, like that snow you see in a school play. I watched it gather on the presents until they were all buried under a blanket of white.

The next morning, I stopped by Johnson's for a cup of coffee and saw Elly Carver and Betty Corwin talking with Bud Johnson in the back of the store. Mary Davis was sitting at the orange Formica table, not saying anything.

"What time did it happen?" I heard Bud Johnson ask.

"I don't know," Betty said, "She says she got there around eight o'clock."

"And she didn't see anyone?"

"No. No one."

At first, I thought someone's house had been broken into. I walked over and Betty Corwin glared at me.

"They're gone," she whispered fiercely.

"Who?" I said.

"The presents. They're all gone."

Elly and Betty kept talking about how awful it was. *What kind of person would do something like that?* Bud Johnson talked about calling Sheriff Perkins, but in the end we decided that nothing had been stolen because the presents didn't really belong to anyone. The whole time, Mary Davis didn't say anything. She just kept sitting at that orange table, staring straight ahead like she was looking at something the rest of us couldn't see.

BILLY WAS THIRTEEN when we lost him. That's old enough to feel the things a man feels. But boys are slower to grow, slower to understand and realize things.

I'd noticed Kathy watching Billy long before he did. Letting her eyes linger on him a little longer, standing a little closer than she had to. Billy didn't notice, not at first, and when he finally did, I'm not sure he understood. He'd known her all his life which probably made it easier for him to not see her in the way that she was just beginning to see him.

Kathy ran with Billy's crowd, made it *her* crowd so she could be near him. She followed him everywhere, and on that night when Billy led those boys down into the cave, she went with him. They say that when the search parties found her and brought her out, she fought them. I even saw the scratches and bruises on her arms. That's the kind of love you have to admire, the kind that deserves a chance to grow.

One morning not long after that terrible night, I found a note in my mailbox, a piece of looseleaf paper with two words written in a careful, childish hand. *I'm sorry.* Even though it wasn't signed, I knew who it was.

I found Kathy sitting alone in the lunchroom the way she had every day for the past six months. Her eyes grew wide when she saw me, and I saw her muscles tense like she was about to get up and run. Then she sank back into her seat, head down.

I slipped onto the bench next to her, careful not to sit too close. "Kathy, honey," I said, "You don't have anything to be sorry about."

That's when she started crying. It surprised me; I'd never seen her cry before, not even right after Billy had disappeared. She cried silently, but in that way that's impossible to hide, her mouth twisted and ugly like she was in pain.

My heart hurt for her, and I put my hand on her back and rubbed it in slow, comforting circles, the way I used to do for Billy when he was a baby. "Sweetheart, don't cry," I said. "It's not your fault." I knew how false my words must have felt to her. But in words of consolation, there's a greater truth at work. So, I said them anyway.

Sometimes I wonder what would have happened if she and Billy had more time. Maybe it's not a proper thing for a mother to wonder about, but I can't help it. We all want our sons to be happy. Even when it's too late for that.

THAT NEXT CHRISTMAS, we did it all over again. We brought our presents down to the mouth of the cave, lit our candles, and sang. Before we left, there was some talk about last year, about whether or not the same thing might happen. Bill Davis got angry and said he was going to wait up all night with his shotgun and shoot the first son of a bitch who put his hands on those presents. As soon as he said it, Mary Davis grabbed her husband's arm like he was already pointing the shotgun and cried out, "No!"

That's when I knew. That's when we all knew what we'd been thinking deep down inside but didn't have the nerve to say. Can you blame us? Even Christ's disciples when they saw his tomb empty didn't realize what it meant at first. We were no different.

I went home and dreamed that we were all standing outside the cave. The snow was falling like bits of lace, and we were singing. I couldn't hear the words, and the melody was unclear, but I could feel the sound of it swelling inside my chest and rise in my throat and come pouring from my mouth. It was the most wonderful thing I'd ever felt. I could see a light inside the cave, not from a lantern or a fire, but like the air itself was made of light, the way the sky just before sunrise looks swollen with it. The light inside the cave was pulsing, and I realized it was pulsing in time with our singing, and the louder we sang, the brighter it grew.

The next morning the presents were gone.

At first, there was some talk about going to the authorities and asking them to search the cave, but it never got any farther than that. The authorities had come and gone the year before, the cave had been searched and the search had been called off. What were we supposed to tell them now? What could we say that anyone else would believe? We could pretend it never happened. Or we could just keep going.

And for three more winters, that's what we did. The presents and the candles and the singing. I think it's fair to say that those were the last happy years of my life. And even though I can only speak for myself, I think it was probably true for all of us.

You might wonder how we could just go on like that and never talk about what was happening and what it meant. Once in a while, some of us would start down that road, but never very far. There was no need to. When something is perfect, why question it?

Then, in the fifth year, it stopped. The next day, and the next, and the next, the presents sat there on the cold, hard ground. They stayed there until the bright paper start to wrinkle and sag in the cold and the freezing rain. Mary Davis ignored our warnings and took to sitting up all night on the ridge above the cave until her husband would come and take her home.

For me, it felt like losing Billy all over again. The past four years had been a sort of gift, a period of grace I could never have asked for or imagined. I'd never thought of it stopping, but now it had, and all the grief that was left over from that terrible time five years before came rushing to the surface.

Every morning when I stepped outside, I saw the same houses, the same roads stretching back and forth to the same places. But it had all changed. Everything looked ugly to me now, flat and lifeless like a bad painting of itself. It may be that miracles run their course like a human life, and that it's no one's fault when they end. But that's not how this felt. I felt like I'd been tricked. When I looked at the people I saw on the street or in the stores or at work, I wondered if they felt like I did. How could they all act like nothing had changed?

One Thursday in late October I showed up at Johnston's for my morning cup of coffee and found the door locked. I figured Bud was just late for some reason but when I dropped by that afternoon on my way home from school, the place was still closed.

Later, Betty told me that Bud Johnson's daughter Courtney had gone missing. Bud had called the sheriff around eight o'clock saying that Courtney had not come home from school. Like her father, Courtney Johnson ran her days and nights like clockwork; up at six thirty, out the door by seven, home by four. Bud had called all her friends, working his way down that list until there was no one left.

Because he had no sons, Bud had not been part of our little town's tragedy five years ago. Those of us who'd lost our boys in that cave had been cut off from our neighbors who had only daughters and had escaped our particular kind of grief. Now, Bud Johnson began to fade away right before our eyes. After a while, people simply no longer knew what to say or how to act around him, so they took to avoiding him. I did too. I'm not proud of it. But I'm no better than anyone else.

Then Rebecca Wallace disappeared in early December. A search party found her shirt in the woods about forty yards from the trail that runs from the back of Bud Johnson's store to the old quarry. All the buttons were missing, indicating that it had been torn off. Broken branches and disturbances on the forest floor were consistent with a struggle. That was the phrase the Maysville paper used—*consistent with a struggle.* One word, cold and scientific. The other, raw and terrible.

Kaitlin Simmons disappeared next. This time, unlike the other two girls before her, someone saw her being taken.

Kailtlin's brother Orin, who was four years old at the time, said he saw it happen. Because he was only four, and because the things he said were so odd, few were inclined to believe him.

Kaitlin had taken her baby brother and their dog for a walk in the woods just after supper like they did every night. Orin said that at one point the dog started baying and howling and took off into the woods after something. When police questioned him, Orin said he saw his sister struggling with someone, though he couldn't identify the figure because its hair was long and covered its face. When asked how he knew the figure was male, the boy said *because it was naked.*

State police combed the woods around Lost River and even entered the cave as far back as they could go, but there was no sign of Kaitlin or the other two girls. A homeless man was found living in a shelter he'd built out of cardboard boxes and tree branches about a half-mile out of town, was brought in for questioning and then taken away. For a while, people felt safer and started letting their girls go out again after dark.

"You know why they didn't find anything in that cave?" Betty Corwin said when I saw her at Johnson's one Friday morning. "They didn't go back far enough."

"You think those girls are down there?" I asked. Betty didn't answer but squinted fiercely out the back window into the green leaves at something beyond them.

That night I spent hours on the computer looking at maps of caves. I knew how large the network of caves under us was, but seeing it laid out in graphs and grids made me feel uneasy. It's strange to think that while we're busy at our jobs or in our kitchens making supper or resting in our beds at night, there's a whole world right below us, one that's been there for a million years and will still be there for another million years after we're dead and gone.

I thought again of the wild stories Billy used to tell about his journeys down into the cave and the things he'd seen there. He used to draw pictures of his explorations and had once shown me a whole roll of wrapping paper that he'd covered with a map and illustrations. I remember how he'd come back from one of his underground journeys with his pants torn and muddy, how he'd spread that big roll of paper out on the floor and lay there gripping a pencil in his hand, adding a new tunnel, a new chamber, a new part of that secret world he loved.

I went into Billy's room and reached up to the back of the closet shelf until my fingers touched something that felt like a scroll. I took it down, feeling like a thief, peeled off the rubber band and started unrolling it.

Seeing Billy's drawings and handwriting again made my heart hurt for a moment, but I shut my eyes, took a deep breath, then made myself look again. I'd forgotten how good his drawings were. Here again was the proof. Scaly, eyeless creatures with fins like dragon's wings, towering waterfalls high as skyscrapers with tiny human figures for scale, and below each drawing, in Billy's careful script, names like *Blind Ghost Fish, Hall of Forgotten Voices,* and *Tunnel of No Turning Back.*

I unrolled the scroll further. In the center of the map was a drawing of a naked girl with her legs spread far apart. Standing between her thighs and towering above her was some kind of man-like creature, his enormous phallus buried half inside her. The girl's head was thrown back and Billy had drawn her mouth stretched wide open in what could have been a howl of pleasure or agony. The man-creature's teeth were bare and clenched, and rays of light were shooting out of his eyes.

I shoved that scroll as far back as I could into the closet shelf, then sat there at the kitchen table with the blood pounding in my ears, trying to get that picture out of my head. Behind my eyes was an empty space slowly filling with a new thought, one that had been there all along trying to get in.

When Billy was eleven, I'd given him one of those action figures for Christmas, the same ones I'd been giving him since he was four or five. A few weeks later I'd found it sticking out of the trash can in his room. When I asked about it, he said, *I'm too old for that now, Mom.* I'd thought he was just being silly. But when I looked at him and saw how his face was starting to change, growing harder and leaner, I knew he was right. There it was, right in front of me every day, and I'd missed it.

The next morning, I met Betty Corwin at Johnson's before heading in to work. We sat at the orange Formica table in back with steam rising from our big Styrofoam cups.

"How old would the boys be now?" I asked.

Betty's expression was startled, almost angry.

"Fifteen, I guess," she said, her lips tight and her voice flat. "Maybe sixteen."

"Seventeen," I said. "Almost eighteen."

Betty looked at me, waiting for me to go on.

"Betty," I said after a while, "Did Neal... did he ever have a girlfriend? A girl he liked?"

Betty kept looking me in the eye, but I could see something inside her flinch. "Rebecca," she finally said in a low, clipped voice, as if saying the names of the missing was disrespectful or unlucky. "Rebecca Wallace."

"Do you think… do you think they ever…"

"No," she said, shaking her head and glancing away, "He was… he was too young for that."

"What about now?"

Betty looked back at me, her eyes wide and fearful.

*"Now?"* she whispered.

"Yes."

Betty kept staring at me, her eyes filling with a fear I recognized. For a moment I wasn't sure if she was going start crying or slap my face. Suddenly she was on her feet, grabbing at her coat. "I have to go," she said, her voice tight and strained.

"Betty, wait…" I said, reaching up to touch her arm. She flailed out and knocked my hand away.

"No!" she hissed, her face angry and terrified. "You're crazy! What the hell is wrong with you? Stay away from me!" She walked away fast and didn't turn around again. A moment later I heard the screen door slam.

I thought about following her and telling her I was sorry. But I wasn't sorry. I hadn't even known what I was going to say until I'd said it. Now it was out there, and I couldn't take it back. I wasn't sorry. I was angry. Angry at myself for not understanding. Like Christ's disciples, like young boys, we're all too slow to realize the truth of things.


THAT WAS THE summer when Kathy came back home. I knew her the moment I saw her. Taller now, the same chestnut hair covering that same sad, cautious face. She was eighteen now, and in college, which was hard to get used to, although it was right there in front of my eyes. The legs that seemed longer than possible, the sudden and alarming breasts. And above it all, those same sad eyes. She surprised me by pulling a bottle of wine out of her backpack. Red, which I don't like, but for her sake I brought out two glasses and we sat at my kitchen table and drank it while the light outside turned rosy and dim.

We spoke of the usual things that a young woman and an old woman talk about. Her mother who was ill. College, which I'd heard was not going well for her, and which she did not bother to hide from me. We still had not spoken of Billy. I was waiting for her to be ready.

After our second glass, she finally said his name. "Do you think Billy suffered?"

*He's suffering now,* is what I wanted to say, but didn't. She wasn't ready for that yet.

So, I poured her another glass and told the story I'd prepared, the one about the light in the cave. Children had seen it, I told her, a light hovering in the darkness far back in the mouth of the cave like the glow of a candle that had broken free, drifting on its own. Sometimes motionless, other times moving like a dandelion seed caught in an invisible current of air.

"Have *you* seen it?" she asked. Her face looked thirteen again, the years washed away by the wine and the fading light. I couldn't risk her going away again. I could tell she was almost there. Almost ready.

"Yes."

I saw the word hit her like a blow, but the look in her eyes was more hopeful than fearful. She asked me if I was frightened when I saw the light and I told her no, no I wasn't. I told her that the light was warm and peaceful and comforting and every other good thing I could think of. When she finally said that she wanted to see it too, I thought *Of course. Of course you do.*

I told her we should go right now while the spirit was on us. But first, I asked her if she wanted to wash up a little. She'd driven a long way, hadn't she? Yes, she said, she had, so I led her to the bathroom and gave her a clean washcloth and a hairbrush to use, sweet-smelling lotions for her skin. I stood in the hallway and watched her brushing her long dark hair until it was almost shining.

I told her to stay close to me when we climbed down the steep trail into the gorge, but of course she knew the way in the dark as well as I did. We reached the limestone ledge at the edge of the river. I could feel the cave breathing its wet, cold breath over my skin. I knew she could feel it too because I could see her hair lifting in the breeze that was pouring up from underground.

"Is this where it happens?" she asked.

*Yes,* I thought, *Yes. This is where it happens.*

My heart was hammering so hard in my chest that I couldn't trust myself to speak, so I raised my arm and pointed into the darkness that yawned in front of us. We were both silent for a long while, and in the silence, I could feel her looking, searching. When she spoke again, still in a whisper, I could hear the rasp of heartbreak in it, and it nearly killed me.

"I don't see it."

"Go a little closer," I said. She turned toward me and, even in the dark, I thought I saw a flash of fear in her eyes. "It's okay," I said, smiling as best I could. She looked back toward the cave, and I could feel her hesitate. I put my hand on her warm, bare arm. It wasn't a push, not really, but it was enough to make her take a step toward that black opening in front of us, then another.

Just before she stepped inside the mouth of the cavern, she paused one last time. "Go on," I said.

She turned once more and looked back at me. I could see the pale oval of her face, like the face of a young deer or a calf in a dark barn. And that's when I realized that she knew. She knew what this was. She knew and she didn't run.

For a moment, I thought I saw a light glimmering in the darkness behind her where I knew there could be no light. Then the darkness slipped around her like a cloak and she was gone.

I turned my back and walked away, back up that winding trail in the dark. I don't remember how I got back, just branches coming out of the blackness to claw at my face and arms, the moon racing overhead behind the trees, following me. When I finally reached the top and saw my car still there, waiting for me, and that empty passenger seat, I bent over and was sick by the side of the road, vomiting out the wine we'd drunk and whatever else was left inside of me.

And that's how I felt for a few days afterward. Empty. Like I'd emptied myself of the thing that had been killing me and was now just waiting for something new to take its place.

The police came with their questions and their stern, sad faces. What was her car doing in my driveway? When had I last seen her? I told them that she'd come to visit, that we'd talked for a while, then she'd gone for a walk. All of that was true. A few days later her face started appearing on flyers on the post office bulletin board and in store windows. *Don't waste your time,* I wanted to say. All those empty plans for the future, college, a family and a home far from here, were a mistake, an illusion. Her path led back to this place, toward a greater purpose. In the end, she had seen that. It was what she wanted.

All of our old girls are gone now, the ones who were around in the beginning. They've disappeared or been taken away by their parents to safer places, far from this one. I don't blame them. People protect their own. That too is part of the way things are.

Still, nature provides. More and more new families are moving here, drawn to the mountains, and the wildflowers, and the cool blue-green river that runs through it like a dream. It draws them, and they come. Like the family who just moved here from Maysville. They have three daughters, six, seven, and nine. Strong as heifers, they climb trees, throw rocks, and aren't afraid of anything under the sun. Their mother shakes her head and smiles, "They may not look like much, but they're going to make fine wives and mothers one day."

And I think, *Yes, they will. Oh yes. They will.*

# The Armor of Light

THERE WERE SEVEN. Seven young men who appeared, one after the other, every two years or so. They all wore the same black suit and white clerical collar that my father wore, but on them it looked wrong. One looked like he was trying to pretend the white collar wasn't choking him. One looked like he was at the end of a leash that no one else could see. One had a habit of keeping his hands behind his back, so that I wondered if there was something wrong with them, or if he had any hands at all. One was an artist who made strange sculptures of sharp, jagged metal that looked dangerous and were titled *Crucifixion #1*, *Crucifixion #2*, etc. One was quiet and overweight and disappeared overnight. None of them lasted longer than two years. None of them were meant to. They were all temporary, like young children with heart defects. Not long for this world.

The idea was for these young men to follow my father around for a year or two, learn from him, and then move on to take charge of churches of their own. I watched them come and go with a mix of curiosity and jealousy. I had no intention of following in my father's footsteps, but there was something troubling about watching him share the secrets of his calling with a series of strangers.

Growing up in the church, there were things that I took for granted. Some of them were hard to explain. Like the special connection I felt between myself and the mysterious power that hid in the shadows above the altar. A small child once asked if I was Jesus, because he thought that my father was God. I laughed, but it made sense to me. I felt like an insider. But there were other things that I was still too young to understand.

At our house, the phone would ring in the middle of the night, then I'd hear my father talking from the bedroom upstairs in his low, even voice. Sometimes I'd hear him come downstairs, start the car and leave; other times, he'd just talk, slowly and calmly, until I fell asleep to the strong and gentle sound of his voice drifting down through the ceiling above.

One night when the phone rang around two AM, I picked it up just to see what would happen. The terrible strangled sounds at the other end were barely human. The next day, my father told me to never pick up the phone when it rang that late at night. He didn't have to tell me. I never did it again.

Years later, when I was grown, I asked him how he did it. How did he listen to human beings at the end of their rope, suffering the very worst things in life? How did he know what to say to them? "It's not what I say," he told me. "It's my presence."

That's when I knew what was wrong with those seven young men who'd come and gone from of our lives over the years. They were like photographs developing in a darkroom, exposed to the light too soon. Pale and raw. Barely human.

The first one was Reverend Carson. He came when I was eleven. Reverend Carson was the first grown man I'd ever seen with a full beard, except for pictures of Jesus and the apostles. He was what people like to call *intense* and appeared to move among us in a sort of meditative ecstatic state. When spoken to, his white-toothed grin would suddenly flash from the middle of his dark beard, and he'd answer in the tone of a benevolent celestial presence speaking down from a cloud. I'm not sure when it occurred to me that he might be acting. But I recognized and understood that need to pretend, to make believe what you wish was true in order to make it real.

One night, Reverend Carson hosted a party for the church teen group in his home. His wife was a big, soft-looking woman with kind eyes who shyly welcomed us into their small house. Inside, I noticed an old guitar propped up in the corner. It was the warm golden color of honey, smokey and dark around the edges like maple syrup, and I couldn't stop looking at it.

"You want to play it?" I looked up and saw Reverend Carson standing over me, gazing down through his wire-rim glasses. Before I could answer, he picked up the guitar and handed it to me. It was heavier than I expected, and I almost dropped it. I recovered and managed to balance it on my knee. I ran my hands over the smooth maple finish, up and down the neck.

After Reverend Carson disappeared into the back of the house, I sat there with his guitar in my lap, touching its smooth finish, pressing my fingers into the sharp hard strings until it hurt. When I'd run through the few chords

I knew, I got up and went looking for him to give it back. I could hear his voice somewhere down a hallway, so I went in that direction.

The door was open into a small bedroom where I found Reverend Carson with his wife. Her face was red and twisted, and I realized with a feeling of shock that she was crying. Reverend Carson was standing very close, bending down over her and talking very fast in a harsh whisper. Before I could back away, Reverend Carson's hand flew out and struck his wife across the face with a loud, hard sound I could feel in my own jaw.

Reverend Carson and his wife both disappeared from our lives soon after that. Later I heard that he'd died of cancer. I remember feeling strangely unsurprised. In a way, it just seemed to make sense. It was as if I knew that he wasn't meant to last.

Soon after I heard that Reverend Carson had died, I had a dream about him. In the dream, he'd come back to show me something. He reached up, pulled the white clerical collar from around his neck and let it fall to the ground. When he took off his wire rim spectacles, there were no eyes behind them, just empty black space. I woke up just as he was taking his beard off. I was glad that I didn't get to see what was behind it.

I thought about that dream when I played Jesus in our church school play. The adults drew a beard on my face with a black eyebrow pencil, wrapped me in a rayon robe and pushed me out in front of a crowd of other kids and grownups sitting in folding metal chairs. After the play, when they were rubbing the beard off with cold cream and Kleenex, I thought of that dream about Reverend Carson, and for a moment I was afraid to look in the mirror because I thought that my real face might be gone.

\*

WHEN I WAS thirteen, my father's assistant was Reverend Douglas. Unlike Reverend Carson, Reverend Douglas was short and soft and pear-shaped. He was also going bald, which made him look older than he was, though everything else about him seemed young and unformed as a baby in the womb.

While Reverend Carson had taken great pains to conceal whatever struggles were going on inside of him, Reverend Douglas wore his struggles on his face. It was the face of the soft, speechless boy I once saw freeze on the high-dive one summer, a look of terror with a trace of determination behind it, the face of someone searching for the courage to fling himself out into space.

The first time my father had Reverend Douglas read the Lesson of the Day from the pulpit, his voice was soft and turned inward, as if he was reading to himself. It almost seemed to cause him physical pain to be up there in front of the whole congregation. His face turned red and his hands shook as he turned the pages.

After the service, I noticed Reverend Douglas alone in the sacristy. He'd taken off his black and white priest's vestments and was standing there, looking at them hanging from a metal hanger. He stared at his empty vestments intently, the muscles of his jaw working as if he was about to speak to them. He must have felt me watching because he turned and saw me. The flush of embarrassment on his face, and the burning shame I felt in my own was the same as if I'd accidentally seen him naked. He moved toward me quickly, eyes blazing with shame and anger. I instinctively threw up my hands to protect myself. But he only shut the door in my face.

That winter, I learned that the Bishop was coming to town. The Bishop was a tall man who used his height like a weapon. He always stood very close when he talked with people, so they had to bend their heads backward to see his face. To see the Bishop and my father in the same room was both upsetting and disorienting. In my young mind, God was my father's boss, so for anyone to interrupt that chain of command felt wrong.

On the night of the confirmation service that the Bishop had come to preside over, my father asked me to serve as the acolyte. Normally, I would sit in the passenger seat next to him on the way to the church, but tonight I sat in the back seat so the Bishop could sit in the front. We were driving down the long back-alley that led to the church when my father took his foot off the gas pedal and the car slowly rolled to a stop. We sat there, not moving, the engine rumbling under us. I remember thinking that it was an odd thing to do. I was sitting in the back seat, but I could hear my father and the Bishop talking in the front. It didn't take long to realize who they were talking about.

"If he's not meant for the ministry," the Bishop said, "Think of how much he must be suffering. The kindest thing would be to put an end to it now."

"But if he *is* meant for it," my father replied, "and we deny him that, think of how much more he'd suffer." The Bishop stopped talking. I could feel him weighing what my father had just said, while the car engine hummed and throbbed beneath us. Finally, I heard the Bishop sigh. "Alright." There was a grudging sound to the Bishop's voice, like a weary judge issuing a stay of execution. I felt my father ease his foot from the brake, and the car rolled forward again.

When we got to the church, I looked at the bulletin, and there was Reverend Douglas's name right next to the sermon. I couldn't believe it. Reverend Douglas could barely make it through the lesson—how was he going to give a sermon in front of a full church? And in front of the Bishop? I wondered who'd done this to him, but I knew the answer. It was my father. My father who had just defended him, who had just argued with the Bishop and won, was now going to throw him into the fire.

Throughout the service, whenever I stole a glance at Reverend Douglas, his face was flushed red, and his lips were pressed tightly together as if he was about to vomit or faint. When I heard the organ play the first notes of the short hymn that came right before the sermon, I felt my heart rise into my throat. I knew that when they reached the third verse, Reverend Douglas was supposed to rise and walk to the pulpit. I couldn't bear to watch, so I closed my eyes and listened to the rumble and moan of the old pipe organ. I thought about how much Reverend Douglas must be suffering, and I wished that I could somehow save him. I remembered some lines from the play I was in, the scene where Jesus is praying not to be crucified. *Father, if it be thy will, let this cup pass from me...* I squeezed my eyes shut, dug my fingernails into the palms of my hands, and wished and prayed as hard as I could. *Father, let this cup pass from him...*

When I heard the organ and the choir stop, there was a silence that felt enormous. I heard a few hushed, urgent voices talking, then a few more. I opened my eyes, not knowing what to expect.

The seat where Reverend Douglas had been was empty, and so was the pulpit. Reverend Douglas was gone.

And although part of me knew that he must have

slipped quietly out of the church while my eyes were closed, part of me knew that I had done it.

I'd made Reverend Douglas disappear.


I WAS FOURTEEN WHEN my father's next assistant came. His name was Reverend Nelson, although I barely heard his name the first time my dad mentioned it. Why should I bother, I wondered. These young men had all begun to blur together, each one fading into the next, on and on. Why should I take the time to get to know this one?

Still, I didn't want to appear rude, so when my father introduced me to a tall, thin young man in the parish hall one Sunday, I held out my right hand. When he didn't reach out to take it, I felt awkward and angry. Then I noticed the empty black sleeve pinned to his side. I felt a hot rush of shame burning in my face, followed by a cold feeling of queasiness. Reverend Nelson just glared at me, his thin lips pressed tightly together. There was something in his face that looked familiar. But I couldn't figure out what it was.

Reverend Nelson spoke very little. He wasn't shy to the point of terror like Reverend Douglas; it was just that he appeared to weigh his words very carefully before he spoke. I didn't like to think that it was Reverend Nelson's missing arm that made me so uncomfortable around him, although it probably did. I think it was the way he looked at me, with a dark expression that looked like resentment, although I couldn't understand why.

In our church, we tended to repeat the same prayers week after week, year after year, until the meaning had worn off of them. *Lift up your hearts,* my father would say, and the congregation's dull rumbling reply, *We lift them up unto the Lord* was physically painful to hear. One

Sunday, my father led the church through a long prayer that I'd never heard before.

*The night is far spent, the day is at hand: let us therefore cast off the works of darkness, and let us put on the armor of light.* The words of this new prayer caught my attention. In that moment, I knew that these words were not just poetry—they were real, more real than anything else. I closed my eyes and tried to picture the armor of light until I could see it, glowing in the darkness somewhere above me. I did what the prayer asked of me. I went deeper and prayed harder, until I could see the armor of light start to descend and fit itself around my body. A warm electric feeling ran through me. When I opened my eyes, I couldn't see it, but I could feel it. I knew it wasn't the kind of thing you can see with the naked eye. I looked around at all the other people on their knees and wondered if any of them were feeling the same thing that I was.

I looked over at Reverend Nelson kneeling in his place near the altar and was startled to see him glaring at me with a look of pure hatred.

After that, I tried to avoid Reverend Nelson as much as I could. When summer came and it was time for me to go to church camp, I prayed that Reverend Nelson wouldn't be there, but he was, standing on the sidelines in his black clerical clothes in the sweltering heat while the rest of us ran around in shorts and t-shirts.

I'd been at camp for almost two weeks when I decided to ask Reverend Nelson why he was angry at me. I don't know what made me think I could ask him that--maybe it was being in a different place, away from everything that I was used to. Or maybe it was because I'd just turned fourteen and felt like I was old enough now to be taken seriously, and not brushed aside.

They kept us busy all day with swimming and volleyball and meals and prayer meetings, so there was no time for me to approach Reverend Nelson until after dinner. It was dusk when I went out to find him. The last light draining from the sky seemed caught in the branches of the trees above. I could hear the voices of boys laughing and calling out all around me in the dark, echoing off the surface of the lake. I was headed toward the open field on the hilltop where I knew the adults would be building the bonfire. I knew Reverend Nelson would be there.

When I got to the field on top of the hill, I saw the huge pile of branches and tree limbs at the center of the field, and one figure circling around it, tossing more pieces of wood onto the pile. The figure had one arm, so I could tell even from far away that it was Reverend Nelson. When I got closer, he looked up and saw me, and the same dark expression came over his face. I'd come here to confront him, but what I really wanted was for him to stop being angry at me. I wanted him to like me. As empty and shallow as that sounds, that was what I wanted.

"Need some help?" I asked.

Reverend Nelson glared at me, then turned his back on me, picking up another long piece of wood and flinging it onto the pile, harder than before. I watched him for a while, not knowing what else to say. I knew that other people would be here soon, and I'd lose my chance.

"Why are you angry at me?" I pushed the words out before I could stop myself.

Reverend Nelson thew another piece of wood on the pile, harder than before. Still not looking at me, he spoke, his voice flat and grim.

"You know why."

"No. I don't..."

"Yes, you do."

I searched my mind but couldn't find anything. I'd never even spoken with him before. This was the most we'd ever said to each other. "I don't know what you mean," I said. Before I'd finished saying it, he struggled out of his black coat, stripped off his shirt, and held out the stub of his right arm toward me. The puckered, angry looking place where his arm should have been made a cold chill go through me, and I tried to hide it.

"You know why I don't have this arm anymore?"

I shook my head.

"Yes, you do. You know why. You were there. You saw it."

Something began to move in the back of my brain. I could feel it coming closer, in flashes. The smooth wooden finish of a beautiful old guitar under my hand. A woman's big, soft eyes, red with weeping.

"Because you hit your wife."

There it was. I'd said it. At first it was only a feeling. Then it was a thought. Now I'd said it out loud, and it was real.

"You think I didn't know you were there?" he said. "I saw you. I saw you watching."

*But you're dead,* I wanted to say, but I couldn't. The world had started tilting a little around me. For a moment, I felt like I might be sick. I saw Reverend Nelson glance down at his ruined arm, a look of disgust on his face. "First, I thought I was the one who was doing this. Then I realized. It was you. It's always been you."

"I haven't done anything to you."

"Yes, you have. Remember that night in church when you wouldn't let me speak? I was scared. But I was ready. You remember."

I did remember—Reverend Douglas's flushed red face, the rumble and moan of the pipe organ, the empty pulpit—

but I was trying not to let it in. The real world was falling apart around me, and I was trying to hold on to the last pieces of it.

"That was my chance," he said. "To prove myself. I could have done it. But you wouldn't let me. You didn't believe I could do it. You didn't give me a chance. You've never given me a chance."

I watched him pick up a large metal can in his one hand, then walk around the big pile of wood, pouring out what was inside it. The sharp smell of gasoline entered my nostrils. When the can was empty, he tossed it aside and pulled something from his pocket. I heard a sharp click and a small flame appeared in his hand. He reached down and touched it to the soaked wood, and in ten seconds the whole thing was ablaze. He then turned back toward me. The firelight made the bones of his face appear to move and change. For a moment, I could see all the different men he'd ever been.

*"That the trial of your faith, being much more precious than of gold that perishes, though it be tried with fire, might be found to praise and honor and glory at the appearing of Jesus Christ."* He said those words softly, gazing into the fire. When he looked back at me, his eyes glittered wet in the firelight. "That was the reading I was supposed to give that night. That's what I was going to talk about. Faith and trial by fire. But you wouldn't let me. What do you know about faith? About what it means to struggle? You've never had to struggle for anything. Everything has just been given to you. Like the armor of light. I saw you take it. You thought it should be yours, so you took it. What makes you think you deserve to have that? Do you know how selfish you are? When you take something like that for yourself, you take it away from someone else."

He stepped closer. I could see his eyes blazing in the dark. "Show me, then. Show me the armor of light. You think it's real, don't you? Prove it. Put your arm in the fire. It can't hurt you now, can it? That's what you believe, isn't it? Go on. Show me."

The fire was roaring higher and brighter now. I tried to remember how I'd felt when I was in that play, wrapped in long linen robes with a grown man's beard drawn on my face, how I'd almost felt sure that I could walk on water if I wanted to. I took my first step closer to the fire, knowing that I was committing myself to a series of actions that I now had to see through to the end. The fire blasted its heat all over the front of my body; the skin on my face, my arms, my chest and legs all began to tighten and sting; one more step and it would start to blacken and split open. I started to raise my right arm and closed my eyes, trying to feel the armor of light surrounding and protecting me, but I couldn't. It was gone. I lowered my arm and stepped back, away from the heat. When Reverend Nelson spoke again, I could hear the smile in his voice.

"That's right. Now I'm not the coward. You are."

I heard him sigh deeply, like some kind of burden was exiting his body with his breath. *"When he hath tried me, I shall come forth as gold..."*

That's when I turned and ran. I ran because I knew what was coming. I ran because I wanted to get help. Most of all, I ran because I didn't want to see. Even when the screaming started, I never looked back. That's when I knew Reverend Nelson was right. I was the coward. Not him.

THAT WAS THE year I stopped going to church. My father never questioned me about it. I think he knew the reason.

When he hired his next assistant, I didn't want to see him. I didn't want to look into a new stranger's eyes and see something I recognized. I wanted to know that it was over, that it had ended that night on the hill. But I couldn't be sure. I knew that the best thing for me to do was to stay away. And that's what I've done.

This world is imperfect. And its people are imperfect. I know that now. It's true about everyone, and I know it's true about me. I'm no different than anyone else. Still, we can be better. I believe that. But we only get so many chances. All of us. Just so many chances to get it right.

I wonder—how many do I have left?

# How the
# World Works

MIKE AND I were born the same year, but it seemed like he was always ten steps ahead of me. If there was an album I hadn't heard, a place I'd never been, a girl I hadn't kissed, Mike had been there, done that. He was also taller than me, a lot taller, so it felt like he'd been looking down on me forever. That's pretty much how he made everyone feel, so by the time we graduated from tenth grade, I was just about the only friend he had left. That didn't bother Mike. While I was trying to figure out how to navigate high school life, his sights were set on more important things.

The summer after eleventh grade, when I was working for a local paint crew, sealing shower stalls with fiberglass, Mike was working as a research assistant on a boat off the Florida Keys. We all joked that Mike was probably just washing down the decks and making coffee for the real scientists. Whatever the truth was, when Mike showed up for school in September, he had a tan like a movie star and a shark's tooth on a leather lanyard around his neck, while I was pale as a fish and had fiberglass particles under the skin of my fingers.

When I asked Mike how he got that job, he acted like he didn't want to tell me. One night after a few beers, he finally opened up about how he'd been mowing his biology teacher's lawn for about a year, then started clearing out his garage and cleaning his pool. He started having conversations with the guy about marine biology; then, after about a year, he finally got invited to come along on that research voyage. I kidded Mike about it, even called him a brownnose.

"At least I didn't have to work a shit job like yours," Mike sniffed. "You know what your problem is? You don't know how the world works, that's all."

I wanted to tell him to get fucked, but I didn't. Because I knew he was right. I didn't know how the world worked. Mike acted like he did, and that same thing that drove me crazy also made me feel safe around him sometimes.

Mike knew how to radiate a sort of serious adult vibe, an impatience with things he considered childish and beneath him—which, at times, seemed like just about everything and everyone. Including me. I put up with it because I knew it was an act. I'd known Mike since we were five years old, and I knew it was important to him to act wiser than everyone else, more experienced, more worldly. I think it made him feel safe. I understood that. We all want to feel safe—although Mike probably had more reason to want that than most of us.

Around the time we graduated from high school, Mike moved with his mother into a local hotel. The story was that their house was being remodeled, but as the weeks and months passed, it became clear that something else was going on. When I drove past their house, I could see that work had stopped. The plastic insulation that had been nailed up to seal missing walls had torn loose and was flapping in the wind.

At first, Mike invited us over to the motel to swim in "his" pool. We went late at night when no one else was around and we had the pool to ourselves. Bugs swarmed around the floodlights above us and danced across the surface of the water, but we didn't care. It was Mike's pool, and for the time being, it was ours too.

One night when we were floating around, beers in our hands, Brad asked me if I thought the water felt warmer. I wasn't sure what he meant, until I saw the way he was laughing.

"Jesus, Brad..." I yelled and swam away from him as fast as I could.

"What's going on?" I saw Mike standing at the edge of the pool, glaring down at us like he was a lifeguard or a cop or something.

"Aw, Brad just pissed in the pool," I said.

"Get out," Mike said. Brad laughed. Mike yelled louder. "I said get out of my pool!"

"It's not your fucking pool," Brad said.

"I mean it," Mike shouted. "Get the fuck out of here, now. And don't come back."

Fewer and fewer people came for those midnight swims after Mike threw Brad out. I guess nobody wanted to be next. I kept going for a while. Then Mike stopped inviting us. Whatever he'd gotten from it at first, I guess he wan't getting anymore.

One day I drove by Mike's house and saw that the workers were back, hammering and sawing and drilling away. I figured things must have gotten better. Then I saw a moving van parked in front of the house, and a woman and two young kids I'd never seen before. I went by the motel to see Mike, but when I knocked on the door to their room, no one answered.

"That poor boy," my mom said when I told her what happened. "That family's had more than enough trouble." My mom was the good-hearted type. Not soft-hearted, but *good*-hearted. But I still didn't expect what she said next. "You find that friend of yours and tell him he's welcome to come here and live here with us. Until things turn around for him."

I stood there letting what she'd said sink in. Mike living here—with us. With me. It was hard to imagine—even harder for him to imagine, I thought. Still, Mike was my friend. I had to try.

I went back to the motel and waited around until I saw a couple I didn't recognize open the door and go inside. I went to the office and asked the clerk who told me what I already knew. Mike and his mother were gone.

That's when I really started to worry about Mike. I didn't know where to find him. School was out, so I couldn't look for him there, and he'd stopped answering my calls a couple of weeks ago. The fact that he hadn't contacted anyone probably meant things weren't too bad for him yet. But I knew how hard it would be for him to ask for help. I also knew that whenever I saw or spoke with Mike again, it would be on his terms, not mine.

One afternoon my phone rang. I knew it was Mike before I picked it up.

"What are you doing tonight?" That was the first thing he said. No *hello*. No *how are you*.

"Nothing. Where are you?"

"Come over," he said. "I want to show you something."

"Where?" He gave me an address I didn't recognize, somewhere on Old Scottsdale Road.

"You want me to bring anything?' I asked. I wasn't even sure what I was offering. Beer, food, money? Warm clothes?

"Nothing," he said. "Just get over here." I thought he'd hung up for a moment. That's what Mike usually did—hang up without saying goodbye. He said one more thing:

"You're not gonna believe this."

Then he hung up.

The address Mike gave me was on the outskirts of town. I didn't know what to expect; maybe another motel, a rented house or room. I followed the directions he'd given me, passing all the landmarks, until I saw lights shining through the trees down below the road on the right. I saw the opening to a driveway, turned in and followed it down.

The trees parted and I saw a huge, split-level house made of some kind of white stone that shone like marble or quartz, bathed in the glow of spotlights. Dozens of huge picture-windows, their shades drawn shut.

*This can't be it,* I thought. It looked like the kind of place where you could get shot for trespassing. I'd already thrown the car into reverse and was starting to back out when the front door opened and there was Mike, squinting into my headlights and waving me in with one hand.

I parked and walked up to him. He looked tired but alert. The urge to hug him came over me for a second, but I knew better.

"Jesus," I said, looking up at the white stone walls. "Who did you have to kill to get this place?"

Mike allowed himself a wry grin, more like a smirk. "Come on," he said, then turned and disappeared into the house. I followed.

Inside, the place was like nothing I'd ever seen in real life. Wood parquet floors that went on for miles, marble columns that disappeared into the shadows over our heads. It reminded me of photos I'd seen of the Playboy Mansion, or the futuristic homes of supervillains in James Bond movies. I half-expected to see bikini-clad girls lounging around on the expensive furniture, butlers serving drinks on silver trays.

"Fuck, Mike, what *is* this place?"

Mike smiled and said nothing at first. He was enjoying himself, making me wait for it.

I followed him down a set of steps into a wide, dark room with floor-to ceiling windows. A huge sofa curved halfway around the room. Against one wall were back-lit glass shelves filled with bottles of every kind of liquor, many I'd never seen before. Against another wall, a massive sound system glowed with silent power, its tiny red lights winking at us.

"Seriously, Mike, what *is* this place?"

"It belongs to a guy I know," he said in that casual, off-hand way of his. "He asked me to house-sit for the summer while he's in Europe."

"What guy?"

"You don't know him," Mike sniffed. He was right—I didn't know anybody who spent their summers in Europe. And I would have bet that Mike didn't either. But here we were.

Mike stepped behind the bar and made us a couple of drinks. Vodka and tonic, which I'd never had before. The metallic taste put me off at first. Then the warmth hit deep in my gut and started to spread outward. By the third sip, things felt looser, friendlier.

I watched Mike go over to the massive CD player and start pushing buttons. "Check this out," he said. There was a moment of deep silence, broken by thundering drums and guitar that sounded familiar. When the voice came in, I knew.

"That's Zeppelin," I said. "What *is* this?"

"It's the new album," Mike said.

"But that's not supposed to come out for six months. How did this guy get the new album before it even comes out?"

"He can get anything," Mike said, like it was the most obvious thing in the world. He drained the rest of his drink and set the glass down. "Wanna see the rest of the place?"

Of course I did.

I followed Mike into another huge room that I realized was the kitchen. There was a long counter in the middle of the floor that looked like it was made of marble surrounded by a dozen leather stools, and a giant copper lighting fixture as big as a car suspended above it. I heard the hum and throb of a refrigerator, but couldn't see one, until Mike pulled open a big door in the wall and frosty air rolled out. Mike walked inside, then came back with his arms full of bread and meat and cheese that he spread out on the marble counter. Then he went back in and came back with a six pack of beer I'd never seen before.

"It's Belgian," Mike said, popping the cap from one bottle and holding it out toward me. "Try it."

I did. It was the best I'd ever tasted.

A low howling sound made me look around. A cat had wandered into the kitchen and was gazing up at Mike. A big yellow tabby, it looked more disheveled than a cat who lived in this kind of house should.

"So, you're cat-sitting too," I said.

I saw Mike's eyes cut to the digital clock on the wall. I'd been watching it too, and I knew it was almost midnight. My Mom would be wondering where I was.

Mike stood up. "I got to get to work now," he said.

"Now? What do you mean? What kind of work?"

"I told you," Mike said, quickly gathering up the plates and bottles. "I'm house sitting. I gotta take care of the place." I watched him toss the bottles and stack the plates by the sink. Then he stood over me, nervously shifting from foot to foot. I realized—he was waiting for me to leave. That was my cue. I stood up and looked around for the way out. It was a big place, and I'd never been here before.

"That way," Mike said, pointing down long hallway. He wasn't going to show me out. That wasn't unusual. But his nervousness was.

"You okay?" I asked.

"Fine," he said. "I'm fine. I'll call you. See you later."


I WALKED BY MYSELF down the long hallway and let myself out. The whole way, I could feel Mike's eyes on my back, waiting for me to be gone.

"Well, that's just strange..." My mother's mouth twisted up at one corner the way it always did when there was something she was trying to figure out. "He's living there all by himself, is he? Where's his mother?"

I realized I had no idea. It had never occurred to me to ask Mike where his mother was.

"Somewhere, I guess..."

"*Somewhere...*" Mom repeated in a mocking voice. "This house. You say it's out Old Scottsdale Road? I've never heard of any house like that out there."

"It's kind of off the road, in the trees. It looks pretty new..."

"And who's this man he's house sitting for? How does he know him?"

"Mike says he's some kind of doctor..."

Mom put away the last dish and turned to face me. "And you're going back there?"

"I don't know," I shrugged.

But I did know. I was going back there. Of course I was.

IT WAS FIVE minutes before nine when I pulled up to the big white house on Scottsdale Road. Every window in the house was ablaze with light. At first, I thought that Mike must have changed his mind and was having a party, until I saw that our two cars were the only ones there. For a moment I wondered if he'd turned on all the lights in the house because he was afraid, but I couldn't imagine what he might be afraid of.

Mike met me at the door. I thought he looked kind of tired and distracted, but I figured he'd just been staying up late, partying by himself. It's what I would have done.

We sat in the big room with the sound system and glass bar, drinking and listening to music. After a while, I remembered what my mom had asked.

"Hey, Mike," I said. "Where's your mom?"

At first, he didn't answer. He seemed lost in the music, distracted. Finally, he said, "Oh, she's around."

*Around where?* I was about to ask, when Mike spoke again.

"Watch this," Mike said. I saw him push a button on the arm of the couch. There was a soft humming noise, and the curtains that surrounded half of the room slowly slid open. Outside the huge picture windows, the branches of trees were lit with colored lights, red, blue, and gold, pulsing and changing in perfect rhythm to the music.

"That's crazy," I said. "How—"

"Don't talk," Mike cut me off, then laid his head back on the couch. "You don't always have to *talk* about everything. Just enjoy it."

I tried to follow his lead and sank back into the huge leather couch and let the music and lights wash over me, but I couldn't relax. Something about it didn't feel safe, but I didn't know what it was. It was a big house, and I was starting to get the feeling that we weren't alone.

I saw a movement from the corner of my eye. I turned and there was a cat staring at me from the doorway. I remembered the one I'd seen here the last time, a big yellow tabby, but this one was gray with a white face.

"So," I said, "You've got *two* cats you've gotta take care of, huh?"

Mike frowned at me like he didn't know what I was talking about. Then the cat caught his eye. "Oh, yeah," he said. "Sure..."

When Mike got up to make another drink, the cat made a frightened noise, crouched down and slipped away. I thought it was strange, but maybe not that strange—Mike wasn't what I'd call an "animal person", and I guessed the cat probably knew that.

"Where's the bathroom?" I asked.

Mike had closed his eyes and appeared to be lost in the music. For a moment I wondered if he'd heard me. "Down that hall," he said without opening his eyes. "Third door on your right."

The "third door on the right" was a lot farther away than in most houses. As I walked down the long hallway over the beautiful parquet floor, I could hear the music getting further and further away behind me. It felt like I was walking into silence. I realized again how big this house was, and I didn't like it. The lights were dimmer and farther apart here, and I found myself passing through pools of darkness between little islands of light.

When I was crossing through one of those areas of darkness, something ran across the floor right in front of me. A scratching sound began, loud and frantic. I looked more closely and there was the same gray and white cat I'd seen in the kitchen, clawing at the front door.

Before I knew what was happening, Mike was there, pushing his way past me and bending down to grab up the cat. The cat howled and hissed and struck out at him. Mike cursed, and I saw a trickle of blood running down his arm, but he didn't let go. Then he was walking away from me toward the kitchen, holding the cat at arm's-length by one of its back legs while the animal thrashed and twisted in the air.

"Mike!" I called out after him, but he kept walking.

*"Don't!"* He turned his head to shout at me over his shoulder. His face was blood-red and contorted with rage. *"Get out of here! Now!"*

Without thinking, I turned and walked fast to the front door, pushed it open and walked to my car, got inside, and locked the doors. I looked back at the lights burning inside the house, and for a moment I almost went back inside to look for Mike. But I remembered the way his face had looked when he turned to shout at me, and I started the car and drove away.


I TOLD MY MOM I was worried about Mike. I didn't tell her about the cat or what happened the night before. I was afraid of what she might think or say. After all, I didn't want to get Mike in trouble. I just wanted to make sure he was okay.

"That does it," my mom said. "You tell that boy he's coming home with you."

Again, my mind twisted, trying to make sense of her words. It was hard to think of Mike living here under the same roof with me. But it was harder to think of him out there on the edge of town in that place. That was the way I was thinking of it now. *That place.*

I started calling Mike, leaving messages. Before, I'd waited for him to call me, to invite me first. But it felt like there was no time for that now. I called him every day for a week—no answer. I knew I should just get in my car and go out there, but something told me he wouldn't let me in. As always, it had to be his idea, on his terms.

One night, my phone rang, and it was Mike. "Come over," he said. Then he hung up.

When I got to the house, I had to wait a while before Mike answered the door. When he finally did, he looked worse than ever. Pale and tired looking, with dark shadows under his eyes. He looked like he hadn't seen the sun in months.

"You okay, man?" I asked.

"I'm fine," he snapped, then turned and went back into the house, leaving me to follow him.

We sat in the same big room again, drinking vodka and listening to music. The trees outside the picture-window pulsed and glowed in different colors like before, but it wasn't surprising to me anymore, and I realized that it was probably easy to get tired of anything, no matter how amazing it seems at first.

"I was just thinking," I said. "I was thinking maybe... How'd you like to come home with me? You know, maybe spend the night. Maybe a couple of nights. You know, like we used to."

I saw his eyes grow wide with surprise for a moment, then narrow. "Why would I want to do *that?*" He spit the words out with so much contempt, it shut me down. I didn't know what to say. So, I didn't say anything. Neither one of us did, for a long time. When I finally got up to go to the bathroom, it was also because it was too hard to be in the same room with him.

On my way to the bathroom, I saw something dart down the long hallway in front of me. A cat. I was relieved to see that it was okay—then I noticed. It was black, not gray and white. It was a different cat. Another one.

I went into the bathroom, which had black marble walls, and a dim golden light that hummed softly above my head. When I stepped out into the hallway, Mike was walking toward me very fast, an anxious look on his face.

"You see a cat?" he asked.

"A cat? Yeah, just a minute ago…"

"Where?"

"Right there," I said, pointing down the hall. Mike ran to the spot and looked around.

"*Where?*" he shouted. "You see where it went?"

"No…"

"*Fuck…*" Mike cursed, then walked quickly down the hall. A moment later, he was back. "Help me…" he said. "Help me find it."

For the next hour, we searched the house. Most of the rooms were shut, so we scoured the hallways and the staircases, looking in every corner. But we never saw the cat.

"He can't get out, right?" I said. "I mean, he's got to be in here somewhere. He'll come back."

"*No,*" Mike said. "We've got to find it!" His face looked pale, his eyes were wide and darted back and forth. I'd never seen him look like that before, and it took me a moment to understand—Mike was afraid.

I followed Mike around for a while, retracing our steps, searching all the places we'd already searched. At one point he stopped, shouted, *"Fuck!"* and punched the wall with his fist. *"Fuck. Fuck. Fuck. Fuck..."* He kept shouting and punching the wall until I saw part of it cave-in. When he stopped, he was breathing heavily, and pressed both hands against the side of his head like he was trying to keep it from exploding.

"Mike," I said, "What's wrong? It's just a cat..."

Before I could say anything more, he moved past me back into the big room. I followed and found him digging through a closet. He came out wearing what looked like gardening gloves, holding a big burlap sack. When he saw me staring at him, he shouted at me.

"Don't fucking stand there! Are you gonna help me or not? Either help me or get out!"

His face looked red now, and I thought I even saw tears in his eyes. I did want to help him. Of course I did. But I didn't understand.

"What do you want me to do?"

"Come on..." he said and went out the front door. I followed him away from the house and up the driveway to Scottsdale Road where Mike turned right and started walking uphill fast. I saw the lights of other houses come into view, but then Mike turned and plunged downhill into the trees. I followed him into the woods, trying to keep up.

"Where are we going?" I asked.

Mike stopped, turned and tossed something to me. I caught it—it was another pair of heavy gardening gloves. "Put those on," he said, then kept walking.

I could hear something making yowling sounds ahead of us in the dark. A cat. *It can't be,* I thought. When we got close to the sound, it stopped. Mike took out his cell phone, turned on the flashlight and shone it down on something on the ground. I couldn't believe what I was seeing, and for a moment I thought I was wrong. But I wasn't. There was a metal trap, one of those wire cages on the forest floor. And inside the cage was a cat. It wasn't the cat I'd seen at the house—this one was big and black with huge green eyes that stared up at us distrustfully.

"Here..." Mike said, tossing the big burlap bag at me. "Hold this." I grabbed the bag and stood there, trying to understand what was going on.

"Mike, what the hell—"

"Just shut up and hold the bag," he snapped. "Hold it open. Right here..."

I did as I was instructed and held the mouth of the bag open right next to the cage. Then Mike opened the cage, reached inside, and grabbed the cat. The cat struggled and clawed at him. It looked like the garden gloves took the worst of it, but I saw the cat's claws connect with the skin on Mike's arm once or twice. Mike cursed and managed to shove the cat deep into the bag. Mike tied the bag closed, stood up and started walking fast in the direction we'd come from. I struggled to keep up with him, tripping over rocks and tree roots.

I finally caught up with him back at the house when he paused to open the door. "Mike...what the fuck is going on? What are you doing?"

He turned and looked at me, and I didn't like what I saw. There was something in his eyes that frightened me. It wasn't threat; it was fear. The same fear I'd gotten a glimpse of earlier. Now it had grown like a wildfire and was threatening to blaze out of control.

"What the fuck is going on?" he asked. A nervous-sounding chuckle burst from his throat. "You want to know what the fuck is going on? You want to see? Alright. Come on. I'll show you..."

Something about the way Mike was talking scared me more than I already was. Still, I had to follow him. I'd been following him since we were five years old, and it was too hard to stop now.

Mike went down a side-hall to a door I'd never seen before and pulled it open. Inside was a long set of stairs that led down below ground. At the bottom of the stairs was another door, a metal one that looked heavy and thick. I could see that it was bolted on the outside. I followed Mike down those stairs, but stopped before I reached the bottom. I just knew I didn't want to get too close to that door.

For a moment, Mike just stood there, still clutching the bag on one hand. I saw him lower his head and take several deep breaths. He put his hand on the bolt, took one more deep breath, then drew back the bolt, opened the door and threw the bag inside.

The darkness moved. I saw it surge forward and start to take shape. A mouth. An eye. A huge hand reaching out. Mike slammed the door and shot the bolt shut. The sounds that came through that door were like nothing I'd ever heard before. Horrible high-pitched howls and screams. The next thing I knew, Mike had me by the arm and was pulling me up the stairs and away from whatever was happening on the other side of that door.

A minute later, I was sitting on the big leather couch and Mike was handing me a bottle of bourbon. I took a long drink and let the heat burn its way down my throat and into my belly. When I felt like I could speak again, I choked out the words.

"What...? Jesus, Mike, what the fuck? What the hell *was* that?"

Mike sat across from me, clutching his own bottle. His eyes looked terrible.

"What do you want me to say...?" he whispered. It sounded like an old man's voice.

"What *is* that thing? What the fuck is going on?"

Mike closed his eyes and let out a long, deep breath. I could tell he was gathering his words, trying to figure out how to explain.

"The guy," Mike began, "...the guy whose house this is. He told me I could stay here as long as I want. That I could do whatever I wanted. As long as I... take care of that thing..."

"Take care... you mean... feed it?"

Mike nodded.

"So... that cat... all those other cats I saw here..."

Mike nodded again, his eyes closed.

"Jesus..." My mind was racing so fast, I felt dizzy. "But... what *is* it? That thing down there?"

Mike shook his head. "I don't know. All I know is... I gotta keep taking take care of it."

"Why? Why do you have to do that? What about the guy? The guy who owns this house? When's he coming back?"

Mike sighed. "I don't think he is. I don't think he's coming back."

"What do you mean, he's not coming back? Why not?"

Mike looked up at me, his eyes red and weary. "Would you come back here if you didn't have to?"

I looked around at the big, luxurious room, at the leather couch, the huge glass bar, and the colored lights glowing in the trees outside. Even now, I could feel the pull of it all.

"But... you don't have to stay here," I said. "Why don't you just leave?"

Mike's eyes grew wider with surprise. "Why would I want to do that?"

"What...? Jesus, Mike, what are you talking about?"

"Look," he said, waving his hand around at the room, at the whole house. "Where else am I going to get *this?* Don't you fucking get it? This is all I'm ever gonna have of this."

He looked angry but I was pretty sure I saw tears in his eyes.

"Mike," I said. "Listen. You gotta get out of here. It... it's not safe. You know that, right? It's not safe. We gotta leave..."

"I can't leave."

"Why not? Why can't you leave?"

"Because. If I leave, it'll die. And if it dies..." he paused, like he was struggling to say it. "If it dies, it'll be bad. Really bad."

I wasn't sure what he meant, but I knew he was telling the truth. He was too scared not to be. I thought about the thing I'd seen down there, only for a second. But a second was enough.

"Mike... what is it?"

He looked up at me, and his eyes had all the weariness in the world in them.

"What does it look like to you?"

"Like... a monster."

"Then that's what it is."

We sat there and drank for a while. I was almost too scared to stay in that house. But Mike wasn't leaving, and I wasn't leaving Mike.

After a while, I called Mom to let her know I wasn't coming home.

"I'm fine," I told her. "I'm okay, really. I'm just gonna spend the night here with Mike."

"You need me to come there and get you?"

*"No,"* I said, a little too loud, then, "No, don't come here. I mean, it's alright. We're alright. We're fine."

She paused for a long moment, like she was trying to make up her mind. When she spoke again, her voice was low and tight-sounding. "Are you boys taking drugs? Because if you are, I'm coming over there right now..."

"Christ, no, Mom! That's not... there's no drugs, okay? It's nothing like that. Jesus..."

"Is it Mike, then? There's something wrong with Mike, isn't there?"

Her words cut straight to my heart, and for a moment, I almost felt like crying. *Yes. Yes, there's something wrong with Mike.*

"No, Mom. He's okay. We're both okay. I just...I'll see you in the morning, alright? Don't worry."

I could hear her making up her mind again. "Alright," she finally said. "But you call me if you need me. You understand?"

"Yes, yes, I understand. Thanks, Mom. Goodnight."

When I got off the phone, I halfway expected to see Mike passed out on the couch, he'd looked so exhausted. But he wasn't asleep. Neither was I.

IN THE MORNING, Mike made us the biggest breakfast I'd ever seen. Scrambled eggs with sharp cheddar cheese and jalapeño peppers, thick slabs of bacon, waffles with fruit and maple syrup and whipped cream, and plenty of coffee, hot, black, and sweet. It looked great, it smelled great, but I couldn't touch it. My stomach was still in knots from the night before. But after a couple of bites, the knots inside me started to loosen and my appetite returned. Before we'd finished, I'd almost started to think that I'd dreamed what happened the night before. Either way, I started to feel better, and I hoped Mike did too. Nothing can be that bad, I thought, when you've got waffles and bacon and sweet black coffee.

You'd think we would have talked about what happened the night before. But we didn't. We spent the day listening to music, talking about albums and bands, exploring the many expensive things and fancy gadgets all around us, all the riches this house had to offer. Of course, Mike and I had always been good at that. Not talking about bad things that happened. Like when his father had left, or when he and his mom lost their house. I'd tried talking with him, but it was always like talking with a wall, a wall that would tell you to back off. I told myself that not talking about those things was my way of helping Mike by giving him what he wanted.

That's what I told myself, so we just kept on going that way. Until it started to get dark.

Mike got quiet as he looked out the window at the light fading in the trees. Then suddenly, like someone had flipped a switch inside of him, he started telling me things. About what he'd been going through for the past couple of months. About how many animals he'd caught and fed to that thing downstairs. How he'd tried using dead animals he'd found along the side of the highway. But the thing wouldn't touch them. That's when he'd realized it would only eat live things. He'd started with squirrels, but they were too hard to catch, so he'd started trapping cats and dogs. But now people had caught on that someone was stealing their pets, and they'd started keeping them indoors after dark. Police cars patrolled the neighborhood every night.

"I can't do it anymore, Rick," he said, shaking his head. "I just can't do it."

"Mike," I said, "Let's get out of here. Right now. You can come home with me..."

"No," he said. "I need you to help me."

"I *am*. I *am* trying to help you."

"No," he said again, "You don't understand. I need you to do it for me."

"What are you talking about?"

"I need you to do it for me. What I've been doing."

My mind froze, trying to take in what he'd just said.

"What? I'm... I'm not... Mike, *nobody* needs to do what you've been doing. Nobody."

"Please, Rick. You can...you can stay here. This can be your place. I mean, look at it."

I felt the pull, but I didn't look. I'd been looking at it too much already.

"*No.* I'm not doing it. Why would I...?" Suddenly I was on my feet. "Mike, this is crazy. It's fucked up. We've gotta get out of here. We've gotta go... *now.*"

"Didn't you hear what I said last night?" he shouted, his face turning red again. "Were you not fucking listening? I *can't* leave."

"Why not? What's gonna happen if you leave? They can't... they didn't threaten you or anything, did they?"

Mike didn't answer at first. He ran his hand over his forehead and turned to look out the window again. Even after everything else he'd told me, I knew there was something else he was afraid to say.

"It's just..." he started, "Sometimes...sometimes I feel like... like if I stop feeding that thing down there... if I stop feeding it, it'll die, and then... bad things will happen."

"Bad thing? What kind of things?"

"Just… bad things, okay? Not just me, but…everybody."

"Everybody? What do you mean *everybody?*"

"*Everybody!*" Mike waved his hand at the window, at the whole world outside. "If that thing down there dies…" Mike closed his eyes and pressed his hands to his forehead like he was trying to hold in all the thoughts that were racing around inside his skull. "Do you…do you remember when we were like seven or eight or something, and we were playing army at the rock quarry? Remember the time you got too close to the edge, and you almost fell in?"

A picture flashed in my mind for a moment, a bright blue sky tipping dizzily over my head, the whole world going out of balance, and the feeling of falling before I even fell. "Yeah…"

"You would've died. But you didn't, right?"

"Yeah. You saved me."

"I didn't save you. That thing. That thing down there. *That's* what saved you."

"What are you talking about? What do you mean it saved me?"

"Look," Mike said, "I don't know how it works, but… there's a reason for that thing down there. It… it protects people. It keeps bad things from happening to them."

"That's crazy! Bad things *do* happen to people!"

"Yeah, well, maybe it keeps them from being any worse than they are. You know that time my mom and I were in that car wreck? And I broke my leg? If it hadn't been for that thing down there, maybe it would've been worse. A lot worse. And when your mom had cancer a couple years ago—"

"Shut up! That's… that's fucking crazy, Mike. Stuff like that… it's just crazy!"

"Yeah?" he glared right in my eye. "You mean like

having a monster in the basement? That shit doesn't happen either, right?"

Whatever I was going to say next just went away, and all I could do was stare at him. He was right. If what I'd already seen was real, what else might be true?

"Rick, listen," Mike said. "I'm tired, man. I'm really… I just need you to take over for me. Just for a while. For a week or two, okay? Then I'll be back and that'll be it. Just a couple of weeks. Please."

I looked at his face and knew two things. I'd heard Mike say *please* maybe only once or twice in my life, so I knew how desperate he must be. I also knew he was lying. He wouldn't be back. Not in one or two weeks, not in a month, not in a year.

*"No."* I looked him in the eye so he'd know I meant it. I saw a rush of anger in his face. Mike had only hit me once in our entire lives, and for a moment I thought he was going to do it again. Then that look of rage faded and he just looked tired again. Tired and sad.

"Alright," he sighed. "Just… just help me do it. One more time, okay?"

I knew I should have said no again, but I couldn't. I felt like I'd just condemned Mike to something long and terrible, so I owed him something. At least that's how it felt to me. I was walking away from this place and what was in it, but he couldn't. I owed him this much.

Mike was right about the police cars. It looked like there was one on every corner. I could see the blue lights flashing through the trees. We stayed off the streets and kept to the woods where we couldn't be seen.

We walked along behind the houses that bordered the woods, passing by the ones with high fences. Mike paused at one backyard. "This is the one…" he whispered.

I watched him peering intently into the darkness. There was one light on by the back door, a small yellow bulb that sent a weak glow over the dry grass.

Mike reached into his backpack and pulled out a long length of thick rope and a plastic bag with something in it that I couldn't see. He reached into the bag and pulled out a handful of what looked like raw meat. Then he stepped closer to that yellow light.

Immediately, I heard a dog growl. The low, deep growl of a big dog. Then I saw it, rising from the ground where it had been resting, a big, barrel-chested German shepherd with a long black snout. I could see its nostrils flaring, probably smelling the meat, I thought. Smelling us.

Mike leaned forward, holding the meat out in one hand, then he tossed it and it landed on the grass about halfway between him and the dog. The growling stopped, and I saw the dog stretch his thick neck toward the meat, nostrils opening and closing rapidly. Then it snapped up the meat and swallowed it in two bites.

Mike took some more meat out of the bag and held it out toward the dog. The dog hesitated, then took a couple of steps closer. Mike tossed the meat behind the dog. When the dog turned to see where the meat had gone, Mike sprang forward and threw the rope around its neck and pulled it tight. The dog exploded into motion, thrashing and scrambling, snarling and twisting its head to get away from the rope. When Mike reached in to pull the rope tighter, the dog twisted its head around and sank its teeth into Mike's hand. Mike cried out and pulled his hand away, cursing.

"Get the bag!" he yelled. I saw a heavy burlap bag that Mike had brought laying on on the ground and grabbed it. I stood there with the bag, not knowing what to do. "Put it over his head!" Mike yelled. I circled behind the dog and threw the bag over its head. The dog thrashed harder, trying to throw off the bag and get at me. "Tie it on!" Mike shouted, "Tie it tight!" I took another piece of rope and wrapped it around the dog's neck while it twisted around, trying to reach me. I could hear its jaws snapping inside the bag.

Mike and I stood on either side of the dog, pulling on our ropes so it couldn't reach either of us. Then we walked it back through the woods to the big white house. The dog tried to dig its paws into the ground, and sometimes we had to drag it, but we finally made it back to the house.

When we got inside, I could see how bad Mike's hand was. The dog had bit it clear down to the bone, and he was bleeding so much it looked like he'd dipped his hand in a bucket of red paint.

"Jesus, Mike..." I said, staring at his wounded hand.

"Fuck it," Mike said, "Come on...help me get it downstairs."

We dragged the dog, still growling and snarling, down the hallway, Mike's hand leaving a trail of blood on the parquet floor. Mike pulled open the door with his one good hand and we started pulling the dog down the stairs toward that big metal door at the bottom. When the dog felt the stairs underneath him, he panicked and started scrambling even more wildly, so we both had to grip the rope that circled its neck and hold on tight. The stairs felt slippery under my feet, and I almost fell once. I looked down and saw that we were walking in Mike's blood.

When we finally got to the bottom of the stairs, Mike looked paler than I'd ever seen him look. He'd left a lot of blood on the stairs, so it was no wonder. "Hold him," Mike panted. I held on tight to the rope while Mike reached up with his one good hand and dragged back the heavy metal bolt—then he pulled the door open.

At first, I couldn't see anything in there, only darkness. A strange smell that I hadn't noticed before reached my nose, a disgusting smell like the unwashed cages of zoo animals, mixed with a sweet stench like rotting vegetation and dead flowers. I could feel something moving toward me, although I couldn't see it yet. Something huge and very old. I knew that was part of what I was smelling—like the smell of old people, but a thousand times worse.

The dog started to whimper again and pull at the rope. Mike wrapped the rope around his hand and held on tighter. The darkness in front of us started to thicken and congeal, until I started to make out a shape, a form coming closer and clearer. I heard a long, wet sound that made me think of a tongue rolling around in a huge, open mouth, and another wave of that rotten animal stench rolled out of the darkness and into my face.

The dog was whining and shaking uncontrollably. It had lost control of its bladder, and I could hear its claws slipping and sliding in its own urine, trying to get away. Again, I heard that long, wet sound, like something living being ripped open. Something opened in front of me, like a flower blooming, a flower made of raw pink flesh mottled with black and brown, like the markings I'd once seen on the gums of an old dog. A sound came out of it, a sort of gurgling hiss of pure hunger that made my guts freeze.

"*Rick!*"

I turned and looked. Standing at the top of the stairs was my mother, staring down at us with a look on her face that was half outrage, half horror.

"What...What in God's name are you boys doing?"

Mike slammed the metal door shut and slid the bolt back into place. "*Get out!*" he shouted up at her. "*Get out of here!*"

That was when the dog broke free and bolted up the stairs. Mom screamed. I started scrambling up the stairs as fast as I could, knowing I'd never get there in time, but the dog pushed his way past her and disappeared. When I reached Mom, she was glaring at us, her eyes wide with terror.

"What's going on?" she said. "What's all this blood…?"

Suddenly, Mike was in her face, roaring. *"Get out! Get the fuck out of here! Right now!"* I saw her mouth working, trying to say something. She stared at Mike's face, twisted red with rage, just inches from hers, and at the blood staining his shirt and dripping from his hand.

Mike grabbed her by one arm and started pulling her down the hallway to the front door that was standing open. I hurried after them, yelling at Mike to let go of her. Before I could reach them, I saw him shove her out the door and watched her stumble down the front step. *"I said get the fuck out of here!"* he roared at her again. Mom recovered her balance, then walked right back up the front steps, drew back her hand and slapped Mike across his face. I could tell how hard she'd hit him from the sound it made.

Everything stopped for a second. Then I saw Mike's face crumple, and before I knew what was happening, he was crying. I'd never seen Mike cry, not even when we were younger. It was like all that crying he'd never done before was coming out now. From the look on his face, I knew it must have hurt him to cry that hard.

Mom reached out to him with one hand, but Mike knocked her hand away and ran off into the trees. She watched him go, then quickly turned back to me, both hands gripping my shoulders, turning me toward the light so she could see me better.

"Are you alright" she asked. I knew she was looking at all the blood on my shirt.

"Yeah," I said. "It's… it's not mine. It's…"

"Come on," she said. I followed her to the car and got in. When we got to the street, she was driving very slowly, craning her neck like she was trying to see through the dark. That's when I knew. She was looking for Mike.

There were blue lights flashing through the trees ahead of us. Mom sped up a little and drove toward them. When we finally turned onto that street, we could see two police cars and a cop standing out on the street talking to a man who looked upset. Even from this different angle, I recognized the house. It was the one we'd taken the dog from.

Then Mike came out of the trees. I saw him before the cops did. He was walking toward the police lights, covered with blood, holding onto a rope with his one good hand. On the other end of the rope was the dog. I couldn't believe it. He must have run after it and caught it somehow. I could see more bites on his wrists and arms. The blue police lights made the blood running from Mike's wounds look black.

I saw the cop finally notice Mike. He stared at him for a moment, then started walking toward him. That's when Mike dropped the rope and slowly raised both hands over his head. More cops got out of their cars and walked toward Mike. Then they were surrounding him, pulling his arms behind his back.

"Wait here," Mom said. Then she stopped the car, got out and walked toward where the police were putting handcuffs on Mike. I watched her standing there talking with them. I couldn't hear what they were saying, but I could see their mouths moving in the flashing blue lights.

I knew why Mike had let himself get caught. He'd done it so he wouldn't ever have to go back to that house again. Or that thing waiting for him there.

After a while, I saw the cops put Mike in the back of one of the police cars and heard the loud *chunk* of the door closing behind him. Mom stood talking with one of the cops for a couple of more minutes, then came walking back and got in the car with me. She sat there behind the wheel for a minute without turning the car on.

"There's nothing I can do," she said, staring through the windshield into the dark. It was the only time that night when I saw her let herself be sad.

I TOLD MY MOM I'd been trying to stop Mike. That's how I explained what she'd seen that night, the dog and all that blood. At least she didn't see what was behind that metal door. I was glad about that.

For the first few days, I kept expecting the police to show up at our door, but that didn't happen. That's how I knew that Mike didn't mention my name when they were questioning him. It was a final gift he'd given to me.

The judge at Mike's hearing wanted to send him home to await trial. But Mike had no home to go to. They might have gone easier on him if he'd told them what happened to all those missing pets. But of course, he couldn't tell them that.

One night my mom came into my room and said she wanted to talk with me. I thought it was about Mike again, but it wasn't.

"You remember those tests I had a few years ago?" she said. "Well, I saw the doctor again on Tuesday and... he says I should start coming in for some treatments..."

I think my brain must have shut down; I knew she was saying things, but I couldn't understand them. When I could think again, she was still talking.

"... because I don't want you to worry, alright? It worked out alright before, and it'll be alright this time. I just... I just don't think people should hide things from each other. Do you?"

I don't think I'd ever felt so ashamed in my entire life until she said that.

Around ten o'clock, Mom said she was feeling tired and went upstairs to bed. I don't know how long I sat there in the dark. Then I got up and went out to the garage. I got a pair of heavy-duty gardening gloves and the longest piece of rope I could find. Then I got in my car and drove out toward Old Scottsdale Road and the big white house in the woods.

I wasn't sure if that thing in the basement was still alive or not. Or if that dog was still around. Even if it wasn't, there were other dogs. Because when someone you love is in trouble, you do everything you can to help them. Even if it means you have to do something wrong.

I'd thought Mike was crazy when he told me why he had to keep feeding that thing. New ideas always sound crazy—like the earth revolving around the sun, or sickness being caused by microscopic animals you can't see. Or the world and everyone in it being protected from harm by a monster in a basement.

The truth is, we don't know how the world works. None of us. We think we know. But we don't.

# These Things
# That Walk Behind Me

YOU KNOW A *grown man isn't supposed to sleep with a light on.*

That's what Robert used to say every night when we went to bed, back when it was one of those little lover's idiosyncrasies that we could still joke about. I told him that I couldn't see well in the dark, that I was afraid of tripping and falling if I had to get up in the middle of the night. That seemed to satisfy him. But it wasn't true.

I've always been afraid of going to sleep. Even when I was very young, I was terrified by the idea of unconsciousness, that there was a precise moment when my awareness was going to be extinguished like a light being turned out. I lay in my bed and waited for that moment, horribly frightened of it, then I'd wake up, surprised to see the sunlight coming through my window. I'd missed the moment I was so afraid of, but the morning light felt tainted by the realization that I was going to have to live through that moment again and again and again.

I make the mistake of telling this to Robert one night as we lay side by side on our backs, our voices floating up to the ceiling in the dark.

"What were you afraid of?" he asks. I listen for some note of tenderness or concern, but all I hear is curiosity. I don't think Robert has ever been afraid of anything in his life, so for him, the question is a purely academic one.

"I don't know," I say. "I guess it was just the idea of losing consciousness. Being completely defenseless..."

Robert is silent for a moment. I can feel the gears in his brain working, coming up with something practical and intelligent to say.

"Defenseless? Against what? I mean, if you were afraid of losing consciousness, of nothingness, then that's just ridiculous. Nothingness means there's nothing there. You can't be afraid of *nothing*."

Robert is right. It wasn't really the idea of nothingness that I was afraid of. It was the idea that there might be something behind it. Something alive and aware that might show its face at any moment. But I can't tell him that. Just like I can't tell him about the grey people.

The first time I saw the grey people, I was in college. It was finals week and I'd been pulling all-nighters, basically living in the library, fueling myself with vending machine snacks and coffee. On my third day without any real sleep, there was a constant, low-level ringing in my ears, and my arms and legs felt rubbery and numb.

I was hunched over one of the long wood tables in the study room late one night when I felt someone watching me. I looked up and saw something from the corner of my eye, standing about twenty feet away next to a pillar. I had the impression of something thin and grey. When I looked directly at it, it slipped out of sight behind the pillar. Not the way a human would move, but with a quick, slithering motion, like some kind of dark fluid slipping down a drain.

I sat there for a moment, trying to understand what I'd just seen. I decided that I must have fallen asleep and dreamed it, so I sat up straight and tried to focus on my book. But the words drifted and pulsed on the page under the ugly florescent light, so I closed my eyes for a moment. Again, I felt like I was being watched. I opened my eyes, and the thin grey thing was there again, closer than before. It quickly slipped behind another pillar with that same liquid motion, but I thought I could make out a long, loose robe, and a face that was somehow not a face.

I looked around at the other bleary-eyed students, lost in their books and papers. None of them seemed to notice. For a moment, I tried to make myself get up and look behind that pillar, but I was afraid of what I might find. I decided to keep my head down and not look up.

A moment later, I could feel it watching me again. This time I knew it was standing right over me. I could no longer read the words on the page, but I forced my eyes to stay on the book in front of me. I knew that if I looked up again, the thing standing over me would show me its face and then take me with it.

When the sun finally came up, I left the library and walked across the campus toward my dorm, and they were everywhere. Behind every building, behind every tree. Watching me. I slept for twelve hours, and when I opened my eyes, they were gone. But there was no comfort in that word. *Gone* meant that they'd once been there. That they were real. And that they could come back at any time.

Sitting at the kitchen table the next morning trying to drink my coffee, I can feel Robert looking at me, inspecting me for flaws. I sit straighter and try to look alert. Robert has been patient with my occasional sleepless nights, my insecurities, anxieties, and quiet spells. But even with the most supportive and understanding lover, there's a point you can't afford to fall below.

"You're not having trouble sleeping again, are you?"

"No," I say. I feel him studying me—Robert can always tell when I'm lying.

"Maybe it's hormonal," he says. "You should try to get more exercise."

More than anyone I know, Robert likes to explain things. Robert is older than me by one year, handsomer by far, and taller by three inches. Five foot eleven, to be exact. Most men would just say they're six feet, but Robert likes to be precise about things. Facts have a sort of moral weight for him, and he chides me when he thinks I'm ignoring them. Working as communications director of a government healthcare agency satisfies his desire for precision and orderliness, as well as his sense of importance. As he likes to say, he's helping people in ways that matter.

*You help people too,* he likes to say whenever he senses that I'm feeling low about the differences between us. *You're a teacher. Teachers help people.* Sometimes I believe him. At other times, his earnest and well-meaning attempts to make me feel like his equal only show me how much less he thinks I'm worth.

"You should go to the gym after school today," he says on his way out the door. Robert's always trying to get me to improve myself. He says he's worried about me, but I know what that means. Worrying about me is a distraction, an annoyance he wishes he didn't have to put up with.

*Don't worry about me,* I want to say. But he's already gone.

*

TODAY A NEW student appears in my classroom, a quiet boy
with a pale, somber face who keeps his eyes cast downward.
There is a young woman with him who I've never seen
before, his case worker, obviously. She sits behind him, hands
folded in her lap, occasionally leaning forward to whisper
something to him, although I never see him respond. At
one point, I look up and see his lips moving as if he's talking
to someone. The other students don't seem to notice until
they're working silently on something. The new boy's voice
stands out in the silence, muttering softly, his eyes shut tight.
I see one or two students nervously glance at him.

At one point, the new boy shouts out a single word
that sounds like *No*. One of the girls sitting close to him
screams, then the whole class explodes into whispers and
nervous laughter. The young woman sitting with the new
boy blushes and leans close to say something to him. The
boy keeps on muttering, eyes shut tight, but I know he's
not talking to her.

"SOUNDS LIKE SCHIZOPHRENIA," Robert says. "Ten's a
little young for that." He says it with the kind of assurance
that I used to find reassuring, but now I just feel a spark
of annoyance.

"I don't know," I say. "I never really like to know what
kind of diagnosis those students have. I don't like to label
them like that."

Robert gives me the kind of patient smile that a parent
gives a child who's prattling on about something they've
heard a hundred times before. "Well," he says, moving to
the refrigerator and digging around inside for a bottle of
wine, "They probably don't even bother to tell you that
stuff anyway, do they?"

Robert pours us each a big glass of Merlot, and we sit down. The wine tastes bitter for some reason, but I take deep swallows, trying to melt the knot of anxiety deep in my chest. I catch Robert staring at me intently. "Are you still not sleeping?" he asks, a concerned scowl creeping across his handsome face.

"I'm sleeping enough."

"What's enough? Six hours? Four?"

I don't answer because I don't like lying to him.

"Dean, you're not, like...*afraid* to go to sleep or something, are you?"

"No," I say a little too loudly. "Why should I be?"

"I don't know. Just... you know... that thing you told me about when you were a kid..."

"Jesus, Robert, I'm sorry I even told you now. God, why do I tell you anything?"

"Okay, I'm sorry, I'm sorry," Robert says, raising both hands, palms-out. "It's just... you know. I want you to be alright."

*You think I don't want the same thing?* That's what I want to say, but I don't. I've said enough already. Probably too much. More won't help.

In bed later, I try to make my breathing as slow and regular as I can to make myself relax. I'm also doing it so Robert will think I'm asleep. Pretty soon, I hear his slow, ragged breathing. I lay there listening and try to take some comfort in that sound.

Three hours later, I'm still awake, staring into the dark. Robert has stopped snoring, so I'm unprotected from all the sounds around me. The long sigh of a car passing by and fading. The staccato pop of wood swelling in the heat. And a new sound from down the hall, in the kitchen. A ceramic clink and scrape that sounds like a coffee cup being clumsily placed in a saucer and picked up again. I wait, certain that it won't happen again, afraid that it will. When it does, the sound is unmistakable.

The third time it happens, I can't stop myself. I get up and walk down the hall toward that noise. I pause outside of the kitchen door and look in. Light from the streetlight outside pours in through the windows, illuminating everything.

There's a man standing by the kitchen counter. He's heavy-set and wears some kind of baggy gray suit that's too big for him. There's plenty of light, but I can't seem to see his face. He picks up a coffee cup, appears to study it, then puts it back down again, making that small rattling sound, over and over. At first, he doesn't seem to notice me. Then he turns his face toward me and slowly smiles, double rows of sharp teeth, long as butcher knives, gleaming in the kitchen-light. At the same time, I see the baggy gray suit that sags in folds around him is skin.

*This can't be happening.* I say those words to myself, closing my eyes and repeating them to push out everything else. *This can't be happening.* I open my eyes again and the thing in the kitchen is still there, grinning at me.

"No." I say out loud, then, louder. *"No."* The thing smiles even wider. A long string of saliva stretches slowly from its lips all the way to the floor.

I turn and walk quickly back to the bedroom. I don't run—I know that running will only make this worse. I get into bed next to Robert, but I don't try to wake him or even touch him. Instead, I lay there and listen for that rattling sound, for *any* sound, but it's quiet now. I watch the door all night, but nothing happens.

\*

"WHAT THE FUCK were you doing in here last night?"

Robert is standing near the kitchen sink, a confused scowl on his face. I'm bleary-eyed and light-headed from lack of sleep, and my heart is beating too fast. I lean against the door frame and try to focus on what Robert is holding in his hand and peering at. It's the white cup and saucer from last night.

"You spill a cup of coffee on the floor and don't clean it up?" I watch Robert scowl harder and bend down to touch a wet spot on the floor. He pulls his fingers away, something sticky and viscous trailing from them. "Jesus, Dean! what the hell..."

"Don't!" I shout. I push him out of the way, and he staggers back against the counter, the white cup and saucer fall to the floor and break.

"What the fuck is wrong with you?" he yells. In his eyes I see anger and something I've never seen in them before. Fear. He's afraid of me.

Now we're both afraid.


*I WANT YOU TO see somebody*. Those are the words Robert uses, the ones I knew were coming. *I want you to see somebody*. I know what that means. I don't argue. I agree, just to keep the peace. Maybe it will help. But something tells me it won't. I don't want anyone else to explain what's happening to me. Not some doctor. Not Dean. Not anyone.

I stay up late, doing my research. I'm learning about the limits of human visual perception. I read about the whole spectrum of invisible light that humans can't see, about infrared light that shines from our bodies, x-ray light that penetrates flesh and bone, gamma light and radio light.

I bring these things up before dinner, trying to sound casual.

"Stop it, Dean," Robert sighs. "Just stop, okay?"

"Stop what?" I know he's on to me, but the reflex to deflect and deny is too strong.

"I mean... you go on Google, you write down a bunch of big scientific-sounding words, then you throw them at me like you know what you're talking about, but you don't. You don't even understand half the stuff you're saying."

Normally, I'd get up and walk away, but tonight my anger flies out at him. "Why do you always have to call me stupid?"

"I'm not calling you stupid..."

"That's what you meant."

"You're not stupid, Dean," Robert says, trying to make his voice go softer. "You're just..." He trails off and looks down, his lips tight. I try to imagine the word he doesn't want to say. *Gullible? Weak?*

Later, I start to wonder if he's right. I don't want him to put a label on what's happening to me and stick me in some kind of box. But isn't that what I'm doing with my invisible spectrum and gamma rays and radio light—trying to put what I've seen into some other kind of box?

BACK IN THE classroom, I try to lose myself in my job, in all the young faces around me, but it's hard. The new boy seems to be getting worse. He shouts out loud at least once every day, flailing his hands like he's trying to push something away. The other kids almost seem used to it by now. They've stopped reacting with startled squeals and nervous laughter. Instead, they stop in the middle of whatever they're saying and wait patiently until the boy's case worker has calmed him down. Their kindness almost makes me weep, then I wonder if it's really kindness that I'm witnessing, or something else.

Today I approach the case worker after class. She's standing by the boy's desk, picking up her things, and looks a little started to see me walk over to her. We've never talked.

"Hi," I say, glancing down at the boy. "I was just wondering... is there anything I can do? You know, to help?"

"No," she says. "Thank you." Behind her polite smile and strained eyes, I can see the part of her that's given up. I glance down at the boy sitting alone at his desk and feel sorrier for him than before.

It must be terrible to have people give up on you.


THERE ARE NO seats on the bus today, so I stand, hanging onto the metal bar as best I can. No sleep now for four days. One moment, my body feels heavy as lead, the next moment, it's so light, I imagine that people can see right through me.

I'm gazing at the window, at the ghostly reflection of the other passengers packed in around me. Then I see the reflection of a face over my shoulder, looking right at me. I freeze, unable to understand what I'm seeing. Two dead eyes like black marbles. A lipless, snake-like mouth that stretches all the way from ear to ear.

I close my eyes as tight as I can and try to concentrate on the rumble and roar of the bus, the voices of people talking around me. Familiar sounds. I open my eyes, and the face behind me is closer than before, just a few feet away, staring at me. He's taller than the other passengers, but they don't seem to notice him. I can't turn around and look. I'm afraid that if I do, he might really be there. When the urge to turn around becomes too much, I shut my eyes again as tightly as I can and squeeze the metal bar over my head so hard that my hand becomes numb. *No. Am I saying it out loud? No!* I hear people around me start to whisper and mutter. I know they're talking about me. When I can't bear it anymore, I open my eyes and the thing is standing right behind me. A long, thin tongue flickers out of its mouth and slides across the back of my neck.

WHEN I WAKE up, there are strangers hovering over me and asking me questions, and a terrible hospital smell all around. My throat feels raw from screaming, but as soon as I can speak, I say, "Robert... Robert Denning." I can't give them his number—the only two phone numbers I've ever memorized in my life are my mother's, and my childhood best friend, and they're both dead now. So, I keep telling them, "Robert. Robert Denning," over and over, until the words are just meaningless sounds.

When Robert finally arrives, his face is flushed red, and his blue eyes are hard. "Christ, Dean! I begged you to see somebody!" Those are his first words to me. I don't know what else I expected of him, but there they are, so I say what I know he wants from me.

"I'm sorry..."

I watch him looking around at the cold, stark hallways, a nervous expression on his face. "Jesus," he says. "You don't belong in this fucking place..." But when he looks back at me, I see a glimpse of the same fearful anger I saw in his eyes the morning I pushed him, and I understand what he really means. *I don't belong with someone who belongs in this fucking place.*

Two men in white walk up to Dean. One of them touches Dean on the shoulder and says something I can't hear. Dean walks away with him, and they disappear around a corner. The other man stays and watches me, an unreadable look on his face. *Don't worry about me,* I want to say. *He's going to get me out of here.* But when the doctor comes back, Dean isn't with him. I understand what's happened before he says anything.

"Your friend believes it's in your best interest for you to stay here with us for a while."

All the breath leaves my body, and for a moment I feel my heart actually stop. *I'm going to die now,* I think. But I don't. Somehow, I don't.


THE TV BLARING—THAT's the one thing you can't get away from in this place. The doctors and nurses come and go, and you can close your eyes if you don't want to see all the other men and women with their vacant, frightened stares. But there's no escaping the sound of the TV. They turn it up all the way, so it keeps battering away at your ears and nerves until you learn to tune it out.

There's a man here who yells at the other patients. An older man, maybe in his sixties, very thin with hard muscles like knots. His head is shaved, and his eyes are bright and wild. I watch him walk over to a middle-aged woman huddled in a chair, shouting angrily and flailing his arms until a couple of orderlies come and take him away. An hour later he's back again, sitting alone in the corner, his bright, angry eyes darting all over the room as if he's looking for someone.

All night long, I can hear someone crying in the room next to mine. I wish I could cry. I wish I could scream or shout, anything to get rid of this tight, terrified feeling trapped in my chest. It hits me that nothing in my entire life has prepared me for this. Nothing I've ever done, nothing I've learned can help me now.

In the morning, I look across the community room and see a frightened-looking man in striped pajamas huddled in one of the ugly, green Naugahyde chairs. His eyes are shut, his lips are moving rapidly. His head jerks and twists as if he's trying to get away from something.

"Ugly motherfucker..."

I turn and see the angry man from yesterday sitting right next to me, glaring at the man across the room. Before I can react, he gets up and strides over to the man and starts yelling and waving his arms threateningly.

That's when I see it. Fading in and out of focus, a figure standing over the man in the chair. Almost seven feet tall, with a face like the skull of a dead bird, long twisted arms and fingers like bare branches that poke and scratch at the man's face while he twists and moans. The angry man shouts and flails at the tall stick-thing, and it turns its head toward him, opens its bony beak and hisses. Two orderlies start to move in, but before they can reach him, the man turns and stalks out of the room, and the tall stick-like thing follows him. The orderlies go back to their other tasks, the man in the chair stops muttering; the tension seems to leave his body and he closes his eyes and appears to fall asleep. I sit there, unable to move or understand what I've just seen.

PLEASE. COME GET me. That's the four-word message I keep typing into my cell phone and deleting—I don't know how many times. I stopped sending texts to Robert a while ago. I couldn't bear to keep looking for his response and not finding it. I still type them. I just don't send them. That way, it doesn't hurt as much when he doesn't answer.

"Why you do that to yourself?"

A gravelly voice speaks close to me. I look up from my phone. The man with the shaved head is sitting right across the table from me, glaring at me with his bright, angry eyes. He nods at the phone in my hand.

"You know he ain't coming back here for you."

*How...?* I look more closely at him. The bones of his ebony-dark face are sharp and highly defined, proud, even beautiful, and I think of the statue of an Egyptian pharaoh. His eyes that continue to blaze at me have small flecks of gold and green.

"My name's Dean," I offer.

"Carlton." He extends his hand across the table. I take it and feel how strong he is. His skin feels dry and leathery and radiant with heat.

He releases my hand and studies me for a moment. "Dean. Tell me. Why is it you don't want something *better* for yourself?"

The tears that burn my eyes startle me, and I turn to wipe them away. *How does he know?* When I look up at him again, he's glaring at something in the room behind me.

"Look," he says. I turn around and feel my throat close with fear.

They're all here. Fading in and out of my vision like objects appearing and disappearing in a heavy fog. The tall, stick-like thing with the dead bird's beak. The grinning man with teeth like butcher knives. The tall figure with the dead black eyes and the wide snake mouth. A dozen others I've never seen before. They bend low over these poor men and women who are trapped here, scratching and stabbing into their soft flesh, hissing terrible words into their ears that make them moan and weep.

"You see them, don't you?" Carlton says. "Don't tell me you don't see them, 'cause I know you do."

My throat is too tight to speak. All I can do is nod. Carlton glares at the creatures tormenting the patients, shakes his head and growls under his breath. "Ugly motherfuckers..."

"You... you stopped one," I manage to say. "I saw you. You made it go away."

"Not now," he growls. "Too many. Some days there's too many, and you can't do nothing."

"But some days..." I say the words carefully, as if they might break, "... you can."

"That's right. Some days you can." He looks at me for a long moment, then leans closer across the table, eyes burning into mine. "Listen," he says, "I ain't never getting out of here. But you will. When you do, remember something. You got work to do. You got real important work to do. You understand what I'm saying."

I look into his wild, feverish eyes. I don't understand, not yet. But I know it's coming. The understanding. Like a train or a storm, it's coming.


ON THE MORNING when they finally release me, the woman who is filling out my papers asks, "Is there someone you'd like us to contact? Someone you'd like to come and get you?"

"No," I say. "No one." When I see the concerned look in her eyes, I remember to smile and say, "Thanks."

In the end, the world outside is not so different from the one inside. You just have to learn to negotiate them both. That's what I'm doing now. One step at a time.

I did see Robert again. He was standing on the street corner in a crowd of people, waiting for the light to change. I saw the thing that was with him. Looming over him, grim and terrible, it had long, twisted fingers like tangled tree roots that pierced the skin of Robert's back and were growing inside of him. I knew that Robert suffered, but I didn't know why or how much until now. I didn't approach him or try to help because I knew he wouldn't believe me. When the light changed, I saw Robert cross the street with the dark thing, and even though Robert was in front, I could see that it was leading him.

There are so many other people out here who need help. More than I ever knew. I look for the ones who I know can't handle it by themselves. The ones who are too old or too young, not strong enough. Like the little boy in the park. I recognize him the moment I see him, the way he sits by himself with his eyes closed and his lips moving, the same way he did in my classroom. I don't need to see the two monstrous insect-like things bending over him and whispering to know how long this has been going on for him—his mother's strained and weary face tells me all I need to know.

I don't hesitate. Not anymore. I walk right up to the two red things bending over him. "Leave him alone," I say. One of them looks up at me, chittering and hissing, the insect features of his face rearranging themselves into what must be an expression of surprise or resentment.

"Leave him alone!" I say again. I hear the mother call out her boy's name, alarm in her voice. In one more moment, I know she'll stand up and run over to protect her child from this stranger approaching him.

"Come with me," I say to the two ugly red things that are now both staring at me. "Now."

And they come. They follow me away from the boy and his mother who I know is now on her knees beside him. "What did he say to you?" I hear her asking. "What did he say?" I don't stay to hear him answer. I keep walking through this world with all these things that walk behind me. I don't need to turn around to know how many there are.

I can't slow down now. I've got work to do.

# The Skin
# You Were Born In

THEY SAY THAT a father's job is to teach his son how to be a man. That was a task I felt unqualified for. I know what a man is supposed to be. But what a man is is still a mystery to me.

When Daniel was two days old, right before they released us from the hospital, the doctor told us it was time to give him the ring. I suppose I'd known this was coming, but I hadn't thought about it very much. Like everyone else, I thought it was the right thing to do. Monica, however, did not feel the same way.

"It's barbaric!" she said.

"Oh, I don't think it's that bad," I said. "Everyone does it."

"I don't care what everyone does. He's our son. We can do whatever we want. Why do you want to subject him to something like that?"

I don't know how I talked her into it, what combination of words and reasons I strung together. I remember saying something about how I didn't want him to feel strange when he was around other boys, that I didn't want him to feel like a freak. And I believe I really meant it. But when they came to take him away and asked if I wanted to go with them, I said no. No matter what I'd said, I didn't want to watch them do it. But I heard it. From all the way down the hall, through closed doors, I heard Daniel scream, a terrible, long scream of pain and outrage that went right through my chest like a spear.

When the nurse brought him back to the room and handed him to me, she pulled back the blanket and showed me the brand new, bright silver ring that passed through the skin of his chest, right over his breastbone. She gave me a little vial of antibiotic ointment and told me to dab the place on his chest five times a day until it healed.

Monica wouldn't do it. She'd stopped talking to me. So, I dabbed the wound on Daniel's chest five times a day like the nurse had told me to do. I couldn't get over how bright and shiny Daniel's ring was, compared to my own dull and tarnished one. I couldn't remember the day when I got my own ring, so I hoped and prayed that Daniel wouldn't remember this day either, that he'd forget all about the pain and how I'd failed to protect him. Like I told you, it was a job I wasn't prepared for.

They say no mother can sleep when her child is crying. It isn't true. I've seen Monica lie in bed like a dead woman while Daniel shrieked and cried in the dead of night. It wasn't always this way. For the first four weeks, she'd wake and nurse him, and when that didn't work, she'd walk the floor until he fell asleep in her arms. It was a beautiful thing to see, and I'll admit that I was jealous. Not of Daniel taking Monica away from me, but of the beautiful bond that the two of them seemed to have.

One night, Monica told me she was done.

"What do you mean, *done*?" I asked her. "Done with what?"

"With this," she said, handing Daniel over to me.

At first, I thought she meant that we'd trade-off these nightly sessions, the way we'd always done with other tasks. But after a few nights, it became apparent that she had no intention of ever taking over this particular task again. It was mine now.

I suppose I should have been angry, or at least objected. But I didn't. I loved it. I loved every moment of it, walking with Daniel's little head pressed close to mine until it felt like our thoughts were passing back and forth between us. It was the most beautiful and perfect thing I'd ever felt.

As Daniel grew older, every night before bedtime, I'd read to him. It was, without doubt, the best part of my day, diving deeply into the stack of favorite books that I kept nearby on the bureau. I loved reading aloud. I used to read to Monica as we lay side by side in bed before she became tired and wanted nothing more than to go to sleep right away. So, this nighttime reading with Daniel felt like a gift, a return to the way things should be. Daniel would sit on my lap and help turn the pages, the top of his head just under my chin, until he grew too big to fit there, and his head rested against my right cheek.

Our favorite book was an old copy of *Fairy Tales of the World*. I loved its heavy thickness, its musty-leaf smell. The illustrations were wonderful; watercolors, woodcuts, and pen-and-ink drawings by different artists, all dead now, their peculiar visions preserved in the yellowing pages. One of them, Daniel's favorite, was a Japanese demon or ghost in a long, traditional kimono, its face an elaborately grimacing snow-white mask framed by a wild mane of serpentine black hair. The demon, fierce and proud, wielded a long samurai sword over its head. I think it was the sword, more than anything else, that attracted Daniel. When he was eight years old and Halloween was a week away, he brought the book to me, pointed to the picture of the Japanese demon, and said, "That's what I want to be."

We worked all week on that costume. I knew Monica had a Japanese kimono-style robe covered with red and gold flowers—not the writhing dragons worn by the demon in the book, but close enough. I went to the costume store and bought white and black makeup for Daniel's face, and a black fright-wig that I teased-out with a comb until it flared-out like a lion's mane. A gold-painted plastic samurai sword completed the effect. When we'd finished putting on the costume, it was amazing. Daniel looked proud, fierce, and beautiful. It felt like this was the way he was always meant to look. He stood in front of the mirror, stunned at first, then energized by his own transformation, roaring and slashing that plastic sword through the air so fast and hard, I could hear it hum.

When I dropped Daniel off at school, I saw gangs of other boys dressed in khaki, camouflage, and military green, their faces hidden by knotted kerchiefs or black ski-masks, plastic machine guns and machetes clutched in their small hands. Daniel stood out among them like a phoenix among crows. I saw him hesitate for a moment, and I wondered if he felt the same misgivings that I did. Then he ran and joined the crowd, and the big school door closed behind him.

When I returned at three o'clock to pick him up, the big doors blew open and all the other boys in their green, brown, and gray uniforms, ran out roaring and barking like wild dogs.

When Daniel finally appeared, walking out of the school by himself, his wig was gone, the kimono torn open and hanging from one shoulder. His makeup was half rubbed-away, the skin beneath it red and raw-looking. I got out of the car fast and ran to him.

"What's wrong, buddy?" I asked, going down on one knee, and putting my hands on his shoulders.

"They... they laughed at me..." he gasped between wrenching sobs. "They said... I looked like a girl..."

I wanted to say *you looked beautiful*, but I couldn't because of the raw pain clutching my throat. It was the hurt of seeing my son wounded inside, pure rage at the ones who'd hurt him. And the knowledge that I was responsible; I was the one who had put the flowered robe on him and tied it around his small waist. I was the one who'd put the wig on his head and painted his face and sent him into that den of little killers. For the second time in his life, I had failed to protect him. And unlike the first time, this was one he would remember.

I think this was when Daniel began to change. It started with his voice. I could hear him trying to make it sound more grown up—not so much deeper, but harder, forcing the gentleness out of it.

One morning I found Daniel standing naked in front of the bathroom mirror, looking at himself. His small body had already started that almost imperceptible process of lengthening, of stretching out toward the future. I saw him glance downward, and I knew he was looking at his ring. It gleamed silver-bright in the bathroom light. As I watched, he reached up and touched it with the fingers of his right hand. Then he looped one finger through the ring and slowly pulled on it, stretching the skin over his breastbone outward. A pang of alarm shot through my guts, and I almost called out for him to stop—then he let go of the ring, and the skin at the center of his chest slowly relaxed back to its original shape. As I'd stood there watching, it felt like I was about to see something terrible and miraculous, something beyond my powers to describe.

I SUPPOSE I COULD have taken Daniel away from here a long time ago, before he turned thirteen. But thirteen always felt like such a long time away.

My neighbor Carl says that what kids need is a stronger sense of direction. In our town, that direction is very clear, but it's not for everyone. Every year, we lose another family, the ones whose boys are about to turn thirteen. My neighbor Carl says those families are the ones with *the wrong mindset,* and he's always glad to see them leave. *Good riddance. Keeps the gene pool pure.*

Carl spent some time out East but came back here because he didn't like the *mindset,* as he called it. "They tell their kids, *you can be anything you want. That's where the trouble starts."*

One day when he was eleven, Daniel came home from school with his lip bloodied. He didn't cry when he told me about the boys who'd beat him up, but he wouldn't look me in the eye. I told him he didn't do anything wrong, and he glared at the ground like he didn't believe me, like there was something down there that he wanted to hurt and kill.

"Everything okay over here?" I looked up and saw Carl standing at the edge of our front yard. I explained what had happened. Carl looked at Daniel who had gone over to a nearby tree and was beating it with a stick. "How old is he?" Carl asked.

"Eleven."

Carl watched Daniel who had dropped the stick and was wandering away, kicking at clumps of grass on the ground. Then he looked at me. "You've talked with him, right?" Carl said. "You've told him all about it?"

"Yeah," I said. The truth was, I had not told Daniel anything about what was coming. Of all the serious talks that a father is supposed to have with his son, this was one I never wanted to have. I told myself that he probably knew anyway that he must have heard stories from his friends at school. Like Santa Claus, or like sex, it seemed impossible that he didn't already know.

Carl glanced back toward Daniel who was still lashing at the tree with his stick. "You think he's ready?"

"He will be," I said. I spoke with that same voice I'd started to hear coming from Daniel, the voice of a man trying to sound stronger and more confident than he really is. *He will be.* What the hell did I mean by that? How was he ever supposed to be ready?

I wasn't ready when my time came. My father had tried. He'd made me join the football team at school when I turned eleven. We ran every day in the hot sun until we fainted, then the bigger boys held me down and beat me in the locker room. *That's nothing.* Those were my dad's words when I told him about it. So, I never told him again. When I turned twelve, he started tying me to a tree in our back yard with thick ropes, saying that if I didn't want to starve, I'd find a way to get out. The first time, it took me a whole day and night, and I'd rubbed half the skin off my wrists and arms before I finally sat down and ate my cold supper. The next time, he tied me tighter.

I never did those things to Daniel. That was one thing that Monica and I agreed on. It wasn't because I thought that measures like these were cruel, although they were. It's just that I never believed they would help when the time came.

On my thirteenth birthday, they'd come for me at midnight, appearing around my bed like figures from a nightmare, bloodshot eyes looking down at me through the holes in their masks. I knew which one was my father because of the black and red ski mask he was wearing, the same one he'd worn to take me sledding when I was smaller.

They loaded me into the back of a van with the other boys, ten of us who'd all turned thirteen since last year, and drove off into the night. I didn't know what to expect. I'd heard the stories, of course, but they were all different. I think the men probably changed what happened every year. They wanted us to be prepared, but not complacent.

What happened next is hard to remember. Sometimes it feels like a dream, though I know it wasn't. I remember how cold it was, the long walk deep into the woods, the flashlights shining on the rocks and roots of trees below our feet, the light of a bonfire casting shadows on twisted tear-streaked faces. I can still hear the boys crying out for their fathers who stood apart in the shadows with their faces hidden. I remembered other sounds that were not human, too horrible to be true. So that night was like a blind spot, a scar on my eye that I couldn't see past, although I could still sense things moving behind the haze if I looked long enough.

WHEN DANIEL TURNED twelve, he brought my old weights into his bedroom and started working out three times a day. I could hear the weights clink and thump on the floor above, sometimes deep into the night when they woke me up. I wanted to go upstairs and tell him to stop, that he needed his sleep. I wanted to tell him that he was wasting his time, that when the time came, none of this would matter. But I figured that would only upset him, or he'd just ignore me. So, I left him alone and learned to sleep through the clink and thump of the weights on the other side of the ceiling above me.

As the months went by, I watched Daniel change himself. His arms and chest grew harder and stronger. That was not the only change. Years earlier, I'd watched my dying father go through a process of removing himself from the rest of us, a sort of deliberate cutting-off of his earthly mortal ties. In his final days, I realized that it wasn't that he couldn't recognize me—he was *willing* himself to not recognize me, to not care. And even though I know it was what he needed to face what was coming, it made me angry. I felt that same anger toward Daniel now. I loved him, but I didn't know how to love what he was becoming.

THE WEEK BEFORE Daniel's thirteenth birthday, I got a call from Monica. She was calling less and less lately, but I'd been expecting this one. Her voice was hard and accusatory.

"You're really going to let this happen?"

I felt the same tightening in my brain, too many thoughts jammed too close to move.

"I don't know..."

"What do you mean you don't know?"

"I mean... it's complicated..."

"It's not fucking complicated. Do you want your son to die? That's all there is to it. Do you want that?"

"No! Jesus, Monica, why would you even ask that?"

"Then *do* something."

She hung up, and I sat for a while, waiting for the blood pounding in my head to slow down. As the tangle of thoughts in my brain began to loosen themselves, one thought separated from the rest and slowly came into focus. We could just leave. Daniel and me. That was all we had to do. Just leave. The clarity of it stunned me.

That afternoon I went to the bank and withdrew fifteen hundred dollars. I would have taken all of it, but I didn't want it to look suspicious. It also would have meant that we were never coming back. I didn't want to think about that now, because I was afraid it might stop me.

I waited till dark before I asked Daniel to get in the car with me. When he asked where we were going, I told him I was taking him out for his birthday dinner. I was praying there was still just enough of the little boy left in him to go along with this. When he walked out to the car with me, I felt a rush of guilt and relief.

I dared a quick glance over at Daniel as we headed down Route 9. In profile, his face looked even leaner and harder than I'd realized it had become. His nose that had already been broken twice in martial arts class reminded me of a seasoned boxer or a Roman gladiator. When we started to get closer to the outskirts of town, I heard Daniel shift uneasily in his seat. "Where are we going, Dad?" he asked, and suddenly he was five years old again. My heart hurt so hard for a moment, I was afraid to say anything. I breathed deeply, swallowed, and said what I'd prepared to say.

"I thought we'd go on a little trip, buddy. You know, just you and me."

Daniel's reaction was immediate and harsh. He didn't have to see the suitcases I'd packed and hidden in the trunk, or all the cash I'd taken from our account and stashed in my wallet to know what was going on.

"Stop the car," he said, his voice cold and hard.

*Tell him the truth,* I thought. "Buddy..."

"Dad!" he shouted, "Stop the fucking car!"

Before I could say anything, Daniel reached across the seat and grabbed on to the steering wheel. I tried to pull it back and felt just how strong he was. The car veered wildly to the right. I stomped down on the brake, and we lurched to a halt, the front two wheels off the road. Before I could say anything, Daniel threw the door open, got out of the car and started walking back in the direction we'd come from. I called his name, but he kept walking, not looking back. That was when it hit me. *He wants this. He wants this to happen.*

Cursing under my breath, I threw the car into drive, made a U-turn and started after him. He must have known I was right behind him, but he kept walking and didn't turn around.

The sharp *whoop* of a police siren pierced my chest. I saw blue and red lights washing over Daniel, illuminating the inside of my car. I stopped and watched the police cruiser roll slowly past me on the left and pause alongside of Daniel.

When I opened the car door and started to get out, the officer turned and shouted, *"Sir... stay in your vehicle!"* I did as I was told. I watched as the officer talked with Daniel, then walked him back to our car. Daniel reluctantly climbed into the passenger seat, and the officer shut the door behind him.

At first, I thought they might let us go home, just to prepare ourselves. But of course, we'd had thirteen years to do that. I knew that one more hour, one more day, even one more year wouldn't make any difference now. You always think you're going to have more time. Time for one more conversation, one more question, one more chance to pause and think and breathe. Even when you know there's not.

We followed the police cruiser at a funereal pace, not too close, but not too far. On the way there, all the words I could have said but never had swelled up inside of my throat and died. Daniel didn't speak either. I risked a glance at him from the corner of my eye and saw him sitting straight with his chin held high, trying to make himself look bigger, older, stronger than he really was. It was a look I knew well, and it broke my heart.

Other cars came out to join us, and soon we were a procession, rolling through the darkened town. Lights flicked on in windows as we passed, hands pulled back curtains, and unseen eyes looked out. I wondered how many boys were watching us, how many mothers, how many fathers. What were they thinking? Were they picturing themselves in our place?

The last lights of town faded behind us, and we drove for a while in pitch darkness. The police cruiser turned off the road, and we followed down a narrow gravel trail. When the cruiser's headlights illuminated a metal gate, chained and locked, we stopped while one of the cops got out to unlock it. In the glow of the headlights, I could see that he'd already put on his ski mask. Then we rolled forward again, tires rumbling over tree roots and ruts in the dirt. We paused for the last car to lock the gate behind us before moving once more, deeper and deeper into the darkness.

This is where an insane thought came to me: Maybe I was wrong about what I remembered. Perhaps my father had never really beaten me and tied me to a tree. Maybe there had been no inhuman, ravening things trying to kill us. No real monsters. No dead boys. *Fathers don't do these things,* I thought. Fathers don't lead their sons like cattle to be slaughtered. Fathers don't hand their sons over to monsters. Of course, they don't. Not really. It was all just a tradition, some kind of game. I almost laughed with relief, but the sound that came out of my throat was more like a gasp or a sob. Daniel heard it and turned and looked at me. It was the first time that I saw him look afraid.

When we finally got to the place, it wasn't the way I remembered it. No bonfires cast flickering shadows, just the blinding glare of headlights from the police car and a few pickup trucks. The trees didn't look as tall or frightening as they once had, and seemed spaced further apart, like they were retreating from something. But the faces of the men, hidden in their cloth bandanas and black ski masks, were the same.

One of the masked figures approached me and spoke in a harsh whisper. *"What the hell are you doing?"* I recognized Carl's voice. *"Here..."* he thrust a black ski mask toward me. A few yards away, I saw one of the masked police officers turn and seem to stare at me. *"Put it on,"* Carl whispered.

I hesitated. I wanted Daniel to be able to see my face. *"Put it on."*

Slowly, with numb hands, I pulled the ski mask over my head. The material felt scratchy and tight over my face and smelled like something that had been buried for a long time.

I looked around for Daniel and found him standing with six other boys. They'd all taken off their shirts and stood huddled close together as if for warmth, their eyes closed and turned away from the blinding lights that made the rings in their chests glitter and shine.

Two men came forward holding a thick rope. I watched them pass the rope through the ring in the first boy's chest, then the next. When they got to the third boy, he made a frightened, sobbing sound and tried to back away, but one of the men held him by the arms until the rope had been passed through the ring in his chest. After that, he stood quietly, face turned downward as if the urge to flee had been drained out of him.

When they got to Daniel to pass the rope through his ring, he held his head high and didn't move or make a sound. I felt proud of him for a fleeting moment, then a surge of panic and shame. There was nothing good about to happen here. Nothing to celebrate or be proud of. But instead of energizing and moving me to act, the shame left me drained and empty, unable to move or speak. I thought of the tree my father had tied me to and how weak and useless I'd felt.

Holding on to the rope, the men led the boys to a large, heavy-looking metal plate on the ground, the kind that construction crews use to cover holes in the highway. A bulldozer rumbled into the light with another masked man at the controls, lowering its blade and pushing the heavy plate aside with a grating, sliding sound. That's when I heard them. The same sounds I had heard in my nightmares for years rising from that hole in the ground. Not human, not animal. Something in-between. It was true. It was all true.

Holding both ends of the rope, the men pulled the boys into a circle around the pit, then pulled the rope tighter until the boys were standing at the very edge. I could see Daniel still standing upright, his eyes looking straight ahead.

The sounds from the pit grew louder. Then the boys began to cry. One by one, their faces crumpled and twisted and grew shiny with tears in the harsh headlights. I could hear at least two of them crying out for their mothers. The men around me grew nervous and impatient, shuffling closer, lowing like cattle. Only Daniel made no sound; his face was lifted toward the light. I suddenly felt rage. Why didn't he get away when I gave him the chance? What was he trying to prove? Who did he think he was?

The horrible, inhuman snarling from below grew louder. Claws scrambled and scraped at the sides of the pit. The other boys stopped crying and began screaming. What could I do? I had no weapon. No power to stop what was happening, no way to stop this thing that had been coming for years. It was stronger than I was. It had always been stronger.

That was when I saw Daniel reach up and take hold of the ring in his chest. He held it tightly in his fingers and pulled hard. I saw the skin on his chest stretch outward, farther and farther.

I want you to picture a boy tearing himself open and stepping outside of his own skin. Picture him growing taller and taller, his hair growing long and wild, fanning out like flames around his fierce snow-white face. Picture him rising taller than the trees, a long sword in his hands splitting the air like a whirlwind and laying waste to his enemies. If I told what I saw, would you think I was making it up because the truth is too horrible to remember? Or would you realize that I was telling you something true, that I was seeing Daniel as he really was?

Could you do it? If it was the only thing left to do, and you had no choice. Tear yourself open and step outside of the skin you were born in. You'd better start thinking about that. Because we always think there's going to be more time. Even when there's not.

# Story Notes

### "Give Me Back My Name"

IN JANUARY 2022, I received an invitation from Tom English to submit a story to a new publication he was starting up called *Nightmare Abbey*. "Genuinely creepy tales… with a sense of dread" was what Tom was looking for. I knew I wanted to write a ghost story—I also wanted it to be a different kind of story.

I started with two questions I like to ask my students: What is a ghost? And what does it mean to be haunted? The answers to those questions are often things you don't know you know until you say them. Before I knew it, I was writing about a man who's changed his identity and is haunted by the life he left behind and by his former wife, who may or may not be dead.

I thought that was all there was to the story until I wondered—what do liars do when their lies are exposed? Answer: tell more lies. Then I wondered—what would happen if the lies he tells begin to come true?

It seems to me that a lie is, more than anything, an act of theft. A lie takes away so much—not just our "trust" in the person who lies to us (although that's bad enough)—it also takes away our sense of how things exist, our vision of reality. A lie can steal our whole world if it is big enough. That's what the ghost-wife demands that her former husband give back to her in those final lines. The fact that he can't do it may be the saddest and scariest thing about this story.

I was finishing the story and trying to find a way to build up to and earn those last lines when it suddenly hit me where I'd heard those words before–the old 'Give Me Back My Golden Arm' ghost story. A simple "vengeful spirit" tale, it was one of the first ghost stories I'd heard while growing up (as it may have been for many folks my age).

I knew immediately that the narrator and his wife should discuss the old "Golden Arm" ghost story. Maybe, I thought, she has to tell it to kids, and she's wondering if it's still relevant and scary enough, then have them wonder out loud about what else it could be besides a golden arm. I put that conversation upfront at the story's start to light the fuse I hoped would burn to the end.

## "Little Gods to Live In Them"

WHEN JULIA AND I were still living on the east side of the Hudson—first in Sleepy Hollow, then in Irvington—they were tearing down the old Tappan Zee Bridge to make way for a new one. Every day, we could hear this rhythmic, almost sub-sonic noise. Thud—thud—thud. We found out that the pneumatic drills were pounding holes in the riverbed. It seemed to last all day and could almost drive you crazy if you didn't find some way not to focus on it.

One day, Julia and I were writing on our favorite couch at our favorite coffee place, Muddy Waters. An older woman, well-dressed, was sitting at a table nearby. It looked like she was waiting for someone—a little anxiously, it seemed to me.

Then the woman was joined by a younger man who strode through the crowd, took her hand, and greeted her warmly. It was clear to me that they'd never met before. The man was wearing some kind of hunting jacket with lots of pockets. The woman sat upright, formal, and a little stiff, while the man slumped low in his chair, stretching out his long legs, making himself comfortable. The contrast was striking.

The conversation between the woman and the man at the table beside us caught my ear. After a while, I started to understand what I was hearing. The woman represented some local citizens concerned about the construction project. At the same time, the man was some kind of public relations representative of the company behind the new bridge. The woman expressed her concerns about the noise, vibration, and potential damage to people's homes. The man listened patiently and said friendly-sounding, reassuring things.

But something about the two of them and their conversation felt strange to me. As I listened, I could detect a trace of anger in the woman's voice—the anger and fear of someone threatened by forces greater than herself. I also understood that the man's calm, relaxed voice was the sound of someone with nothing to fear because he knows he has all the power.

After a while, the man got up and left. The woman stayed behind for a while and then left, too. I felt I'd just stumbled into a small part of a larger story, so I decided to go home and try to write the rest of it.

The man had seemed so controlled, so unnaturally relaxed and friendly. Almost inhuman. What if he wasn't human?

That's when the story took off. More questions followed. What if the bridge he was building wasn't really a bridge? What if it was something else—some strange, secret thing impossible to define or understand?

Other ingredients found their way into the story as I wrote it: a memory of the first solar eclipse I experienced as a small child, small roadside hokura shrines in Japan, and later, after we'd moved across the river into this 160-year-old house, a homeowner's anxiety at the inevitable destructive effects of time and decay on the things we value and love.

I distinctly remember reading a poem about the hokura or Shinto shrines that appear in the story, in which the line "little gods to live in them" appears. The phrase stuck with me, and I knew I wanted to use it as the title—but when I went back to look for the source, I couldn't find it, no matter how hard I looked. I even started to wonder if I might have dreamed it.

### "The Devil Will Be at the Door"

IN FEBRUARY 2020, Mark Beech, editor of Egaeus Press, invited me to submit a story for his new anthology. Called *Crooked Houses*, it was supposed to be a book of stories about haunted houses—but Mark was encouraging writers to return to a "pre-Victorian" model of ghost story, in which the ghost can't be reduced to a simple human drama, like murder or some other kind of violent death. Instead, Mark wanted ghosts that were some inhuman, elemental threat. More monstrous and primordial. I pondered Mark's guidelines for a while, and the message I finally got was this—Be terrifying.

I read somewhere (in an essay about scary movies) that nothing is more frightening than fear. I tried to think of a time when someone else's fear had frightened me badly—I didn't have to think very long.

When I was in college studying psychology, a professor in the folklore department told us that he had a recording he wanted us to listen to. This professor was famous for books of traditional ghost stories that he collected from elderly people in the Appalachian region. Occasionally, someone would contact him with their own stories of actual hauntings. Eventually, he decided that these personal accounts were folklore or folklore-in-the-making, so he started recording those stories too.

There was one interview in particular that he wanted us to listen to—he said he wanted to get "a psychological perspective on it."

That's how a colleague from the psychology department and I ended up sitting in the university library with headphones on, listening to this reel-to-reel tape of a man and a woman talking about their house being haunted or possessed. Truthfully, I can't remember very many details from their story—but what I'll never forget is the sound of pure, raw terror in their voices. The longer we listened, the more I could feel their fear creeping inside my body like a virus. After a while, my colleague and I turned the tape off and just sat there, waiting for the effect of those voices to loosen their hold on us.

That was the kind of relentless, contagious fear that I tried to bring to this story. The story the man tells on the tape is made up, as is the face-to-face encounter with him and, of course, the rest of the story. The beginning, about my father telling that horrible, gory jump story to a busload of kids, is 100% true—there's a busload of adults my age who can vouch for that.

Then there's the title... it comes from a song I remember hearing on the car radio as a very young child, driving down the twists and turns of 31-E into Eastern Kentucky. It was a country song, one of those old-school bluegrass ones with three chords and high-lonesome harmonies:

*Don't go to Matt's cabin, don't go to Matt's cabin,*
*The Devil will be at the door.*
*Don't go to Matt's cabin, don't go to Matt's cabin,*
*You'll never be seen anymore.*

That spooky song and those words gave me a taste of the same relentless terror I felt years later listening to that tape, and I knew I had to use them as the title of this story. Here's the funny thing–no matter how hard I try, I can't find any information about that song anywhere. It's as if it never existed, like the house in my story.

*Crooked Houses* sold out its first print run in a matter of weeks and went into a second edition. Then, in 2021, I got an email from Ellen Datlow asking to publish "The Devil Will Be at the Door" in *Best Horror of the Year Volume 13*, my first appearance in that venerable series—so I must have been doing something right.

### "Angelmutter"

SOMETIME IN THE late 1950s, my mother was driving through the mountains of West Virginia late at night, her brand-new baby (me) in the car with her. She'd run out of baby formula and was desperate to find some, so she pulled off the road in some tiny mountain town and went into a little country store with me in her arms. A group of older men sitting around looked up at her, staring like she was some alien creature. One of the men spoke to her in a strange accent she could barely understand: "Ayer ye lookin' fer the wimmen-folk?" My mother got what she was looking for and made it out alive—unlike the unfortunate woman in my story, who does live but never makes it out.

I once met a woman who claimed to be terrified by the idea of nursing a child at her breast. The thought of it was more disgusting and horrifying than almost anything she knew. She became the inspiration for the main character in my story. I started with two strong elements—a main character (very unlike my mother) for whom motherhood is fraught with trauma and feels almost monstrous, and an actual monster who exists not to kill or destroy but to nurture and sustain the damaged lives that are brought to it.

I wrote "Angelmutter" for *Twisted Book of Shadows*, an anthology that Christopher Golden and James Moore were putting together for Haverhill House Publications. Soon after submitting the story, I got an email from Christopher Golden, explaining they were taking the unusual step of reaching out to me before the official submission window was closed because they wanted the story and didn't want to risk losing it (which was enormously gratifying, of course). After the book came out, I was on a panel with Chris Golden and Jim Moore at the Merrimack Valley Halloween Book Festival. We were discussing "Angelmutter" when Jim Moore turned to me and said (on mic) in his coolest deadpan manner, "That's one fucked up story, David." I took that as a compliment—I still do.

## "That the Sea Shall Be Calm"

ONCE EVERY FEW years, I really love to sit down and whip up a tale told in a good old 19th-century diarist's voice—or, I should say, my approximation of that voice. In my previous collection, that story was "The Last Testament of Jacob Tyler," a story told in the voice of a ruthless mercenary involved in the Anti-rent War in 1840s New York. In this book, I decided to write in the voice of a scientist on board a 19th-century scientific voyage in the Pacific.

This story was originally intended for a themed anthology of horror stories about the sea. I started looking for interesting nautical legends–particularly strange and dangerous entities encountered and spoken of by sailors. I skipped right past the sea serpents and mermaids (although I do love sea serpents, I'll admit) until I found a legendary creature I'd never heard of before—the Klaubertermann, a creature from German mythology who protects sailors and makes repairs on their ship in secret—however, if any sailor sees the Klaubertermann, that means the ship is doomed. I asked myself, what would happen if a ship rescued a man lost at sea, and the sailors became convinced that he was a Klauberterman, a harbinger of death and destruction?

For this story, I took a deep dive into research. I studied the voyage of the HMS Challenger and read the logs and records of the crew and expedition members. I researched facts about food spoilage, provision shortages on board long sea voyages, and hallucinations and "miraculous sights" experienced by sailors lost at sea. I even got into the nitty gritty of oceanic depth measurements and plotted the actual route my fictional ship would take, including the correct distances and travel times. By the time I was through, my head was swimming with nautical facts and figures, but it all paid off, and I enjoyed every minute. "That the Sea Shall Be Calm" was finally published in *Supernatural Tales*, whose editor David Longhorn has also been known to enjoy a good seafaring tale.

### "The Man Outside"

I'VE WRITTEN PLENTY of stories about places that frightened me or made me uneasy, but this was the first time I've ever written a scary story set in a place that I love and feel safe in.

Julia and I have been going to a cottage in the Shawangunk Mountains for ten years or more. We write, read, take hikes, cook, and burn lots of firewood—it's one of our favorite places on Earth. So it's strange that I used it as the setting for this very strange and disturbing tale. Maybe the idea of something terrible happening in such a good place was fascinating.

I wrote the story in one sitting, in a very stream-of-consciousness way. It felt like writing down a bad dream—in fact, a bad dream may have been the original inspiration for this story—but I find that dreams tend to fade once you've written them down until you can't remember the dream, only the words on the page.

In the first version I wrote, there was no background mention of the wife's encroaching dementia (or the old couple's son)—it was only about the nightmarish events taking place that one night in the cottage. At first, I'd hoped to make it a kind of brief, surreal prose-poem—later, the need for narrative crept in, and I added the background bits about the wife's dementia, plus the son and his alarm at the father's casual attitude about his wife's disappearance.

Still, even with these traditional narrative elements added, I think a lot of the original surreal nightmarishness still carries over, especially in that ending. Writing this story feels like the closest I've ever come to having a nightmare while awake and writing it down as it happened.

## "Where the Monsters Are Lonely"

THIS ONE STARTED as a much shorter story (called "The Worst Thing"). That original version also started with the scene where the school kids find Warren's shelter in the woods. It also contained the narrator's high school memory of the night ride with Warren (and ditching him by the side of the road), then the daughter going missing, and the final confrontation in the woods between the narrator and Warren.

It was Julia who suggested that the single high school humiliation wasn't enough, and that the narrator should have harmed Warren in a much more serious way to inspire him to take the narrator's daughter and to cause the narrator's powerful feelings of guilt and fear. I added the element of the narrator and his friend framing Warren for arson.

The new element of not only framing Warren for arson but also failing to come forward to prevent him from going to prison felt so heinous that it threatened to overwhelm the rest of the story—also, it was hard to believe it was something that the narrator could just carry around and merely "feel bad" about. Then Julia suggested that the narrator's guilt (plus his drug use on the night of the arson) could cause him to have partially blocked the memory, a memory that I could reveal piece by piece as the story goes on.

The school field-trip in the woods at the beginning of this story is almost 100% true, including the young students discovering the strange-looking shelter of woven sticks, and me shouting at them to get away from it because I thought a homeless person might be living there. Unlike the one in my story, that shelter was empty.

The character Warren was based on a boy I went to high school with. Like Warren, he was a quiet, intense loner with a reputation for turning red traffic lights to green with the power of his mind. I did take a ride with him one night like the one described in the story—and yes, all the traffic lights turned green, basically freaking all of us out. We did not, however, ditch him by the side of the road or taunt and abuse him in any way—I think we were far too scared of him to do anything that stupid.

### "When the Circus"

My FIRST WIFE worked in a bar across 34th Street from Madison Square Garden when I moved to New York City in the early eighties. I often hung out and met people like me who'd come to the city to become writers, musicians, actors, artists, etc. There was a lot of drinking, plus other things. (It was the early eighties, after all.)

One night, I was sitting by the big plate glass window, looked up, and saw elephants—huge, real–live elephants walking by. This was back in the day when the Ringing Brothers circus used to march their elephants through the Holland Tunnel all the way to Madison Square Garden—but no one had told me that, so for a few moments, my sense of reality felt seriously twisted.

I thought of those elephants again when I came across

an anthology calling for "new urban legends." The editors asked for all stories submitted to be explicitly linked to a specific urban setting. They also said we could use an existing urban legend or make our own. I remembered that nocturnal elephant parade through the streets of Midtown New York City. I'd also read old news accounts of circus fires, especially train fires when elephants were injured and killed during transport, and those fed into the legend I was concocting.

Lenny's character is based on two guys I knew back then. One was the bartender at the bar where my first wife worked, and the other was a former drummer for a famous punk rock band who held court at the Ear Inn—both "real New Yorker" types who considered it their duty to educate ignorant hicks like me on how to survive in the city.

The refrain of "Don't look" came to me like someone had spoken it in my ear and held on until the very end. (I knew almost from the start that it would be the last two words of the story—well, two of the last three words, at least.)

### "Eyes Like Small Black Stones"

A FEW YEARS AGO, Julia and I were looking for inspiration for new stories. We decided to go to our local vintage shop and look through old photographs to see what caught our eye and sparked our imagination. We found a wicker basket full of old black and white photos curled around the edges like dry leaves. ("Dead people's pictures," I think we called them.) Three struck me right away. One was an older man wearing a wool suit and a broad-brimmed hat that looked like it was from the forties, sitting on a hillside with a younger woman and pointing toward something off-camera. The second one, which looked like it was from the same era, was a young boy who looked about six years old, glaring at the camera with a look of hard-eyed, hateful mistrust. The third was a swan, floating in the water, strangely out of focus and with some kind of glare on the lens that made the swan look ghostly and ablaze with light. I knew I wanted all three of these photos—and I knew that all three were from the same story.

The older man in the wool suit looked imposing and in command, like a retired general. Even when relaxing on the lawn with his family, he looked like he was pointing out the direction of troop maneuvers. From him, I created the manipulative racist patriarch in my story. The little boy in the second photograph had so much cold anger in his round, pale face, I knew that something inside him was broken and that he was the kind who could end up causing as much harm as he suffered himself—he became the old general's troubled grandson. And that radiant, ghostly white swan became the supernatural hot spot of the story, the force of chaos strong enough to rip apart the order imposed by these flawed humans.

I'd also recently been shocked and more than a little heartbroken to discover that an older man who I knew and respected had fallen under the spell of the political insanity in our country and held beliefs that I found repugnant. For a while, I couldn't make sense of it—how could this otherwise kind, intelligent, warm-hearted man hold such cruel and destructive ideas? I tried to rationalize it and explain it away, but in the end, I couldn't. Much of that heartbroken cognitive dissonance went into the character of the patriarch's daughter, although I like to think that I didn't go quite as far into denial as she did.

That this story was set in and around Washington, DC, is no coincidence. That was where I spent every summer of my childhood in the homes of certain elderly relatives where the name "Roosevelt" was still spoken like a dirty word, and the vocabulary of casual racism was used without thought or apology. That was the world that the patriarch in my story represented and the one he was bent on defending to the end—it was a pleasure to kill him.

The story exploded into a kind of novelistic kaleidoscope, with its shifting POVs and flashbacks. It became so unwieldy that I had to put it away for a while. About a year later, Julia and I were on holiday in Gloucester, Massachusetts, driving around and talking about a new Egaeus Press anthology calling for stories about birds. Julia had started a bird story—I hadn't yet, but I wanted to. As we passed by a lake, Julia looked out the car window and said, "Look... swans!" And just like that, I remembered my swan story and decided to finish it.

Mark Beech thought the bird connection was a little "secondary" but still loved the story enough to take it, and it was published in the Egaeus Press anthology *Ornithologiae* in 2022. Later, Ellen Datlow was kind enough to ask for it to be included in *Best New Horror of the Year, Volume 15*. So, this strange, formerly unwieldy story of mine has done pretty well—it just goes to show that it pays to believe in the weird ones.

### "Lost River Boys"

CAVES HAVE ALWAYS played a big part in my imagination. I was raised in Kentucky, and caves were all around. As a school kid, I was taken to see the mummy of the native American boy who'd been trapped in a rockslide inside Mammoth Cave. I'll never forget the ancient brown leathery skin stretched over his stick-like bones or that moment deep in the cave when they turned out the lights and showed us how dark darkness can be. So, of course, it was only a matter of time before caves began to appear in my writing.

Several years ago, I imagined a small Kentucky town named "Lost River," where every local boy had disappeared into the local cave one night. I thought about the impact a tragedy like that would have on a small rural community and the different types of characters who'd be affected and involved. All those characters started coming to life and speaking to me.

My favorite voice, and the one who started speaking to me first, was a fifty-year-old woman named Ellen Duncan. I knew that she was a schoolteacher and that her son was one of the boys lost in the cave accident. I knew she was very smart and strong and dedicated to her students and her son. I also knew she was an alcoholic. Once she became real to me and started talking, all I had to do was listen and write it down.

Over the years, I've created a whole cast of different characters and various members of the community with their own stories to tell, but it's Ellen that I find myself returning to, like in this story. As usual, I didn't know what she was going to do at the end of the story—until she did it. I thought it was a little harsh myself, but it was her decision, not mine.

For years, finding anyone who'd publish these stories was hard. I'll confess that I sometimes wondered if it was because they were too "rural"—specifically, too "southern." I was very grateful when Tom English, editor of *Nightmare Abbey*, started giving my Lost River stories a good home.

## "The Armor of Light"

MY FATHER WAS the rector of the only Episcopal church in a small southern town. Growing up in that church and watching him do his job was probably the most formative experience of my life. It's hard to explain to others what it's like to see the daily human drama that goes on "backstage" in a church, plus the power of the whole ritual aspect, the visceral and mind-changing absorption in music, prayer, and story.

I remember how I felt when I first saw *The Bishop's Wife* and *The Holly and the Ivy*. Those two old movies gave me my first extended glimpse into the kind of life I recognized. I wanted to do the same in my writing. I tried writing straight autobiographical essays at first, but when I decided to tell about my early church life through the lens of horror and fantasy, I found a way to get closer to just how strange it could be.

As a kid, I was fascinated with the series of young men who served as "assistant rectors" in my father's church and how they all came and went, one after the other, in a mysterious way. They all seemed to share certain core attributes—a repressed social awkwardness and an intense discomfort inside their own skin. In some ways, I thought it was almost like they were all the same guy—and as soon as I realized that, I had the whole basis for this story.

I wrote the first paragraph of this story as a free stream-of-consciousness write. As soon as I wrote it, I knew I had to keep going and make it a whole story.

## "How the World Works"

FOR HORROR WRITERS, there's nothing like a manuscript call for a themed anthology to illuminate the gaps in their work. Some can be intimidatingly specific. For example, "Stories about zombie gunslingers." Now, zombie gunslingers may be a cool idea, but chances are, you probably don't have a story like that on your hard drive. That's not surprising, given the layers of detail required in a guideline like that.

But what about "monsters"? "Monsters" should be a primary color in every horror writer's palette, right? So, imagine my surprise when I realized I had no monster stories. That just didn't seem possible. I like monsters— the fictional kind. Cryptids, too (which are sort of semi-fictional, depending on who you ask). But, with one or two possible exceptions, I'd somehow never written a monster story. I decided to correct that right away.

I don't remember exactly how I created the monster in this story. I know that I was thinking about the symbiotic relationship between some monsters and humans—from prehistoric ritual sacrifices for appeasing harvest gods to Victor Frankenstein and Henry Jekyll's dysfunctional bonds with their monstrous creations. What if a teenage boy had to "pet-sit" a monster? Why would he even do that? What's in it for him?

I was also dealing with the death of someone who'd been my best friend from the time we were five years old till we were twenty-five. In some friendships, there's a follower and a leader. My friend was the leader, and I was his willing follower—until I wasn't willing anymore. Soon after his death, he started to reappear in my fiction. He'd probably been appearing in my fiction long before that.

Every time there's an intelligent, domineering, controlling character whose life intersects with my main character's, that was my old friend in disguise. Our relationship was nowhere near as dysfunctional as the one between the two boys in this story, but the parts that *were* dysfunctional ended up going into the writing. (I did help him out once with a housesitting job when we were teenagers, but there was no monster involved—just a monster-sized dog, but that's another story.)

Probably the most remarkable thing for me about writing this story was the narrator's mother. She was originally supposed to play only a "bit part"—but she had other ideas. Writers like to say that their characters sometimes "talk" to them and tell them what to do—this one would not shut up. She pushed her way deeper and deeper into the story, the same way she pushed herself into these boys' lives. I'm really glad she did because she brings a level of real-life surprise and heart to the story that wouldn't be there without her.

### "These Things That Walk Behind Me"

THIS STORY STARTED when I followed Ray Bradbury's advice and wrote a list of things that scared me when I was young. One of the first things on my list was falling asleep–I was terrified of it when I was small. That loss of consciousness and falling into darkness felt a little too close to dying for me. I gave that fear to my narrator and let him try to explain it.

The hooded phantoms the narrator sees when pulling the all-nighter in college are the same ones I saw. That whole scene is true, word for word. I'd never had such a convincing and terrifying hallucination before and haven't since (lucky for me).

The character I've called "Carlton"—the man who seeks out the narrator in the psychiatric ward and speaks to him about the gift and responsibility they both share—is based on a real man I once knew.

I worked in the mental health sector for twenty years, leading writing workshops for mental patients. It was an amazing and humbling experience, and I met and worked with some unforgettable people. One of the most unforgettable was the man "Carlton" was based on. A schizophrenic, he was very symptomatic, manic, and incoherent. The longer he wrote, the calmer and more coherent he became. Then he'd begin to say the most startling things, these sudden flashes of insight into whatever you were thinking or worrying about—things he had no real way of knowing. At first, I thought I was just imagining it—when I mentioned it to a woman who worked at the psychiatric center, she said, "Oh yes. He does that all the time. Everyone here knows about him."

In most horror stories, the protagonist either survives by defeating or escaping the monsters or is defeated by them. In this story, I decided to give the protagonist a different kind of victory by having him go even deeper into the things that used to frighten him.

There's a story about a Tibetan Buddhist master who prayed to be reborn in hell so he could offer help and comfort to the hell-beings trapped there. I don't believe I was consciously thinking of that story when I wrote this one—but I think a little of it came through anyway.

### "The Skin You Were Born In"

THIS IS A story about fathers and sons—one particular father and one particular son, of course, but I think there are things in here that most fathers and sons will recognize. If you're a father—the father of a son—one day, you will realize that your son is not you, not some kind of version of yourself. And that truth, like many other perfectly obvious truths, can be incredibly difficult to grasp. As a father, you may try to resist this truth, even fight it—until one day when your son reveals himself to you in all his beauty, strength, and otherness. That's what I'm trying to find a new way to talk about in this story.

# Acknowledgements

IN HIS BLURB for my first collection back in 2020, Steve Duffy (a marvelous writer and great guy) wrote, "This is David's first collection, and I'm happy to recommend it, on the strict understanding that he comes up with another, as soon as he likes." I'm very glad to say that I'm now finally able to honor his request.

I'm very grateful to Steve Berman, editor of the great Lethe Press, who pleasantly startled me by knowing my work when I first reached out to him, for his love and support of literary horror, and for bringing this book (and so many others) into the world.

In the realm of what I call "grown-up horror fiction", John Langan has been one of my guiding lights. To have his generous words introduce these stories is an honor and a thrill I could not have expected or imagined a few years ago. (I also could not have imagined playing guitar back-up to his rousing rendition of 'Werewolves of London' at a reading in upstate New York last October, but that is another story...)

Small presses and magazines are the lifeblood of literature and deserve our respect and support. My thanks to the editors who first published many of the stories in this book: Mark Beech, Tom English, Christopher Golden, David Longhorn, James M. Moore, C.M. Muller, and Matt Schumacher. A special thanks to the great Ellen Datlow for reprinting two stories in this book in her *Best Horror of the Year*, Volumes 13 and 15.

I'd like to thank Daniel Braum for a long, informative, and encouraging telephone conversation about publishing, while sitting on a bench under the trees outside Two Alice's coffee shop in Cornwall on Hudson, and for all his supportive words and deeds before and since.

A special thanks to all you readers who've chosen to give your precious time and attention to these stories. I hope you'll find them worthy.

And as ever and always, my thanks to Julia Rust, a brilliant writer, actor, and teacher who I'm lucky to share a home and this life with. My thanks and this book are for her, with all my heart.

# About
# The Author

DAVID SURFACE LIVES in the Hudson Highlands of New York State in a 160-year-old brick home that he shares with the author Julia Rust. His first collection of short fiction, *Terrible Things*, was published in 2020 by Black Shuck Books. He is co-author with Julia Rust of *Angel Falls*, a YA-crossover novel published by YAP Books - Haverhill House Publishing; their new novel, *Saving Thornwood*, has also been accepted for publication by Haverhill House. David's stories have appeared in *Best New Horror of the Year, Supernatural Tales, Nightscript, Shadows and Tall Trees, Nightmare Abbey, Phantom Drift, Chthonic Matter* and other publications. His newsletter, 'Strange Little Stories' features a new strange-but-true story by himself and a new guest-author every month. You can learn more about David and his writing at davidsurface.net

# Previous Publications

These stories first appeared in the following publications:

"Give Me Back My Name", *Nightmare Abbey, issue 1*, 2022

"Little Gods to Live in Them", *Nightscript, volume VII*, 2021

"The Devil Will Be at the Door", *Crooked Houses: Tales of Cursed and Haunted Dwellings*, Egaeus Press, 2020

"Angelmutter", *Twisted Book of Shadows*, Haverhill House Publications, 2019

"That the Sea Shall Be Calm", *Supernatural Tales 41*, 2019

"Where the Monsters are Lonely", *Chthonic Matter Quarterly*, Winter 2023

"Eyes Like Small Black Stones", *Ornithologiae*, Egaeus Press, 2022

"These Things That Walk Behind Me", *Nightmare Abbey*, issue 2, 2023

"Lost River Boys", *Nightmare Abbey*, issue 3, 2023

"The Skin You Were Born In", *Phantom Drift 10*, 2020

"When the Circus", "The Man Outside", "The Armor of Light" and "How the World Works" are original to this collection.

www.ingramcontent.com/pod-product-compliance
Lightning Source LLC
Chambersburg PA
CBHW020431030726
47495CB00006B/1747